# LOVE OF FINISHED YEARS

## A Novel

## Gregory Erich Phillips

**SPB**

Sillan Pace Brown Books
Portland, Oregon

Praise for
# *Love of Finished Years*

*"A wonderfully satisfying read."*
*-- Chanticleer Reviews*

*"What a truly wonderful story! I've read it three times, and with each reading I find myself caring about the fabulous characters and their lives even more."*
—P.J. Alderman, New York Times Bestselling Author

*"From the riveting opening that takes place in NYC's Lower East Side's sweatshops until its gripping conclusion, this enthralling novel vividly portrays the desperate times of German immigrants landing at Ellis Island in 1905 in search of a better life. A timely read ... it illuminates the issues that we are experiencing a century later...Phillips reminds us that love, light, and perseverance can help us find a way to overcome almost any obstacle."* —Chanticleer Reviews

*"I do hope the author has a sequel in the works...a beautiful novel that is set in a fascinating time in our nation's history."* -
--Linda S., Boulder, Colorado

~~~~~

**Grand Prize Winner of the**
**Chanticleer Book Awards**

Sillan Pace Brown Publishing
An imprint of Sillan Pace Brown Group, Inc.
Portland, Oregon

www.SillanPaceBrown.com

First Edition, **ISBN**-13: 978-1-64058-011-4

**ISBN**-10: 1-64058-011-5

1. Historical Fiction 2. World War One - fiction
3. 20th Century NYC – fiction 4. Women's Suffrage
5. German Immigrants – fiction

Published in the United States of America by
Sillan Pace Brown Publishing, a member of Sillan Pace
Brown Group (USA), Inc., 2018

*Come to me in the silence of the night;*
*Come in the speaking silence of a dream;*
*Come with soft rounded cheeks and eyes as bright*
*As sunlight on a stream;*
*Come back in tears,*
*O memory, hope, love of finished years.*
—"Echo," Christina Rossetti

# PART I

# CHAPTER ONE
# AN OLD GERMAN WEDDING

*September, 1909*

The tenement steps were still dark as the teenage girl descended from her fourth-floor apartment. She held on to the shaky banister, quickly measuring the uneven steps. In the last four years, she had climbed down them so many mornings that she could have done it with her eyes closed. She knew each sag, each crack.

Elsa tried to tell herself this morning was no different from all those others, but she couldn't shake the knowledge that if she failed today, everything would change.

As she opened the front door, a faint gray light entered the dusty building. The crisp air of early autumn bathed her face. There were no electric street lamps here on 3rd Street, but she could see the glow from Second Avenue. She headed that way. Despite the darkness, the Lower East Side was quickly coming to life.

Physically exhausted but mentally alert, she pressed on into the city. She was accustomed to weariness—it had become her way of life.

At sixteen, Elsa knew most people took her for an adult. With her brown hair, fair face and broad shoulders, she blended easily into a crowd. Much as she might long for her sister Sonja's slender frame and delicate face, she had begun to appreciate the strength that helped her cope through these times.

It was good that Sonja's factory days had come to an end.

The events of this week had pushed Elsa's strength to its limit. These were supposed to be days of joy. Now it was up to her to save her family from another disaster.

The windows on Second Avenue began to show signs of life. Shadows moved around inside unlit apartments. Dawn still came early enough to prepare for the day by natural light. In another week or two, precious cents would need to be spent to dress by gaslight.

Elsa hurried down the sidewalks of the Bowery as the city awakened. The morning sun shot between the buildings to her left, casting a long shadow beneath the elevated railway.

Two boys pushed a cart loaded with lettuce and cabbage heads, as an eager dog danced between its wheels. Soon a second cart appeared, and before Elsa had walked another block, ten or more carts were in position for business along both sides of the street. Shop windows started opening below painted signs or embroidered banners in both English and Yiddish. Merchants in loose trousers and suspenders, most wearing yarmulkes on their heads, appeared in the shop doors. Young boys ran across the street in front of Elsa, their shoulders loaded with fabrics, bound for one of the many family-owned clothing factories that dotted the neighborhood. Soon the horseless carriages began to *click-clack* down the rough street, carrying the "swells" from uptown.

Elsa's gaze was drawn from the street-front shops to the tenement windows above, where small clothiers would soon begin work in their apartments. She couldn't help wondering whether those family operations would offer an easier life than the shirtwaist factory where she and her mother spent their days. But these smaller shops maintained tight ethnic distinctions. While many of the clothiers had emigrated from Germany, they all spoke Yiddish. A German-speaking girl like her was as foreign as a native-born American.

Even at her factory, Yiddish was the primary language of

the workers. But the business was large enough—and diverse enough—to give her a chance to learn the language and culture of her new country. She spent her days among not only Jews but also Italian and Irish immigrants, a handful of black Americans and others. She and her mother were the only Christian Germans. How could they have known they would emigrate just as the majority of the city's Germans were *leaving* lower Manhattan?

Elsa arrived at the police headquarters on Centre Street just as it opened. The ornate building looked alarmingly out of place amid the humble shops and tenements. She wondered whether that was intentional—an attempt to intimidate outsiders like herself. She refused to be deterred. Her family depended on her. Everything she had worked for could crumble if she let timidity get the better of her now. She marched up the steps between two snarling stone lions and into the police station.

An hour later, she walked out with her mother.

"*Was hast du zu ihnen gesagt?*" her mother asked.

"I told them the truth," Elsa replied in English. She knew her mother could understand her, even though she spoke little English herself. "I told them your daughter's wedding is Sunday. They did not have the heart to keep you in. Then I told them something that probably is not true . . ." She looked pointedly at her mother.

"*Ja?*"

"I promised you would not do it again. Look at this!" Elsa held up the release form she had signed in the station. "Nina Schuller. Arrested for disturbing the peace." She slapped the single page. "You have a record now, mother."

Nina threw up her hands. Elsa couldn't help but laugh, even though she was still upset with her mother for landing in jail overnight. She folded up the page and stuffed it into her skirt pocket.

"Come." Elsa urged her mother forward. "We must take

the train. After what happened yesterday we cannot be late."

They paid uptown fair at the nearest elevated station. The factory was a mile northwest of their apartment. It was rare for them to take the train, even in the dead of winter—the daily fare would add up fast. But considering the temperaments at the factory, they were already at risk of losing a half-day's wages.

"Could you not have waited a few more days"—Elsa scolded once they were seated on the train—"until after Sonja's wedding? I was lucky to get you out. You would have been fired."

"I might still get fired today. But everything we have worked for is at stake. You saw what happened yesterday. They beat poor Clara! Was I supposed to just stand there?" She grabbed Elsa's arm." There will be a strike soon—not only at our factory, but at all the garment factories. A women's general strike."

Elsa scowled. She admired her mother's tenacity and her will to improve life for the women in the factories, but she herself hoped to escape this life another way.

"I am doing it all for you," her mother added. "I am growing old. I do not care for myself. Sonja . . . I always knew she would marry. But you . . ."

Yes, once again, the reminder that she wasn't as likely to marry as Sonja. Elsa felt the pang every time her mother alluded to it.

"You have prepared yourself for an opportunity in this country. You learned the language and the customs. I was angry at first, but you did what you had to."

Elsa looked across at her mother sitting on the train bench beside her, and then glanced down to where her hands rested in her lap. The veins on the tops of her mother's hands were pronounced; her fingertips sharply calloused from the precision of her work. Elsa's own hands would look that way at a much younger age than her mother's.

"You cannot do it alone," her mother said. "America is ready to give women a real chance, but we must fight for it."

"After the wedding. Once Sonja is with her new family, you and I can fight together. If it comes to a strike, I will stand beside you. We have survived together before. We can do it again."

Elsa wrapped her arm around her mother and smiled. After all they had endured in America thus far, a strike, even as winter approached, didn't seem so daunting.

The train ground to a halt at Washington Square. The two disembarked and rushed to enter the factory. They took their places at their workstations: Elsa at the loom, Nina at the cutting table.


The end of the factory shift was only the beginning of that day's work for Nina and Elsa. They had hours of wedding preparations to do and only two evenings to complete them. Nina's arrest on Thursday had hindered their plans. Now it was Friday, and most of the merchants closed their shops at sundown for the Sabbath. They walked the long way home via Avenue B where a German grocer was still open.

The next day, after another full shift in the shirtwaist factory, they came home ready to begin cooking in earnest.

"How many people will be there?" asked Elsa as she began to chop asparagus.

"At least forty. Maybe every German in New York. There has not been a wedding in the community yet this year. No one wants to miss it."

"*Darf ich euch beiden helfen?*" asked Sonja.

"*Nein,*" insisted the mother.

"I will not have you working all night. You must look fresh and beautiful tomorrow. Try to sleep."

Sonja withdrew, but Elsa could hear her sister bustling around in the second room of the apartment. Elsa knew her sister felt restless being made to sit idle as others worked. She would have felt the same way.

She watched as her mother's eyes followed Sonja. Elsa understood Nina's concerns for her older daughter. Sonja had suffered greatly here in America. Elsa had watched her spirit nearly break. Her life would be better now with her husband and his uncle at their uptown bakery. Sonja deserved a good man like Christof.

As the iron pot began to heat on the stove, the smell of asparagus soup permeated the apartment, bringing back nostalgic memories of northern Germany. This was the first time they had cooked asparagus soup in the traditional way here in America, using white asparagus. Christof's uncle, Gerd, had procured it from a cousin's farm, all the way from Pennsylvania. Elsa slowly stirred the broth to a boil, dropping in onions, sausage and kale. As the soup simmered, they prepared the batter for *Pfankuchen*. Every large bowl they owned, plus a few borrowed from neighbors, was filled with batter, then covered and stacked. The German pancakes would be fried up on the churchyard stove tomorrow.

The gaslight burned past midnight in their apartment. Finally, everything was ready.

Early the next morning, Elsa went down to the street to hire a cart. After bartering with an Irish boy, she brought him upstairs to help her carry down the pot of soup and bowls of batter. Together they pushed it four blocks to St. Mark's Lutheran Church. Gerd Steigenhöffer was already there, unloading baskets of bread from his bakery in Yorkville. The Irish boy asked Elsa for a cup of the soup. She refused at first, but finally gave him a ladle-full. He did look pretty hungry.

Nina had almost finished dressing Sonja when Elsa got home. She stood quietly in the doorway, watching as her mother carefully laced up the front of Sonja's white dress, tying a bow at the top of the bodice, below her collarbones. The transparent sleeves draped softly down Sonja's arms, gathering at the cuff. The dress was beautiful, traditional, and hadn't come cheap. Nina turned her daughter around to face her.

*"Oh, du bist so schön,"* Nina murmured, reaching up to touch her daughter's face, then arranging her brown curls over her shoulders.

*"Danke, Mutti."*

*Elsa* smiled as she watched the tender moment. She was happy for her sister. But there was also sadness in hearing her mother's words—she doubted she would ever hear her say *"You are beautiful,"* to her. Her mother was always honest, and Elsa liked her that way. And it was true—she *wasn't* beautiful. She'd been a plain child, and even as the years had brought a woman's shape to her body and more maturity to her face, she remained so. She didn't expect some miracle to suddenly alter the plainness and strength that so contrasted with her sister's beauty and grace.

Elsa forced her thoughts from herself. Today she wanted to take joy in her sister's hopes. Sonja's dreams would be fulfilled. Her own still had time to grow.

Soon a throng of guests poured into the rickety tenement to escort the bride to the church. The procession sang and shouted through the street, to the amusement of neighborhood onlookers, and to the suspicion of several policemen. They arrived at St. Mark's just before the midmorning service. The pastor and all the German parishioners weren't surprised by the boisterous crowd—they had been anticipating this day for weeks. Almost everyone stayed in the church for the wedding ceremony immediately following the usual Sunday service.

Only one of four parents was present at the wedding. In Germany that would have raised eyebrows. But not here. Separation and loss were a way of life for recent immigrants. Elsa knew her mother was grateful for the way Gerd Steigenhöffer took an active role in the ceremony, as if he had been the groom's father.

The loss of Christof's parents along with so many others in the *General Slocum* steamboat fire five years ago still stung the local German community and St. Mark's parish in particular. Although Christof had remained in his family's Lower East Side apartment after the disaster, he was eager to move uptown after the wedding to help run his uncle's bakery.

After the ceremony, everyone went outside to the tables. Elsa did most of the serving herself. *Spargelsuppe, Pfankuchen,* and a roasted boar provided by the groom's family made all who could remember nostalgic for their homeland.

Gerd's cousin pulled out a violin and began to play. Another guest produced an accordion. As soon as everyone had finished eating, they pushed the tables aside and began to dance. Only the older people knew the folk dances from Germany, but everyone joined in on the polkas, even the children. Gerd and Nina had taught the bride and groom how to dance the *Kleiner Schottisch,* much to the delight of the older guests. When the song ended, they applauded the newlyweds. Then the musicians tore into another fast polka.

Elsa paused from clearing the dishes, watching as pairs of guests joined in the dance. Suddenly she saw Gerd coming toward her with outstretched hands. She held her stack of dishes protectively in front of her.

"Come, Elsa. Join the circle with me."

"Oh, no. I do not know—"

"It is easy." He gently took the dishes out of her hands and set them on the nearest table. "I will show you."

Before she could protest further, he tugged her by the hand into the dance. Her heart beat wildly as she joined the dancing circle. She tried to keep her eyes on Gerd's feet but soon forgot. He flew around the churchyard with agility that belied his years, and Elsa's feet barely touched the ground. She forgot her timidity and laughed with delight.

Gerd clapped happily after her as she returned to the

tables. Elsa smiled from ear to ear. She could scarcely remember having so much fun.

Gerd rushed over to the violinist and whispered something. The musicians nodded vigorously before Gerd turned back to the crowd.

"The bride is for sale!"

Two old women pushed Sonja to the center. She removed one of her shoes and placed it on the grass beside her. The men came one at a time to buy their opportunity to dance with the half-shod bride, each dropping something in the shoe.

Elsa was happy for her sister but she would miss her. The Yorkville neighborhood seemed a long way away. Although she and Sonja had grown into very different people, they remained close. She had few other friends.

She felt her mother's arm wrap around her shoulder.

"It is just you and me now," said Nina.

Elsa nodded slowly. They'd come across the ocean as a family of five. How quickly it all changed.

"Lots of changes," said Nina, as if divining her daughter's thoughts. "But look at all the work you have done and where it has brought you. Your courage inspires me. Your opportunities will be different from Sonja's, but they will come. This is the land for it."

Elsa knew her mother was right, but there again was that little sting—one more subtle reminder of the difference between herself and Sonja, which anyone could tell with a single glance at the sisters.

Was America really the land of opportunity? She thought back wistfully to the farmland and green forests of Germany. What a contrast to the smelly ship, Ellis Island, the clothing factory, and the apartment where she had spent her teenage years. Everything on this side of the Atlantic had been strange and difficult. The few native Germans in the neighborhood were moving away as fast as they could, replaced by Slavic Jews, Irish, and Italians. Most of these people here today didn't even live very close. Many she hadn't seen in the pew of St. Mark's for two years now. Elsa heard less of her native language every day. Even her mother was finally learning English, out of necessity.

The afternoon grew late. A slight chill permeated the sunny day. As Elsa gathered the plates and watched the waning celebration, she felt her childhood drifting away from her.

What if her opportunity never came? Might she still be working at the shirtwaist factory at her mother's age? Perhaps she would be lucky and meet a man to take her away from it all, as Sonja had met Christof. But was that even what she really wanted?

# CHAPTER TWO
# ELLIS ISLAND

*October, 1905*

Little Elsa was tired of standing.

For relief, she lifted one foot after the other. It helped a little. She tugged at Sonja's hand.

"Are we in a line?" she whispered.

"I think so."

She tried to see around her parents. There hardly seemed to be any order to the throng. Though obscured by the tall bodies around her, the room was huge.

"Why is everyone pushing?"

Her father turned and pointed an irritated finger at her. *"Sei ruhig!"* The stress was evident on his sweating face. "You do not need to understand."

Her mother turned back toward them, her face placid and determined. Little Anton fidgeted restlessly in her arms. The baby had been coughing since they came off the ship early that morning. "There is nothing we can do but wait. None of us know how long it will be."

Elsa hung her head and dropped imperceptibly back from her parents. She hoped they would reach wherever they were going soon. The long voyage had been frightening. So was this strange ordeal. She wished they were back in Germany.

She felt Sonja squeeze her hand and glanced up. At least Sonja still glowed with excitement. Elsa felt encouraged.

Above the tall people around her, Elsa could see the high windows in the walls, foggy from the condensation of damp bodies and ocean air trapped in the stuffy chamber. A few fans spun near the ceiling, but they didn't seem to do much good. The room smelled just like the ship. Pressing through the queue, her eyes dropped back to the dirty wood floor, caked with a thin layer of dust and salt.

Finally, the family reached the desk at the front of the line. Elsa's legs ached. She just wanted to sit down.

A man in a tight uniform and funny cap looked at the papers her father handed him. His mustachioed face was void of expression as he glanced at each member of the family, then at their set of papers. Elsa felt sorry for him. They would soon be done here and on their way into the city. But he had to sit here every day, smelling this smell and dealing with people who didn't want to see him.

He handed the papers back to her father, Tobias. No words had been exchanged. Then he pointed to another line on his right. Elsa thought she would cry.

That first glimpse of New York from the ship this morning already seemed so long ago. Elsa remembered how the sun had risen on the departed eastern horizon, brilliantly lighting the iron buildings of the city. Her view had been brief, as taller passengers quickly enveloped her, abuzz with the excitement of a long journey's end. After that thrilling moment, this waiting felt all the more tedious. She should have known better than to have gotten her hopes up.

Over the next hour, the family endured a series of medical examinations. Men and women came through the lines to check the immigrants for various physical ailments. Elsa wondered whether they were doctors. They didn't look like doctors.

Suddenly a gruff-looking man was forcing her mouth open and inserting a stick. Elsa choked as he forced her tongue down for what seemed a very long time. It didn't actually hurt so much as it repulsed her. Finally he released her mouth with a grunt.

He performed the same task with the same stick on her family members, then motioned to another of the officials. Elsa couldn't understand what they were talking about, but they seemed concerned. The first man kept pointing at the baby, who couldn't stop coughing. One of them took a piece of chalk and made a mark on each of their sleeves.

Each subsequent examination went poorly. Their education and skills were deemed unimpressive. This surprised Elsa. She and Sonja had both attended a few years of school. Her father had been a successful cart maker in Germany. But it seemed cart makers weren't in great demand in New York. Elsa could sense her father's anger and frustration.

As the grueling day came to an end, the Schuller family was shown to a room with two bunks. Elsa knew their day at Ellis Island hadn't gone well. Her eyes kept returning to the chalk mark on her sleeve. It worried her. What did it mean?

It felt good to finally lie down, but Elsa couldn't sleep. She and Sonja lay on the top bunk while their parents and the baby lay below.

"Isn't it wonderful to be in America?" Sonja whispered, loud enough for Elsa but not their parents to hear.

"I do not like it."

"We will leave this place soon. You and I will have to work at first, but soon we will go to school again. I know that is what you want."

A vigorous infant cough sounded below. Elsa waited until Anton was finished. "I hope so."

But all she could think of was the comfort of their little house in outside Hamburg. For the first time, she wondered whether maybe she didn't want to be in America. She had no choice about it. But she wondered why they were here, and why only now, after Anton was born. Life hadn't seemed so bad in Germany.

Elsa decided not to dwell on her worries and chose instead to dream about this new life. She imagined the education she would get in America, and dreamed of the kind of woman she could become. She had heard so many grand stories and hoped some of them were true. She lay awake long after Sonja relaxed into sleep.

The next day there were no inspections. Elsa didn't know what they were waiting for. She grew restless and could tell that her parents were restless as well. While the time on the ship had been long and wearisome, at least they were always moving this way. One had only to go out on the deck and look at the passing water to feel the progress. There was no progress now.

Late in the afternoon, Elsa slipped outside. She walked around to the back of the Registry Room and sat on the ground with her back against the wall of the building.

The gravel sloped down from her seat to the lapping water. The water here was gray, just like the sky. Even the buildings of New Jersey across the water took on the color of the gloomy afternoon.

People passed by where she sat but didn't seem to notice her. She knew she wasn't an interesting child to look at.

Elsa's expectations for this journey had been smaller than the others'. She sometimes enjoyed letting her dreams carry her away, as she had last night before falling asleep. Usually she forced herself not to. It was too painful to hope for things that never came about. Would their lives really be better in New York? Was this all worth it? It had terrified her to leave behind everything she knew except her family. Yet she watched it all with wonder. It was too strange to even feel real.

"I am surprised I found you out here."

Startled by the voice, Elsa looked up smiling at her sister. Sonja slid down the wall to sit beside her.

"You found a good spot. Look." Sonja pointed across the bay. Elsa brought her head close to her sister's arm, as if there were something in particular to see on the adjacent shore.

"What do you want when you are older?" Sonja asked.

"*Ich weiss nicht.*" Elsa realized that Sonja had been pointing at their future.

"Do you think about what you will become in America?"

Elsa closed her eyes. There was a gentle breeze coming in from the water. It felt refreshing against her eyelids.

She had thought about it. She'd been thinking about it just then. But she didn't know how to put her thoughts into words.

"I think about it all the time," Sonja said. "I will have a little house in the country, with a green lawn and some trees."

Elsa smiled at the image. The thought of warm green lawns was so enticing. It had been a long time since she had sat on grass. She breathed deeply, wishing she could smell freshly cut grass, but only the scents of the sea filled her nostrils.

"My house will be in a town," said Elsa. "Not like Hamburg. A smaller town like where *Oma* and *Opa* have the farm." She paused.

"I want some children."

"How many?"

"Five or six."

"That's a lot."

Elsa frowned. "I suppose I will need a husband, too."

Her sister laughed. "Yes, Elsa, I think you will need a husband. Pick a nice one who will help you with your five or six children."

"How many children do you want?" asked Elsa.

"Two would be enough."

"What sort of husband do you want?"

"One with a house in the country."

They burst out laughing, and neither could stop for a while. It felt good to laugh.

After a few minutes, Sonja said, "I know it will happen."

"How?"

"We have always been taught that God is looking out for our best interests. You do believe that, right?"

Elsa nodded.

"And that is why he wants to give me my house in the country."

Elsa said nothing. Sonja's logic didn't make sense to her, but she assumed her older sister was right. She always assumed this.

Sonja's dreams had always been large and grand. She had shared them with Elsa many times, both on the ship and before they left Germany. Elsa's dreams were smaller. She had always expected to accomplish a little less than her sister.

She didn't mind this. In fact, she eagerly embraced the prospect of following in her sister's shadow. It felt more comfortable than to think of forging ahead in the world alone. Sonja had taught her to dream. She expected Sonja would also teach her to achieve. She wouldn't mind following in her sister's path to her own, less impressive destiny.

Elsa glanced toward her sister, then back toward the gray water. Perhaps her dreams were less impressive than her sister's, but she was more comfortable with her own dreams. Sonja was counting on too much—the will of God and the luck of a future man with means. Elsa wanted dreams she could work for and bring about herself.

What would *really* happen to them once they got into the city? They would be just as poor, and now also hampered by unfamiliar culture and language. Even the smallest dreams would be hard-won.

"We should go back inside," said Sonja. "Mother will be preparing dinner soon."

Elsa doubted much preparation was needed for the

inevitable canned meat and salt crackers. But she was hungry and had grown accustomed to the meal.

Together they walked through the registry room toward their bunks in the hospital dormitory. Sonja took Elsa's hand as they pushed through the throng. People were packed so tightly together that one could hardly move, yet it was a lonely place.

As they neared their two bunks, Elsa thought she heard animated voices. Soon she realized with surprise that they were speaking German. Two officials stood with her father.

Sonja grabbed her arm. "*Warte mal.*"

The sisters slipped behind the next set of bunks and watched.

"The boy has a fever." It was their father's voice. "He needs a doctor. Without help he may die."

"What is one baby to me?" said the official in poor German. "I would rather he die here than go and infect Americans."

The officials weren't taller than their father, but held their heads in a way that suggested they knew they were in control. It seemed to Elsa that only one of the two understood German.

"He is not contagious," their father argued. "I am not sick. My wife and daughters are not sick. You are not sick. Just bring a doctor, *please*. I will give you anything to let us into the city."

The man translated this last comment to his associate, who grinned maliciously.

"What could you give us?" asked the one in German. "Your daughters?"

The other man said something in English, and they both laughed loudly. Elsa was almost glad she didn't understand.

They left, walking right past Elsa and Sonja, the non-German speaker glancing indifferently at the sisters.

Despite the ambivalence of the Ellis Island officials, a doctor finally came to see the baby later that day. His fever was rising; Nina had to force him to eat. The doctor left without a word. He obviously couldn't speak German.

Days continued to pass, one by one, each more tedious than the one before.

Elsa could hardly stand the wait. She wished her father would *do* something, but he had never been that kind of man. This journey had been the only ambitious thing he'd ever done.

Where was he now? Hopefully he was working to get them released from this place, but she doubted it.

Elsa sat down next to her mother on the lower bunk. The baby was mercifully asleep in her arms, spared for now from his coughing fits.

"Mother, why did we come to America?" she asked.

Nina looked at her daughter with surprise. Elsa immediately bit her lip. She was not supposed to ask that kind of a question. Fortunately, her mother didn't seem in a mood to reprimand her.

"There are opportunities in this country that we would not have had in Germany."

"Father's uncle is waiting for us. Is that right?"

"Perhaps. Your father wrote to him, but we left before receiving a reply."

"Will Father find better work here?"

"We hope so."

Elsa didn't expect to be told anything more. But after a short sigh, her mother continued, speaking more freely than Elsa was accustomed to.

"I know that our little house in Germany seems better now than what we came to, but life was hard for us there. We tried to protect you and Sonja from knowing that. Neither your father nor I had any inheritance. Your father did well enough with his cart shop, but what could you and Sonja hope for from that? You would have had to marry, and that is not always certain."

"I will learn to speak English," Elsa said. "When we go to

school in America I will study so hard. I will learn to read and write, then I will learn a trade."

Her mother smiled. "I hope we can give you that opportunity. All of us will have to work very hard."

"I like to work."

"Yes, you are a good worker when you feel like it. You need to learn to work just as hard when you do not feel like it."

Elsa watched her mother's eyes look out across the dormitory beds, then back at her.

"You are growing up, *mein liebchen*," she said. "I can see that you will look a lot like me when you are older. You will be strong but not pretty. Sonja will have an easier time marrying than you will."

Elsa had tried to imagine herself growing up beautiful even though with each year the mirror made another destiny ever more clear to her. Her mother had evidently decided she was old enough to face the truth.

"But you married Father," Elsa said.

"I was fortunate. What your father wanted from a wife, I was able to give. I have further been fortunate that I have a husband who is not cruel to me and who does not drink or cheat. The simple life with my children has been enough for me."

Elsa listened with surprise. This was the most candidly her mother had ever spoken about her own marriage.

"Would that be enough for you?"

Elsa didn't answer. Both remained silent for a long time. Finally Elsa voiced the silent question that had been on both of their minds for months.

"Why did we not come to America until Anton was born?"

Her mother took a long, drawn breath. "I do not know."

Elsa knew. Her resentment toward her father grew. He hadn't wanted this opportunity for his daughters. If he had, they would have made the journey years ago. He'd only wanted it for his son. Had he ever even wanted his girls to begin with?

"Pray for your brother, Elsa. He cannot die. You remember how sick I got when he was born. Because of that I can bear no more children. For that reason, we all need Anton to live."

With a start and a cough, the baby woke up.

Elsa understood her mother more clearly than if she had answered her pointed question. Tobias Schuller had his son after all these years. This had sparked the impulsive journey to the *land of opportunity*. If Anton were to die now, there was no telling how her father would respond.


Elsa knew exactly when Anton died.

She didn't need to hear his breathing stop, to hear her mother begin to weep, or even to see him go limp in her arms. She would never forget the keen wave of death in that moment.

They were swaying on the water again. The tall buildings grew larger as their barge approached the Battery. After more than a week on Ellis Island, they were finally allowed to enter the city.

It was too late.

Elsa rose from her seat and walked a short distance away. She didn't want to hear her parents' cries. She had grown to love her brother in his short life—how could she help but love him? Yet she also had so much cause to resent him. So while she was sad for his death, she didn't cry.

Anton's death would affect them all. The loss of a loved one hurt, but this loss would run deeper. With Anton dead, her father no longer cared about America. Elsa was only just beginning to comprehend how her brother had been the only glue keeping the family from descending into chaos.

## CHAPTER THREE
# A NEW CAREER

New York was terrifying. Everything seemed strange, loud and ruthless. Cold towers loomed in the distance, higher than Elsa ever dreamed buildings could rise.

Tenement owners greeted the barge at the Battery, loudly promising cheap and beautiful apartments. Tobias silently led his family through the gauntlet of salesmen. Elsa barely noticed the transaction that coldly and efficiently removed the baby's body from their care. There was no time to grieve or even to say good-bye.

Someone directed the family to Avenue B. That street, they had heard, was the center of Little Germany and very close to the address they had for Tobias's Uncle.

They walked east with their luggage, around the bottom of Manhattan Island, under the Brooklyn Bridge and the towering construction site that would become the Manhattan Bridge. Everything that surrounded them was moving at an alarming pace. Elsa smelled unknown foods and heard the sounds of unfamiliar industry all around her. The people looked strange. Every block or so, she transferred her suitcase from one hand to the other, but it barely seemed to help. She was exhausted when they reached the Lower East Side.

Expecting to find a supportive neighborhood of German speakers, they were in for a harsh awakening. No German shops lined the streets. No trace of their language could be heard. Elsa recognized English and Yiddish, but there were other, surprising-sounding languages. At the address where Tobias expected to find his uncle, a gruff Jewish woman tried to send them away. He showed her a letter with Hans Schuller's name and address. She shook her head at the name, but directed them to St. Mark's Lutheran Church on 6th Street.

It was there that they finally met a German—Pastor Reus—and learned of the sad state of *Kleindeutschland*. Elsa collapsed into the seat offered to her at the rectory, dropping her load.

Pastor Reus explained that while there were still a number of vibrant, German-speaking blocks in the neighborhood, Germans had been rapidly leaving the area, moving across the river to Brooklyn or uptown to Yorkville. With great sadness, the minister told them about the disaster that had occurred the previous year, when over a thousand German Americans, mostly parishioners at St. Mark's, died in a fire on the *General Slocum* steamboat on their way to a parish picnic on Long Island. In the year since the tragedy, hundreds of the surviving Germans had left the neighborhood. Their apartments were being filled by new immigrants, mostly from Eastern Europe, Italy, and Ireland.

Pastor Reus remembered Hans Schuller and thought he had moved to Brooklyn about four years ago. Tobias thanked the pastor and told him they would forge on, but Pastor Reus encouraged them to stay in the neighborhood. Apartments were cheaper here, and work was supposedly plentiful. He accompanied them to the office of a local landowner, Mr. Andretti, and introduced them to the Italian in English, then returned to his church.

Andretti led the way to his tenement building on 3rd Street, between First and Second Avenues. The fourth-floor apartment had two rooms, and there was a working toilet off the hall, to be shared with the other three apartments on that floor. The landlord communicated that their rent would be twelve dollars a month. Elsa didn't know how to judge the value of this sum, and she could tell her father didn't, either. But they had few options. The day was growing late, and the air felt like rain. They needed a place to stay. Tobias agreed to take the apartment.

All they had were deutsche mark coins, but Andretti was kind enough to accept their money for the first month's rent, and to calculate the exchange rate. What he took was almost half the money the Schullers had left from their trip. Elsa watched the transaction, assuming they were being cheated. But her father didn't argue with the landlord. He didn't know the words to question, even if he had known the true value of deutsche marks when converted to dollars.

The landlord shut the door, leaving the four of them standing in their empty apartment. The walls were covered in cracked and yellowed wallpaper.

"*Na ja. Es ist gut,*" said Nina with conviction, dropping her suitcase onto the warped floor boards.

In the morning Tobias, Sonja, and Elsa went looking for work.

The fall air was cool and filled with unfamiliar smells. Elsa's senses were overwhelmed as she followed her father through the strange streets to the place Pastor Reus had told them to go to look for work.

Hopkins & Co. served as the employment hub of the Lower East Side. Ignorant immigrants stood in wait outside the office, trying to look impressive. Only a few factory bosses came that day. From the scores of hopeful workers, only a few were chosen. With new ships arriving every day, the factories were well staffed. Elsa and the other two stood in confusion, not understanding how the process worked and unable to ask.

Elsa didn't pay much attention to the proceedings. Even when a boss walked down the line examining everyone, she didn't expect anyone to notice her.

A strong hand grabbed her arm. She jumped in fear. A strange man lifted her chin and gazed into her eyes. Then he turned and walked away, motioning for her to follow.

She held back, looking up at her father for help, but he pushed her forward, waving her after the man. She had no choice but to go. He walked into the office and filled out the necessary paperwork with Hopkins, then left the employment office, heading north at a quick pace. Elsa followed, sometimes forced to run in order to keep up with his long strides. The man was very tall, and though his height made him appear to be thin, he was a big man. There was a solemn sternness about him. He never smiled, but neither did he seem cruel.

Elsa stared at everything she passed and tried to keep a count of the blocks.

The factory wasn't far, for Hopkins had placed his office strategically. Elsa gazed at the ten-story monstrosity before her and cringed. She wished she could read the sign, so that she could tell what new trade she was about to learn. The man was already through the door. She hurried in after him.

Inside the building, they entered an elevator. What a strange and frightening contraption! She jumped and clutched the railing as it lurched upward. Floors passed quickly against the iron grating.

Once they stepped onto the open eighth floor, it took Elsa a few moments to understand that this was a clothing factory. The strange machines that twisted back and forth at the hands of the workers didn't look like any sewing mechanisms she had seen. But the cutting and stitching tables solved the mystery for her.

She smiled. She already knew how to sew. This was the perfect new career. Most importantly, she *had* a job. Her father didn't even have a job yet. She felt proud and mature.

It was warm in the large room, despite the cool morning outside, and the fact that all the windows that broke the concrete walls were flung open. The bustle of machines and the women who operated them warmed the place up and kicked dust and cotton puffs into the air. The wood floor was strewn with scraps and thread.

She followed the boss to a loom on the other side of the large open room. It was the only machine with a single worker. He said something unintelligible and pointed to her designated spot.

The girl at the loom looked up and smiled cheerfully at her as the boss walked away.

"Hi," she said, immediately putting Elsa at ease. It was the first kind gesture she had received from an American.

Elsa had never seen anyone like her before. She didn't look like people in Germany, or like those she had seen in America thus far. Her skin was dark, and her hair was thick and black. She was the only person of her race in the factory.

The girl asked Elsa something.

"*Deutschland,*" she said, not knowing how else to communicate with the American girl.

"*Deutschland?*"

"*Deutschland. Europa,*" Elsa repeated, shaking her head. "America."

The girl laughed. Tapping herself, she said, "Beth." Then more slowly, "I'm called Beth."

Elsa finally understood and identified herself the same way.

Beth began to show Elsa how to work the loom. The process was complicated, and Elsa was soon confused. But Beth was a good teacher. She spoke constantly as she showed Elsa the job. Though Elsa couldn't understand, she associated the words Beth used with the motions she made. Thus, the first English words she learned were "thread," "weave," "spindle," and "loom." It turned out she wouldn't be sewing after all.

Elsa liked Beth. She was pretty and seemed confident. Her face shone with warmth. She had a small frame. Elsa sensed that Beth was older than her, even though they were about the same size.

Alone as she was, behind a barrier of language, now that she had a friend, Elsa began to feel excited about America.

Leaving the factory that night, Elsa felt she might be able to succeed in this land. Her back ached and her fingers stung from ten hours on the loom, but she had a new skill and had already learned a few words of English.

She walked back toward Hopkins & Co. by the light of the street lamps on the Avenue, wondering whether she would be able to find her way home. Her family hadn't known where her job would be, or when to come look for her. It was only her second day in the city, and nothing was familiar.

But she no longer felt like a child. She felt mighty, thinking about the wonderful person she had become. She was a screw in the vast machine of clothes-making. Beth had shown her, pointing to other parts of the factory, and even sometimes to their own garments, how the cloth they spun was cut and sewn into ladies' blouses there in the same factory. She tried to imagine the ladies who would wear clothes made from the very cloth she had spun today. Her job was a simple step in the process, but she would perform it with joy.

The streets teemed with activity and life. Workers like her made their way home, while others looked to be preparing to go to work at night. The tenements glowed with the light of family dinner tables. Beyond, to the west and to the south, tall buildings towered above the tenements, no longer seeming as ominous as when she'd seen them yesterday. Many were still rising, reaching ever higher into the sky with construction crews buzzing like ants on the top floors even at this late hour.

Perhaps this was indeed the land of progress, industry and wealth, as her father had told them so many times on the ship. Elsa began to understand the draw—why so many had left satisfactory lives in Europe to be a part of it. Surely some great future awaited her, too. Once she learned the language and could go back to school to learn to read and write, she would be able to make a fine woman of herself. Today had been the first step.

She found her way home without difficulty and marched proudly upstairs, thinking of the sixty cents she had earned.

The apartment was beginning to look like a home. Nina had purchased two beds, bedding and basic cookware. After also buying a few days' worth of food, they had hardly any money left.

The mood upstairs was glum. Neither Tobias nor Sonja had been as successful as Elsa. They had left Hopkins & Co. at noon to return home. After the few tasks of putting the flat in order, they'd had nothing left to do but brood on their loss.

But Elsa felt proud. If only for today, she was supporting the family. Her sixty cents a day would pay for rent and buy food. It would allow them to survive. Maybe, though her father had lost his son, he would be proud of his daughter who worked like a man. She hoped so.

Yet as the days turned into weeks, Elsa could feel her father distancing himself from her, as well as from her mother and Sonja. Elsa knew how hard he'd taken Anton's death. It was hard on her mother as well. But Nina coped through her love for her daughters, while Tobias silently pushed his family away.

Elsa remained the only worker in the family for almost a week before Sonja was hired by a cannery. It was another week before Tobias finally got a job at the construction site for the new Manhattan Bridge. Elsa tried to understand how demoralizing those early days were for her father . . . not only to have his son die but also to watch his daughters go off to work while he sat idle.

Tobias's spirits seemed to improve during his first weeks of work, but soon he became depressed and distant again. He complained that the work was harder than any he'd done before, that he wasn't built for the strain of construction labor.

The rains had started, and soon the snows would come. He came home with hands chafed from grasping wet cables hour after hour, day after day.

As winter cast its darkness over New York, so too, did Tobias pull a cloud of darkness over his family. Elsa grew to wish for some sign of emotion in her father, even anger. Nothing was worse than to be treated as if she weren't there.

The combination of Tobias's, Sonja's and Elsa's wages equaled almost seventy dollars a month. They calculated that after rent, food, clothes and other expenses, they could save about twenty dollars a month. This sum in their minds quickly grew into the dream of one day buying their own home.

Saving money, however, proved difficult. By the second month, they were already in Andretti's debt. By the time the debt was cleared, it was winter. Food was more expensive in winter, and they needed warmer coats. Tobias needed costly leather gloves to survive his work out in the elements.

Then they discovered how badly they needed coal. They hadn't budgeted for coal. During the winters in Germany, wood was plentiful. In recent years Elsa had accompanied her father as they took their cart to the forest to gather wood for the fire. The thought of buying things to burn seemed absurd to her. Tobias clearly felt the same way, for he resisted purchasing it as long as he could. But try as Elsa might not to complain, the cold meals were tedious, and it became unbearable to pass a night in their flat without a fire. In the end, it was her mother who went out to buy coal and the first warming fire in their tenement apartment was burning when Tobias came home from work that evening.

By the time spring came, they had hardly saved a penny.

# CHAPTER FOUR
# SHATTERED HOPES

There was a particular evening late in March when Elsa finally felt that winter was over. Standing outside the factory, she glimpsed a hint of light still shining in the sky. How she looked forward to spring.

Sonja's job at the cannery was farther from the apartment than hers. Elsa waited each night in front of the clothing factory to walk home with her sister. During the first few months, she always thought Sonja looked exhausted when she trudged into view. Elsa doubted her sister's work was harder than her own. It was the loneliness of the career, not the difficulty of the work that bowed Sonja's back. But today, when she saw Sonja coming, Elsa noticed that her posture had changed. She had developed an attitude of complacent endurance.

"Do you know if we have saved any money yet?" Elsa asked as she fell into stride beside her sister.

"Why does it matter?"

"I thought . . . now that Mother is working too, perhaps Father will let us go to school."

Their mother had begun to sew at a clothier's shop run by a German family out of a nearby tenement. She only worked a few days per week, when a large order came in.

"Give up your dream of school," said Sonja. "It will only make you unhappy."

"You did not used to think that way."

"Things have changed. Give up your fantasy of school. It is all we can do just to survive."

"Remember all those things we talked about on the ship? All those dreams we had?"

"America is not what I thought it would be. You need to learn that, too."

Her words crushed Elsa. She said nothing else for the remainder of the walk, but occasionally looked over at her sister's face. Who was this girl who only a few months ago had dreamed of the little house in the country? Had she really lost hope in America so quickly?

Elsa felt betrayed. Sonja was the one who was supposed to forge the way for them both. Elsa knew she wouldn't have the courage to go and ask her father about school alone.

Elsa cried silently that night, turned away from Sonja on the small bed they shared. She arrived at work the next morning weary and sad.

"What's wrong?" asked Beth.

Elsa explained her dilemma in the simple, halting English Beth had taught her.

Beth listened as Elsa related her problem, her hands continuing the rapid motion of weaving. When they spoke they seldom looked at each other. The foreman made frequent passes through the rows of looms to make sure the children remained focused.

While Elsa thought the factory boss looked like a good man, the foreman frightened her. He had a bushy beard and sinister eyes. His lips were always curled in a crafty smile. He would come up quietly behind the girls and look over their shoulders to inspect their work. Sometimes he got so close Elsa could feel his breath on her neck.

After his pass by their loom, Beth inclined her head slightly toward Elsa.

"I went to school for a few years."

Elsa glanced at her friend in shock. "You never told me that."

"You never asked." Beth smiled. "I didn't need to work until my father died. Since then, my mother has helped me continue learning. She could teach you to read and write."

Elsa was ecstatic. All through the winter Elsa had assured Beth she would be leaving the factory soon to begin school. Now she found she had a brilliant woman working beside her all along. As soon as the thought came to her, Elsa realized how much Beth had already taught her. That she could already speak some English was thanks entirely to Beth's instruction.

"We have a Bible and a hymnal," Beth continued. Elsa had no idea what a hymnal was, but assumed it was a very special sort of book. "I learned to read from them. If you come to my apartment after work, Mama can teach you. I already asked her."

"You did?"

Beth smiled again.

Elsa's heart pounded. How grand it would be to understand the signs she saw everywhere. But her parents would be furious if she didn't come straight home after work.

"I want to. But I am afraid."

Beth nodded. "I know. But you know you need to do this. If you don't learn, then you may be working in this factory for the rest of your life. What is the worst that could happen if you come?"

"I will get beaten."

"Would that be worth learning to read and write?"

"Yes." Elsa's answer came without hesitation.

"Then come. Come with me tonight, before your parents have the chance to object. Mama works closer to home than I, so she will already be there when we arrive."

Elsa's fingers shook with excitement. The threads wouldn't obey her touch, and she felt like the foreman's eyes were always looking her way.

The mid-morning sun came in through the high windows,

through the grated shadow of Beth and Elsa's loom, to light the dust that hovered in the air. Elsa tried to focus by watching the rhythmic movement of the shadow.

She was afraid to go with Beth but this might be her only chance to get the knowledge she craved. It seemed like the day would never end. When their shift was finally over, they waited together until Sonja came into sight.

She stopped and stared suspiciously, first at Elsa, then at Beth. Suddenly, for the first time in her life, Elsa needed to assert her will. Her heartbeat quickened, and she bit down on her lower lip. She glanced at Beth, but her friend couldn't help her. This was her task.

As she hesitated, Sonja spoke first.

*"Komm' jetzt.Wir gehen nach Hause."*

"I am going with Beth tonight." Elsa was relieved to finally get the words out.

"What?"

"Her mother is going to teach me to read."

"You cannot do that. Mother will beat you."

"I must go with Beth."

"I will not have this." Sonja looked angry. "She will beat me, too, if I do not bring you with me."

"Tell them I was gone before you arrived."

"You arrogant girl! I will *make* you go home with me."

She reached for Elsa's arm.

"Come with us, Sonja."

Sonja froze. She didn't know much English, but she understood this simple phrase of Beth's. She looked at Beth, then back at Elsa. Elsa thought she saw a flicker of hope in Sonja's eyes. Quickly, her eyes dropped.

"Go on. I will not stop you."

She trudged away. Elsa watched her leave, wondering how Sonja could have so quickly given up her dreams.

She turned and hurried after Beth.

Beth lived in the opposite direction from the factory, west, near Sheridan Square. It was a shorter walk than her own daily trek, but Elsa knew it would be a long walk home later for her beating.

Elsa thought Beth's tenement building looked much nicer than her own family's, both inside and out. Beth explained that originally this was supposed to be one of the *worst* neighborhoods in the city. That was why the city council designated it for black families. But the residents had built it up over the years, so now it rivaled nicer neighborhoods. Unfortunately, it now looked like an attractive place to live, and those who had done the work of improving their neighborhood were being pushed out by white people.

Elsa sensed the cohesiveness of the neighborhood. It felt different from Andretti's, where the residents would never think to improve the building themselves.

As soon as the girls entered, Beth's mother bounded forward from the back of the flat.

"Oh, oh, I'm so glad." She clapped her hands, and then hugged her guest.

Elsa wasn't used to being hugged—she would have pulled away but the woman's embrace was swift and enveloping.

"I'm Josephine. Now you sit down right there so we can get started. The sooner we send you home the better it will be."

She directed Elsa toward a chair at a small table. Josephine pulled up another chair beside her. Beth sat on the floor.

It was a small room, made to seem smaller by all the pictures on the walls and little keepsakes on counters and shelves. One or two pictures might have been of family, and there were several images of Jesus. But most of the pictures looked like they had been cut out of a magazine or catalogue only because they were pretty. It gave the room lighthearted warmth that put Elsa at ease.

She couldn't understand how Beth's mother had seemed to know she was coming. She hadn't told Beth her dilemma until that morning. It dawned on her how much she had already revealed of her family's situation to her friend.

Josephine laid a Bible open in front of Elsa. She set a piece of paper beside it. On the paper she wrote the vowels and made Elsa say them, then showed her where the letters fit within the titles of the Bible books. They started with the prophets: *AMOS, EZEKIEL, ISAIAH,* and *OBADIAH* were the first Bible books Elsa learned to recognize. She remembered hearing about Isaiah in church but hadn't heard of the other ones.

"We don't have a Bible book that starts with the last vowel," Josephine explained. "But there is a very important place in the Bible that starts with the letter *U*. It was called *UR*." She wrote it on the page, using, as she had thus far, only capital letters. "There was a man who lived there named *ABRAHAM*."

As she wrote the new name, Elsa excitedly pointed back at *AMOS*.

"Yes," Josephine said. "And look. Abraham has the letter *A* in his name three times."

With that, she began to explain how the letters connected with one another in the words.

By the time Elsa left, her head was full of stories: Abraham's journey to a new land, the prophets and their adventures, and many more. She promised to come back every day after work.

It was very late when she returned to her tenement. The building was dark. She was exhausted and hungry after her long walk but didn't expect any dinner. Josephine had offered her food, but she had been taught not to accept charity.

The apartment was quiet when she entered. Her father slept, and Sonja pretended to sleep. But Nina was waiting up for her.

Elsa endured the belt in silence. It didn't anger her. She had been rebellious and deserved it; it was her mother's right to punish her. What angered her was that her father didn't even seem to notice her absence. Her mother cared—and was worried. That was why she punished her.

Elsa's heart went out to her mother as she took her whipping. How hard it would be to feel she was losing control over her life after working so hard for a stable family. Elsa was just beginning to work toward her own dreams.

She stumbled into bed, exhausted and in pain, but happy. The throbbing of her back paled in comparison with the thrill of her new knowledge and the hope of new opportunities.

Once their mother was in bed in the second room, Sonja pulled out a piece of bread she had hidden under the blanket and handed it to Elsa. She accepted it gratefully. After biting off each piece, she held it in her mouth to soften it so her mother wouldn't hear her chewing. It was enough to sustain her into the next day.

The next two nights progressed exactly the same way. Elsa came home late, endured a whipping, and supped on whatever morsel Sonja had managed to hide for her. On the fourth night the whippings ceased. By the next week, a cold meal began to appear for her, and she knew she had succeeded.


Nina was beginning to forget Germany.

It was sad, for she had loved her homeland and had little to love about America. Yet it was a necessary thing, because there was no going back. This was home now, whether it felt like it or not.

They had been here almost a year. Even though the German population of the Lower East Side had shrunk considerably, they'd managed to find enough German-speaking families to feel as if they had a community. Nina still couldn't speak English. She had little opportunity even to *hear* English. Her limited work was in a German family's home. She did all her shopping at the German grocery, the German baker or the German butcher. Yet even with these signs of familiarity, she felt the slow loss of traditions and customs that her family had treasured for centuries. Would her daughters ever have a chance to know them?

What would happen at Sonja's wedding... and then Elsa's ... if they were lucky enough to marry? Would they marry German men who respected their traditions? Even if they did, would they remember enough to teach their own children the ways of their homeland?

Nina hadn't worked today. She sat in the large room of their apartment, mending her husband's socks. This room served as kitchen, living room, workspace, and bedroom for the girls. She and Tobias had a small, separate bedroom. The walls were covered in faded green paper, which cracked at several places near the ceiling. Against the outside wall, a faint, yellowing streak ran down from the upper crack, where a trace of moisture oozed through.

She never had any second thoughts about marrying Tobias, despite his shortcomings. A woman like her needed to marry. They had both been the younger children of farming families, with no inheritance and no skills other than farming. Tobias had managed reasonably well, learning to work with wood and metal. Once his oldest brother could no longer afford to keep him on at the farm, he had moved to the city and opened a cart-making trade. It was a better choice than to join the army as the two middle brothers had done.

Nina was only vaguely aware of the politics that had sparked a population boom in the early years of the new German empire. But she felt the poverty that families like hers had suffered as a result.

It was her blessing that Tobias admired strength and resolve in a woman more than beauty. Though he didn't show her affection, she knew he respected her. She never had to worry about him being drawn away by another woman—he wasn't that type of man. Their marriage wasn't an arrangement of love as much as a partnership for survival.

It had been hard at first. What young woman doesn't dream that her marriage can live up to the youthful fantasy? Early in their marriage she would cry herself to sleep after Tobias mechanically had sex with her. Soon she accepted things as they were and knew she was lucky to have a husband who wasn't cruel to her. Yet even now, it hurt. She was acutely aware that he hadn't touched her sexually since her last pregnancy.

Sonja would be home soon, she thought. She usually waited for Sonja before she began to prepare dinner. Tobias would come about an hour later. Elsa . . . who could say when she would return?

All through the spring and summer, Elsa had gone to see her new friends after work. Nina did wish they could afford to send her and Sonja to a real school, but it was impossible. So Elsa did what she needed to do.

Nina didn't regret punishing her those first few days. Children weren't supposed to make decisions on their own, even if the decisions themselves were defensible. What might it lead to?

Discipline was the only way she knew to keep control of her family. She never considered that it might not work until that night when Elsa took her belt without a quiver. She had expected it and made her decision despite it. Nina had suddenly felt powerless. How could she stop her daughter from doing anything if she no longer feared punishment? Rebellion had never been Elsa's way. She had always been the model of obedience. Her act had been so out of character.

It angered Nina at first, but in time she realized how right her daughter was. Poor Elsa got nothing from her family—not education, not tradition, and lately, not even affection. Of course she would look elsewhere. If she didn't, it would destroy her.

Sonja's footfall sounded on the stairs outside the

apartment. Nina rose to begin preparations for dinner.

After it was ready they waited with the stew on the stove until the coals began to burn out, then they supped together in silence. Their eyes met several times during the meal, but neither dared to voice the thought on both their minds: something was amiss.

Tobias had worked late before. The bridge construction had ramped up as the worst of the summer heat subsided. Perhaps he had been forced to work another extended shift. But something *seemed* wrong that evening.

Only after Elsa returned did Nina really begin to worry. Tobias never went to the saloons to pass the evening with the other workers. He diligently saved every penny he earned. Could he have finally gone the way of whiskey, like so many others? If he had, would that be any worse than his silent, sober neglect?

She went to bed but couldn't sleep. After another hour she grew angry, then fearful.

With a sudden flash of dread, she rose and looked behind the sink for the jar where they kept their money. It was empty.

That was like him.

If he were to leave them, he would plan ahead and take what he wanted. Then he would leave without causing a scene, for he feared her more than their daughters did. It irked her that he had pulled it off without her ever suspecting his deceit.

Nina stumbled back to bed, shaking with despair. She didn't even know whether she would miss him. He had put food on the table, a roof over their heads, and given warmth to her bed—not much else. Yet after all these years she had grown used to being with him.

Now they were three women alone in a city eager to ruin them. Did the man feel no duty toward the girls he'd fathered? Was she, now that she was incapable of bearing a child, a useless weight to him?

She lay motionless, her eyes fixed on the dark ceiling. The

foundations of her world seemed to crumble around her. No longer could she count on the protection of a husband or her children's obedience.

Another winter would come soon. She would need a permanent job, but even then, their savings were gone. Should anything go wrong, they would be destroyed. They were unskilled, uneducated women. Only the youngest even spoke the language. Women like them weren't expected to live in this world without a man.

The very injustice of it spurred her to do *something*. She wouldn't let Tobias drive her to the depths of despair that he had reached. She would provide for her daughters as long as she lived—they needed her.

She laid awake the remainder of the night, wondering whether her daughters yet sensed their own peril.

# CHAPTER FIVE
# WINTER IN NEW YORK

By early December, it was clear it would be a cold winter in New York.

It frightened Elsa to see that now, of all times, her mother seemed weak. Often before, she'd wished her mother would soften. Not now.

It had been two months since Tobias left them. The day after, Nina went to stand in the lines at Hopkins & Co. Middle-aged women weren't the most common laborers, but Nina was clearly strong. She was hired by a warehouse near the shipyards. Her pay was far less than what Tobias had commanded, but more than what the girls earned. They weren't able to save much money on their three salaries, but they kept up on their rent and expenses.

The little things had to go wanting. Elsa knew her mother had been planning to buy a sewing machine, which while expensive at first, would have saved them money over the years when compared with buying their clothes ready-made. Now that they were all working, no one had the time or energy to sew clothes by hand.

Their meals became simpler, as groceries were reduced to the staples. Once the spices and treats they had in their kitchen were gone, they couldn't justify buying more. Salt became the last flavoring on their meals that winter.

Elsa continued her after-work studies with Josephine. In nine months, she felt she'd made incredible progress. Through the words of the Bible she'd quickly learned the name, sound, and symbol of each letter and how to combine them. Josephine had a story for each letter, making them easier to remember. Once Elsa was able to put letters together and decipher words, she wondered at their meanings. When she grew weary of deciphering the words herself, Josephine would read a fascinating story from the Bible while Elsa followed along with the text.

She remembered some of the stories from her younger days. Others she heard regularly at church. But when Josephine told a story, it took on new life. Elsa always asked questions. Her lessons were so captivating to her that Elsa often forgot she was learning.

The most rewarding moment for Elsa was when she began to realize she could read other things than the Bible. The signs she saw on street-posts and shop banners began to make sense. Even when she didn't know the words, she recognized the letters and knew how to say the words. Best of all, the few German shops left in their neighborhood used the same letters. How magical it felt when, for the first time, she read a shop's sign, pieced together the letters, and realized she was learning to read in German as well as in English.

Christmas passed without fanfare. Hearing the old German carols at St. Mark's and seeing the lighted tree made Elsa nostalgic. But Christmas was welcomed more for the two consecutive workdays off than for the celebration of tradition.

During the brief holiday, Elsa perceived that the weakness she'd seen in her mother stemmed from more than a heavy heart. Her breathing was labored and she began developing a cough. She slept far longer than usual. Yet the day after Christmas, she trudged back to the shipyards, determined to beat this latest affliction.

Elsa was afraid, and she saw the fear in Sonja's eyes as well. Elsa remembered the sound of this cough—it had killed their brother.

After an especially frigid day less than a week after Christmas, Nina's coughing hardly stopped all night. It reverberated through the tiny apartment. Elsa lay awake beside her sleepless sister. A heavy snow had begun to fall, quenching all noise from outside. By morning there were several inches on the ground.

"Please stay home," Elsa urged her mother in the morning.

"We will be ruined if I do not work."

So they all marched out into the dark morning, the snow still swirling in their faces. Nina headed east toward the river, while Sonja and Elsa walked northwest.

By the time Elsa reached the factory, her shoddy coat was soaked through with melted snow. The inside of the factory was muggy from all the evaporation off wet bodies. The closed windows were steamed over. Elsa took off her coat and laid it on the floor beside her workstation, hoping it would dry by the end of the day. Summer or winter, the work always made her hot and sweaty. The girls worked in only their blouses.

At the end of the day, Elsa told Beth she wouldn't be able to come for her reading lessons for a few days. Then she hurried past home in the direction of the shipyards. The snow had stopped but was slick and icy on the sidewalks. Wet pools crunched under her feet where the carriages had splashed mud up onto the snow. Her worn shoes were soon wet. None of them had been able to afford new boots or coats this winter. Soon she spotted her mother's figure, slow and hunched as she struggled through the snow. She stopped and heaved with the weight of a cough.

Elsa ran forward as best she could in the slick snow. Nina relaxed against her daughter's shoulder. Elsa felt more and more of her mother's weight against her as they neared home and ascended the tenement stairs. Sonja helped them over to the fire she had lit and replaced their wet coats with warm blankets. Elsa collapsed on the floor by the stove, exhausted as

Nina collapsed into a chair.

Though she sat by the fire well into the night, Nina's face remained ashen. Sonja had made a warm stew, but Nina could barely eat it. None of them slept much that night.

In the morning, Nina still couldn't eat and could barely stand. Still, she tried to dress herself for work. Elsa, with Sonja's help, forced her back into her bed.

"How can you lift cargo when you cannot even stand?" Elsa said.

"I must work. I will not leave you to starve like your father did."

"It will kill you."

Nina was too weak to resist for long. She collapsed back on her pillow as her coughing turned to tears.

"Oh, God, what will become of us?"

"I will go to talk to your boss," Elsa said. "I will tell him how sick you are. You have been good at this job. He will hold it for you."

"That does not happen," Nina said, even as her exhaustion overcame her will. She relaxed, staring blankly at the ceiling as her daughters prepared to leave. Sonja lit another fire to keep her warm.

Elsa hurried toward the shipyard. She tried to run, but the streets were too slick. Meanwhile, since Elsa's shirtwaist factory was on the way to Sonja's cannery, the elder sister promised to tell Elsa's boss why *she* would be late.

Elsa's haste had been unwarranted. She arrived at the docks before her mother's boss, waiting anxiously until he arrived. The big man looked down at her with scorn, thinking she had come for a job. Elsa surprised him by addressing him in near perfect English. She identified her mother.

"She is very sick. We would not let her come for fear it would kill her. Surely you heard her coughing."

"Yes. She sounded terrible."

"A few days of rest should be enough for her to get better.

Will you hold her job for her? I know she is a good worker."

"We will see."

Looking into his eyes, Elsa had little confidence.

She had a sudden vision of them becoming destitute. Her stomach clenched into a sickening knot. She tried to believe things would go back to normal after her mother recovered . . . if she recovered.

By the time Elsa arrived at the clothing factory, it was an hour past her assigned start time. She took off her coat and laid it on the floor, immediately falling into work alongside her partner. Taking long, slow breaths, she endeavored to regain her cool. Beth said nothing; pretending work progressed as usual, even though working the loom alone for an hour had yielded poor results.

The foreman wasn't fooled.

Elsa shuddered as she felt his breath behind her neck. She tried to keep her hands busy on the loom so he wouldn't be disappointed by her work. Surely even *he* would have sympathy for her family's plight. But he wasn't looking over her shoulder to check her work. He was looking down her blouse and noticing how rapidly she was growing up.

Elsa was confused by this. Though she felt her breasts developing—often painfully—she couldn't comprehend men's desires and stimulations. She'd felt that last year's blouse was growing too tight but they couldn't afford a new one now. While she knew her mother planned to buy her a brassiere in addition to a new blouse, Elsa's chest developed at a faster rate than their meager savings.

"Come into the office, girl," said the foreman.

Elsa sighed and stopped her work. Beth had a look of fear on her face, but Elsa wasn't afraid. She had been whipped once before at this factory. She had been whipped frequently by her mother. Pain was a trial, but she didn't fear it.

Alone in the office with the foreman, Elsa steeled herself for a beating.

"You were very late today," he said.

"Did my sister not come to explain?"

"Oh, she did." He picked up his switch. "But tardiness cannot be excused for any reason."

Elsa began to fear that she would get fired as well as beaten. She stood waiting as he came toward her, tapping the switch against his hand. She turned away from him, expecting the whip against her back.

Instead of the switch, she felt his bushy whiskers against her neck, then his hands cupping both her breasts. Horrified, she tried to twist away from him.

The foreman held her firm, pushing his waist against her and breathing heavily against her neck. He slipped one hand inside her blouse, while with the other tried to turn her face toward him for a kiss. She resisted, but that only seemed to make him more determined. His lips and tongue touched her ear, as his hand squeezed her breast inside her blouse. Elsa gagged.

The office door opened.

"Ernest, what the hell are you doing?" shouted the factory boss. The foreman released Elsa and turned toward his manager. He stood silently for a moment, without a trace of guilt, and then walked away. Elsa cowered against the wall, her arms clutched protectively across her chest.

"Get back to work, you hussy."


Elsa focused her mind and all her hours away from the factory on her mother. The excitement of learning English and the allure of the Bible stories had been temporarily forgotten. She even pushed aside thoughts of the horror at the factory, though the incident lingered, an undercurrent to everything else. She could not escape a confused feeling of shame.

Rest and protection from the winter elements were enough for Nina to improve. Pastor Reus had given them some medicine that slowed her cough, allowing her body to begin to heal itself.

After four days in bed, she returned to the shipyards, but she found no welcome at the warehouse. When Elsa and Sonja returned that night, she told them how her boss gruffly gave her four dollars and pushed her out the door. He had gone to Hopkins & Co. for her replacement the very morning of Elsa's visit. Nina assured them she would find work again quickly, but Elsa doubted it would be easy. Still, Elsa reminded herself that her mother might have died. That fear was gone now. Somehow, they would survive together. January was a slow time for hiring, and the cold and hungry of the city were especially desperate. Nina stood in the lines at Hopkins & Co. with a hundred others, all competing for a handful of jobs. Not even the German tailor where she had worked earlier that year needed her help now.

Nina's last four dollars had already been spent on coal and food; they would be relying on the girls' wages until Nina found work. They each earned sixty cents per day. After paying the rent to Andretti, and for their portion of gas and water, they would have a little more than three dollars left each week.

Three dollars to feed three people, provide coal for each day's fire, and replace their tattered clothing as winter grew worse. They decided to save their coal for the coldest nights, leaving their stove bare and eating their meals cold when they could endure it.

But every night was cold that year. A harsh wind battered the East Coast through the winter. The snows were frequent. Old people tried to remember the last winter of its kind.

They pulled the bed that had been Tobias's and Nina's from the second room up close to the stove and slept in it together for warmth. The stove only gave slight warmth when the coal was rationed. They took turns lying on the side of the bed closest to the fire. Outside the wind whistled in the darkness like a rabid beast, beating at the windows and sliding its fingers through every crack in the walls. Elsa dreamed of the cold as a living monster intent on devouring them.

Elsa's boots had sprung holes on the sides as the soles began to peel away from the leather. She could see her wet sock poking through. She stole a handful of thread off her loom and wrapped it tightly around the front sections of her boots. This protected her feet for a few days until the thread wore through. She made this same cheap repair twice more before finding some wire on the street. More durable than the thread, the wire lasted her the rest of the winter but hurt her feet until her calluses molded to the new surface.

Compared to the blistering cold outside, the warmth of her sweatshop labor offered a strange relief. Yet the factory had also come to disgust Elsa. Every time the foreman passed by she ignored him, hoping he would forget and not try something again. Yet the very sight of him or the sound of his voice made her want to vomit.

They went on because there was nothing else to do. Elsa and Sonja worked their long hours for the pittance on which they survived. Nina stood in the lines at Hopkins & Co. as more people arrived each day, while few were chosen.

As she grew accustomed to the new and meager reality of survival, Elsa's anxiety turned to anger. She blamed her father for everything, even the sickening experience with the factory foreman. If he'd supported them like he should have and let her go to school, that never would have happened.

Anger was easier to carry than fear or shame. Anger was easier to feel, an antidote to fear, and a mask for the shame she otherwise would have been unable to hide from her friends and family.

After her mother's illness, Elsa no longer went to study with Beth and Josephine. Hard as the late-night walk was in good weather, she couldn't think of doing it in the snow. Even when the weather improved for a day or two, she felt guilty about doing an enjoyable activity while her mother and sister suffered. That winter she only made the walk to Sheridan Square once a week, on Sundays after church at St. Mark's.

It took some time after her father left for Elsa to tell Beth and Josephine. Similarly, after her mother lost her job, she hadn't intended to tell them about her family's plight. They were just as poor, and she didn't want them to try to offer her charity. Worse still, she didn't want to feel pressured to accept when they offered to let her share their meals. How could she, when her mother and sister sat hungry at home? But Beth worked beside her every day, and Elsa wasn't good at concealing her emotions. Finally, one Sunday in early February, she told them that her mother had lost her job.

"You must not let yourself become bitter," said Josephine.

Elsa wasn't surprised that Josephine heard the anger in her tone. It was her anger that allowed her to talk about things without divulging everything. But the words themselves surprised her. She thought it was perfectly within her rights to be angry.

"Your father has given you many reasons to feel angry," Josephine continued. "It goes deeper than his abandonment. He should have let you go to school. He should have shown you love. His abandonment began long before he actually left. Now he has left you practically to support yourself. It is okay to feel angry for a while. But in time anger becomes bitterness, and bitterness can destroy a person. If you let it take hold of you, especially at your age, you may never be able to get rid of it. You must forgive him and focus on caring for your mother and sister. They need you so much now."

Elsa didn't want to forgive her father. She didn't want to forgive the foreman, either. She was still in too much pain.

Josephine must have sensed her thoughts. "When you refuse to forgive someone, you hang onto the things they did to you. Failing to forgive means wanting to hold onto the pain.

Why would you want that? Anger can lead to positive action. But bitterness internalizes the sin that someone else did until it becomes your sin, too."

Elsa didn't really understand. But she didn't want the pain to last. Maybe she would try to let it go.

"We will pray for you, Elsa. And you should pray, too. Pray for your father, and for anyone else who has wronged you. That is the most effective way to forgive."

Josephine opened the Bible that lay on their table. "Let's look at the place where Jesus taught his disciples how to pray. You probably say The Lord's Prayer in German every Sunday. I will teach you to read and write it in English, and then maybe you can teach Beth and me to say it in German."

She smiled warmly at Elsa, lifting the mood from their serious dialogue. Elsa slid closer to her, eager to learn. Her studies had become her favorite activity in her life—the one bright spot in an otherwise bleak and horrific winter.

Hunger had become their constant companion. They could only afford to eat what kept them alive—no more. For Elsa, the constancy of cold was only broken by the steamy discomfort of the sweatshop. Nina had it worse than her daughters, as she walked each morning in search of work, then sat alone each afternoon in the cold, lonely apartment. For Nina and Sonja, they had no time to relax, no opportunity to forget their struggles. For Elsa, her only respite was her weekly visit with Josephine and Beth.

A new fear haunted Elsa that winter. Although the foreman didn't touch her again, she always felt his eyes on her, as if he were waiting for his next opportunity to corner her alone. Several times when she saw him near the factory entrance at quitting time, she made Beth wait until Sonja arrived to walk home with her. It was still too cold and wet to walk to Beth's house on workdays.

In February, word circulated that anyone who had been sexually abused by the foreman Ernest should talk to Rachel at Aisle 16. Rachel was one of the few adult women working on their floor.

Elsa had never heard that phrase before. She didn't know enough about sexuality to know whether what he'd done to her constituted a violation to her virtue. She became very quiet at her loom after hearing the cryptic message.

Beth seemed to notice right away. When they were given a short break to eat lunch, she confronted Elsa. "What happened that morning the foreman took you into the office?"

Elsa burst into tears. All her feelings of shame rose to the surface.

"I thought so." Beth embraced her. "Will you talk to Rachel?"

"Should I?"

"Have you told anybody about it?"

"No."

"Not even your mother or sister?"

"I can't tell them." Elsa was mortified that Beth knew. How could she tell her mother and sister?

"Don't be embarrassed," said Beth, stroking Elsa's back. "You did nothing wrong."

Beth was right. Why did she still feel so ashamed?

"You should tell Rachel what happened," Beth said.

"I will get fired."

"Maybe *he* will, instead. It is worth the risk to keep him from hurting other girls like he hurt you."

Elsa lifted her head off Beth's shoulder and wiped her eyes. Did Beth realize that if she lost her job, she really would starve, along with her mother and her sister?

The lunch break was over. They walked back to the loom.

"We've been there, too, my mother and I," said Beth as her hands resumed work. "People like us are always a small step away from destitution. There are no laws to protect us, no well-meaning citizens looking out for our welfare. At least there's someone in the factory looking out for us girls now. I've been here four years, and I know you're not the first girl who's been molested."

Elsa didn't answer. She wished the whole thing could just be forgotten. Why did Beth have to stir it up?

"Tell your mother what happened. Ask her what you should do. Then you will know you didn't make the decision alone."

Beth could tell her mother everything, but Elsa had a different relationship with her mother and was from a different culture. She didn't think she could possibly tell her mother. Yet after a few days of pondering, Elsa decided she should. Even if her mother were angry with her, punished her, and blamed her for the incident, it would be better than keeping it inside. All winter, it had been festering inside her. It was close to turning into bitterness, like Josephine had told her it might.

Elsa had underestimated her mother.

The trials of the last six months had changed them both. Nina had grown to see her daughters more as women than children. Elsa was growing up faster than her mother could manage.

Elsa saw through her tears that her mother had swallowed her own.

"This was my worst fear for you and Sonja," her mother said. "I don't know how to protect you anymore from the evil of this world. But one thing you must not feel is shame. All the shame is on this man."

"What should I do?"

"Talk to the woman. Our security is a small price for the justice that may come. We must be willing to work for the change we want to see."

The next day, Elsa recounted the incident to Rachel at

Aisle 16. She was the third girl to come forward. Rachel assured her she would remain anonymous. Elsa doubted it; the head boss had been a witness.

Two weeks later, when the boss summoned her to the office, Elsa was sure she would get fired. At least she didn't fear being alone with him.

"I always try to run a fair factory," he began. His tone was gruff, but his attitude was strangely defensive. "I have no tolerance for shenanigans from my workers."

Elsa tilted her head. Josephine's lessons hadn't exposed her to any Irish slang words.

"I hold this factory to a high moral standard," he continued. "That I have employed your loom partner, a colored girl, for several years should be evidence of this factory being a fair and progressive place. We pay our girls just as much as our boys."

Elsa found this statement insincere, since the only men working in the factory were foremen. No boys worked there since girls would do the work for less.

"For that reason, I want to apologize for my foreman's behavior some time back. Ernest has been fired, and I assure you that his actions in no way reflect the Triangle Shirtwaist Company as a whole."

"Thank you," she said, relieved both that her job was safe and that she wouldn't see the horrible foreman again.

Yet even through her mix of emotions, Elsa recognized the boss's feigned morality. Whether or not the police had become involved, Rachel had stirred up enough of a scandal that firing the foreman had become the easiest course of action. Elsa assumed she was the only one of his victims that the boss personally knew of. He was only being kind to her now in an attempt to limit the damage.

"I can see that you are struggling this winter." He paused, unsure what he wanted to say. "I cannot increase your pay, but let me know if there is something I can do to help your family."

Elsa was stunned that he would ask such a generous question. If it was only in hopes she would stay quiet about the incident, she didn't care.

"My mother needs a job," she said quickly. "She has worked in a clothing factory before and will work hard."

"Hmm. We only employ a few older women. They are more expensive, you know."

Elsa was about to blurt out that her mother would work for a child's wage, but held her tongue. If he was in a generous mood today, why not push her luck?

"Let me see what I can do," he said.

Elsa went back to her loom. Hope fueled her labor for the rest of the day. Could her courage to come forward actually have saved their family?

As she was walking toward the door that night, the boss caught up to her.

"I can use your mother at the cutting table. She can start tomorrow. I'll pay her a dollar a day."

# CHAPTER SIX
# THE SHIRTWAIST STRIKE

*How far we've come,* thought Nina as she sipped from a cup of *tea,* of all things.

"This is the first time I have had a friend over for tea since . . . well, since Germany. Thank you, Rachel."

"No, thank you," Rachel said. "Our lives seldom give time for such things. But perhaps we can change that. Promise you will join me in the march on Sunday."

"I will. But I cannot allow my girls to join. They have more to lose than I do."

"I understand."

Nina enunciated slowly, sometimes pausing between words and phrases. Her English was mostly correct, if not comfortable. She had been learning to speak it from Elsa.

In the two years since Nina had started working at the Triangle Shirtwaist Factory, she and Rachel had become as good of friends as their hard working conditions allowed. In Nina, Rachel found an ally in her passion to make life better for the women who worked in New York City's factories. Elsa's experience with the foreman had shaken Nina and made her determined to do something about it. Rachel subsequently drafted her into the burgeoning workers' rights movement. Nina relished this chance to point her energy in a new direction.

In recent months, the movement had coalesced into an organized Women's Trade Union League. This coming

Sunday there would be a march from the Bowery to Broadway in support of the union.

"You have made this apartment quite the home," Rachel said, looking at all the decorations and small improvements Nina had added over the months.

Nina glanced around, too, then down at her teacup, which symbolized the changes as much as anything. These last two years had been better for them. Money was still tight, but they had managed to buy some proper dishes, a table cloth, and window shades, as well as a third bed so Elsa and Sonja no longer had to share. But what Rachel was pointing out were the little things that had gradually been collected. Each item alone seemed small, but when added together, they made this humble flat a reflection of their lives. During the early days, this had been a home of suffering. Their shared struggles had bonded them together and transformed it into a home of love. Lately it had finally become a home of joy.

Nina knew Rachel Shapiro lived alone in an apartment on Allen Street. That apartment had seen her promise as a young mother with a hard-working husband. Then suddenly it was the home of a childless widow after her husband and baby succumbed to the same epidemic of influenza. That had been seven years ago. Nina felt a connection with Rachel because of their shared suffering. They had each lost a husband and a child. Yet Nina still had two living children to work for. Rachel's apartment was now merely a place to lay her head. Her life and passions were away from her home.

"Where are your daughters tonight?" Rachel asked.

"Elsa is studying her reading with Beth's mother. She speaks perfect English but thinks there is still more for her to learn. I did not understand this at first, but I support her now. She is trying to make something better of her life. Is that not the very thing we are working toward? Elsa works for the same thing, in her own way."

Rachel nodded.

"I certainly would not speak English yet if not for Elsa."

"And your older daughter?"

Nina smiled. "Sonja is being courted."

"Indeed?"

"A young German man from the neighborhood has taken an interest in her. I am hoping there will be a wedding before the end of the year."

Will you be sad to lose her?"

"I will miss her, yes, but it is necessary. Sonja needs to marry. Factory work has been hard on her. She is frail and tender. Our struggles have nearly broken her spirit. We have been here for three and a half years now. It has made me stronger, and made Elsa stronger. But Sonja cannot keep on with this life. This man she has met can give her a better home. She will soon be nineteen. It is a good age for a girl to marry. Christof is German and a Christian. It would be a good match."

"I hope she finds happiness," said Rachel.

Nina sensed that Rachel shared her own thought: marriage hadn't given either of them happiness. Society held it up to women as an ideal—the goal and culmination of youth. It was the same here in America as it had been in Germany. For Rachel, marriage gave a few happy years followed by tragedy and loneliness. For Nina, the loneliness of having Tobias beside her gave way to the loneliness of having him gone without a trace.

It was this harsh reality that inspired Nina to fight for working women's rights. It made her angry. Poor women should have opportunities other than husbands.

"I should go," said Rachel. "It's late. The way they are working us now, I need my sleep."

"Yes. My daughters will be home soon. Sonja will surely have stories to tell."

\* \* \* \* \*

After church that Sunday, Nina made her daughters spend the day with their friends—Elsa with Josephine and Beth, and Sonja with Christof Steigenhöffer and his family. She joined Rachel and the others from the Women's Trade Union League at the Bowery.

Nina knew she was risking their recent security by involving herself in the women's union movement. They had managed to save a little money but couldn't afford for her to lose her job. She still had a responsibility to her daughters.

If Sonja really did marry Christof, she would feel bolder. Elsa could take care of herself; she had proven that. The best thing she could do for Elsa was to stay in this fight. If no one fought for women's rights, what chance would Elsa have to actually use the knowledge she had worked so hard to acquire?

Nina marched through the city that day with several thousand women of the garment industry, carrying banners in English and Yiddish. Their demands for better wages, shorter hours, and an end to abuse from the bosses were met with enthusiasm by the crowds that lined the streets. But the protest occurred on a Sunday. When Nina and the other women got to the factory the next morning, the bosses were unmoved. What the women did on their day off was up to them. The fact that they were all back at work on Monday proved to the bosses that the women's march to have been mere vanity.

Still, Nina felt elated after the march. Seldom had she had so much fun as when marching with all those women. Having only just begun this fight, she hadn't expected immediate success.

Rachel, though, was despondent. She told Nina they had made no progress at all. After the thrill of the march wore off, Nina also realized they would have to do more—risk more—to make any real progress. The next time the League met—the Sunday after the march—a fiery young woman named Clara Lemlich proposed a women's general strike. *That* would get the bosses' attention.

Shortly after Nina got home from the meeting, Christof and Gerd Steigenhöffer came to call at the Schullers' apartment. Christof formally requested permission to marry Sonja. Nina happily gave it. Gerd produced a bottle of beer he had brought in anticipation of Nina's answer. The five Germans commenced a spontaneous celebration for the upcoming union of their families.

The atmosphere at the Triangle Shirtwaist Factory had grown tense. In the months since the women's march, Clara Lemlich had been distributing fliers among the workers, calling for the general strike. Rachel advised Clara that she needed to start preparing the women to be out of work for a few weeks, maybe even months. Unless they were ready for this sacrifice, a strike would not succeed.

Less than half the women in the factory knew how to read, but the message of Clara's fliers was clear. It was all the women talked about. The pamphlets made the rounds in all the clothing factories. Though their source remained anonymous, the bosses had gotten their hands on the incendiary material. They cracked down, forcing the women and children to work faster for increased production. They lengthened the hours to eliminate leisure time. Heavy locks were installed on the iron doors, and the women were forced to remain inside for ten or eleven hours at a time. Even a bathroom break had to be approved by a foreman.

As hard labor grew even harder, some of the women became resentful toward the Women's Trade Union League and its leaders, Clara in particular. Without a belief that things could get better, they didn't appreciate the firebrands who made things worse. When the bosses began to secretly inquire as to the source of the pamphlets, several women were more than willing to give them Clara's name. Rachel was implicated as well. The foremen began watching both closely, waiting for an opportunity to incite an altercation.

Nina had continued to support the Women's Trade Union League and attended all the meetings, but her focus was on Sonja's upcoming nuptials. Less than a week before the wedding, she had no idea how quickly things were coming to a head.

After a day in which the women had been locked in the factory for twelve hours with barely enough food and water to sustain them, and with even the windows locked against escape attempts, Rachel convinced them to form a picket line to protest.

In the morning, the women gathered outside the factory but refused to go in. Clara worked at a nearby factory but had heard of the incident and joined the workers of the Triangle. She had written a new pamphlet for distribution. Among other things, it demanded nine-hour workdays, regulated breaks and proper ventilation in the factories. These fliers were given not only to the women but also to the bosses and foremen, and to any passers-by. Even those women who didn't support the movement stayed in the picket line, more afraid to cross their sisters than their bosses.

The enthusiasm was short-lived.

Suddenly a gang of hoodlums fell upon the women with switches and baseball bats, corralling them toward the factory entrance. The intimidation alone was enough to force obedience. Very few women were actually hit or whipped. Once inside, the foremen escorted the women to their places.

Clara, however, was singled out and dragged into the street by the hired thugs.

Nina instinctively rushed over to help. She yanked one of the hooligans off Clara before the police appeared to stop the fracas. All the other women were inside the factory or peering out from the doorway. Only Clara and Nina remained in the street.

The factory boss walked up. "Arrest these two for insurrection."

Clara was badly injured. The police commander sent her to the hospital, while Nina was taken to the police station.

For the women of the Triangle Shirtwaist Factory, another twelve-hour day without fresh air awaited them. The angry foremen were quick to punish any failure or perceived disobedience. Elsa had seen her mother's arrest but was forced into the factory. By the time she was finally released from duty the police headquarters had closed for the night. She couldn't get her mother out until the next morning.

Adrenaline alone powered both Nina and Elsa through those endless workdays and the long nights in the kitchen preparing for the wedding. Neither stopped to think how much it had taken out of them until they got home Sunday night after Sonja was married. Both of them went immediately to bed.

Elsa came down with an inevitable cold a day later. But there was still no time to rest. Work at the factory went on.

Several weeks after the wedding, the strike finally came. Nina knew she and Elsa would be able to endure it. If Sonja had still lived with them, she might not have had the courage to walk out on her job as winter approached. But as it was, she knew it was the right thing to do and was proud to have Elsa standing beside her.

The wedding guests had been generous, so despite what they had spent on preparations, Nina thought they had just enough money left to last the winter, if it came to that.

Twenty thousand women had walked out of their garment factory jobs. The strike lasted the entire winter. Despite the financial hardship it placed on many women, a spirit of camaraderie sustained them. Nina and Elsa took in two women who lost their apartments because of the strike. Rachel filled her once lonely apartment with as many as a half dozen refugees. When the strike ended in February, they knew they had won a major victory for women workers.

The workweek was shortened to fifty-two hours, pay was increased, and provisions were enacted to ensure equal treatment of union and non-union employees. More importantly, the women of New York City, and indeed, of all major US cities, felt the empowerment of having stood successfully against oppression. From that point on, other victories—such as the right to vote—seemed to be only a matter of time.

Despite the success of the strike, Clara Lemlich was permanently barred from New York City's garment industry. Her leadership had made her something of a celebrity, however, so she had the support to continue her work as a reformer and suffragist. Though they initially went back to the Triangle Factory after the strike ended, Nina and Rachel were advised by women of the union to look for other employment. The bosses were still angry about the money they had lost that winter, and hadn't forgotten who the strike instigators were. Rachel knew a number of clothiers in the Jewish community and was able to get Nina a job, as well as one for herself. Nina found it frustrating—having so recently learned English—to now hear nothing but Yiddish all day long. But a job was a job, and she was thankful to have one where she wouldn't be abused.

So once again Elsa was alone at the factory where she had spent almost every day of her American life. But things were very different. She was now sent home at a regular hour, and earned a dollar and ten cents a day.

The loom was gone. Due to the lowered hours and increased wages, the factory managers deemed it unprofitable to weave fabric as well as to assemble clothing in the same facility. Bolts of fabric now arrived daily from mills in Massachusetts. Elsa was assigned to a sewing machine on the tenth floor of the building. She knew how to sew, so she didn't mind. But it saddened her to be separated from Beth, who now worked at the finishing table on the ninth floor.

# CHAPTER SEVEN
# TRAGEDY AT THE TRIANGLE

As quitting time approached, Elsa looked forward to the evening with her mother and Pastor Reus. Thanks to the successful strike, work on Saturdays ended at four forty-five. It made a huge difference, leaving time for an enjoyable evening. The factory windows were open now. Elsa could sense the springtime air growing warmer each day.

With her increased leisure hours, Elsa continued to visit Josephine one or two nights per week, but it was more to see a friend than to learn reading. The truth was, Elsa had learned everything about the English language that Josephine could teach her. Josephine had realized it first and told her. Elsa had been slow to agree, but now she knew it was true. Still hungry to learn, Elsa had sought other ways. Pastor Reus had a good little library at the rectory. He lent her books in both English and German that she could use to push her reading skills and further her knowledge of both languages. Tonight's visit was to hear about some work in translation that the minister thought would suit Elsa. The type of opportunity she had been working so long for might finally have arrived.

The smell of the warm outside air was overcome by the smell of hot, overworked sewing machines, and the persistent smell of sweating bodies. This afternoon, the sewing machines seemed almost to be burning, so strong was the smell.

Elsa leaped from her seat. That smell wasn't the machines. Something really was burning.

"Fire!" The panicked cry came from across the room.

The entire top floor of the factory seemed to realize what was happening at the same moment. Shrieks of panic erupted as girls abandoned their work and ran for the exits.

Smoke filled the floor before anyone saw a flame. The fire had started one floor below. Soon orange tongues were lapping at the wooden floor, spreading fast as it caught paper patterns and dry fabric.

Elsa looked around her quickly. The elevator gate showed an empty shaft. A girl stood there, repeatedly pulling the call cord. The stairwell was on the other side of the floor. A dozen or more girls had already converged on the iron door, only to find it locked. The foreman was nowhere to be seen. Amid the crackling of flames and the screams of despair, Elsa could hear the scratching of panicked fingernails against the immobile iron door. Her head swirled in terror. The heat in the room became choking.

Elsa ran toward the window. Another girl was pulling herself up toward the fire escape stairs. Elsa boosted her feet to help her through, and then lifted herself up to the catwalk outside. She shuddered as she looked ten stories down. Flames had engulfed the fire escape below and were quickly moving higher. Girls who had escaped from the inferno on the ninth floor were rushing down the stairs to the street, but flames now blocked the way. Suddenly a girl flew out the window below, crashing to the hard sidewalk below. Another girl jumped, then another. Their bodies lay flat and still.

Elsa screamed. The horror momentarily paralyzed her, even as flames began to lap at her feet.

Other girls came through the window onto the fire escape. Elsa's panic broke. She climbed up to the roof. Only a few more girls made it up after her before the heat melted the fire-escape ladder.

On the roof of the factory, dozens of girls ran about in a panic. Flames curled up the sides of the building. Safe only for a moment, Elsa didn't see any escape by which they could survive. Fire trucks had appeared below but she doubted they would be in time to save her or the other girls on the roof.

Their savior, however, was already at work.

"Hey!"

Elsa heard the shout through the din, coming from the taller building of New York University next door. She looked up as a professor and several students pushed a painting ladder out their window. It wobbled precariously in the air.

Elsa scampered to the edge of the roof and waited, leaning over as far as she dared to grab the other end of the ladder and brace it against the roof of the Triangle factory. Girls began to stream across to safety.

Elsa held the frame of the ladder with shaking hands, trying not to look down at the yawning gap between buildings as she half climbed, half crawled across. The professor pulled her in through the window. She collapsed in a corner of the university office and began to cry.

Some girls crowded toward the windows to watch as the rescue continued, but Elsa, who had seen those girls who leapt to their death splayed out on the sidewalk, didn't want to see anymore. She could still hear the screams, the crackling flames, and occasionally a crash from inside the factory. She watched the girls coming through the window one after another, hoping against hope for Beth's face to come next. Working on the ninth floor, Beth's best chance would have been to go down rather than up, yet Elsa still hoped and prayed.

The stream of girls across the ladder slowed. The last girl to be dragged through was already unconscious, her hair singed and smoking. The window went quiet. After another minute, they pulled the ladder back in, its end black from the flames.

Elsa turned her head against the wall, weeping from both sorrow and relief.

After recovering her senses, she followed the other survivors to the street. It was a relief to see the familiar faces she had worked with, yet she wondered about every face she didn't see. The firemen began to bring covered bodies out of the building. Elsa's hopes of seeing Beth again fell, as dozens upon dozens of white-sheeted corpses streamed out. Eventually there was nothing to do but go home, hoping to see her mother before news of the disaster reached her.

She tried to hold out hope, but in her heart she knew Beth was dead.

One hundred and forty-six girls had died in the fire. They were found suffocated by smoke, singed against the locked doors, as skeletons hunched over sewing machines, or dead on the sidewalk from their jumps in desperation to escape. Most of the dead had been on the ninth floor.

News came that the Triangle Shirtwaist Factory would never reopen. Its owners were tried for negligence, with the primary grievance being the locked doors. Yet in a trial that left the families of the victims outraged and disillusioned, the owners were acquitted of all criminal charges. A civil settlement resulted in a payment to the families that averaged seventy-five dollars per victim.

Elsa had been hesitant about the translating jobs Pastor Reus discussed with her, because she hadn't wanted to leave her mother alone. She was also nervous about taking on something new—where she would be all on her own. But the fire at the Triangle Factory changed everything. She couldn't bear the thought of working in another factory. The flames may not have reached her body, but her heart was scarred by the tragedy.

Pastor Reus began to submit her name for consideration, but it turned out there was a good deal of competition. He had been optimistic for Elsa until she needed to actually apply for the jobs. Yes, there was a need for German to English translators in New York City. But there were still a lot of

Germans in the city. Most of them lived uptown in Yorkville—where Sonja and Christof had moved to—or in Williamsburg, across the river in Brooklyn. Elsa's command of both languages was excellent, but she hadn't been formally trained. Employers were doubtful of a lifelong shirtwaist-factory worker who claimed advanced linguistics.

The pastor himself had some work for her. He still gave his sermons in German, but the St. Mark's parish was shrinking. He knew he would have to start preaching in English soon, since he wasn't ready to retire. Elsa began translating his old sermons into English. He couldn't pay her much, but it was better for her than to have to return to a factory.

After a year, an opportunity finally came. An attorney on Long Island had seen an increase in work for German importers and had an ongoing need for translation of legal documents. He had also just lost his housemaid to marriage and hoped to find an educated German who could fulfill both functions. He began his inquiries in the German community in Williamsburg. Pastor Reus had been circulating Elsa's name for some time, so when John Graham, Esq., began to make inquiries, the St. Mark's pastor was informed right away.

Elsa had mixed feelings. She had hoped to find something in the city, where she could stay close her mother and sister. This job was far out on Long Island. If she took it, there was no telling when she would see her family again.

She told her mother about the job and her thoughts after meeting with the pastor. Nina had been waiting for her in the churchyard. The trees that had surrounded the church when they first arrived in New York were mostly gone. Construction buzzed from every direction as more tenements rose on the surrounding blocks. They began to walk home as they talked.

"You must go," Nina said emphatically. "This is everything you have worked for. These chances do not come often. For people like us, once in a lifetime is as much as you can hope for."

"But what about you? I do not know when I will see you

again."

Nina smiled. "My greatest joy will be to see that you and Sonja are happy. Knowing you will not spend your whole lives the way we have spent these seven years... that is enough for me."

"Perhaps in time the family can find you a job on Long Island as well," Elsa said. "Then you can come be near me."

Nina smiled and took her daughter's arm. "Look at me, Elsa. I am illiterate and unskilled. Now I am also growing old. This is *your* opportunity, and that makes it sweet to me." She paused. "My place is here, with the women of the union. Look at all we have done. The next fight is to win women the right to vote. I want to stay here with my sisters. The best thing I can do for you now is to stay in this fight and win you rights that I never dreamed were possible."

Elsa nodded, understanding, but already feeling bereft.

Nina reached up and touched her daughter's cheek. "Look at you, *mein liebchen*. You are a woman now."

Elsa smiled, appreciating her mother's compliment, even if it paled in comparison with the *"du bist so schön"* she'd told Sonja on her wedding day. Now nineteen, Elsa felt like she knew how she would look as a woman and was satisfied. She had grown into her face. Her awkward frame had developed into a womanly figure that, while strong, was beginning also to exhibit an adult grace. She would never be conventionally beautiful. Still, she sensed that people were drawn to her in a way she didn't fully understand.

Pastor Reus contacted the attorney on Long Island, and Elsa was immediately offered the job. This once, she was the perfect fit. There weren't a lot of preparations to undertake. Her belongings fit into a single bag. Besides her sister's family, she didn't need to say many good-byes.

She saved the hardest good-bye for her last day in the city.

Josephine welcomed her at the door of her apartment with tears in her eyes. She squeezed Elsa into a tight, loving hug. As a young girl, Josephine's hugs had made Elsa nervous. Now she had grown to love and depend on her mentor's embraces. They held each other for a long time that morning, communicating what no words could say. When they finally released each other, both were crying.

"I will miss you so much," said Elsa. "I hope you know how much you have meant to me."

Josephine nodded.

"I never would have had this opportunity were it not for you."

"I'm so proud of you, dear." Josephine wiped the tears from her eyes. "It has been lonely, you know, since Beth's been gone. Without your visits I . . . I don't know."

"Do you have people here to look out for you?"

"Oh yes, dear. My neighbors have been so loving. I have the folks at church. I have a brother, too, over in Queens. He comes to see me sometimes. I'm still sad, but I'll be okay. I have my faith. God's with me. I know I'll see Beth again, by and by."

Elsa smiled.

"Although I'll miss you, knowing that you're off somewhere good, doing what I helped teach you to do, will be a great comfort to me in my old age. I had hopes for Beth, but there's a limit to the chances colored folk can make for themselves. I had high hopes for you, too, and now here you are."

Josephine walked toward the shelf. Taking down the Bible that they'd spent so many long evenings studying together, she brought it over and pressed it into Elsa's hands.

"Take this. I want you to have it now."

Elsa shook her head. "Oh, no. I cannot take your Bible."

"It will give me joy to know it's with you. Precious things like this are supposed to be passed on. Remember me, and remember Beth when you read it."

Elsa felt the weight of the old Bible in her hands. The black leather cover was cracking and faded in some areas.

Who had owned it before Josephine? How long had it been in their family? How could she take it away from them?

Yet suddenly, Elsa realized that she *had* to take it. It would be a gift to Josephine as much as a gift toward herself. Josephine had no one left now that Beth was dead. She didn't have much that she could pass on beyond her time, but what she had taught Elsa *would* carry on. Elsa understood that she was now Josephine's legacy. The Bible was a symbol of that. While she initially thought it would be selfish to accept the gift, in fact it would be selfish to refuse.

Tears welled in Elsa's eyes as she held the Bible to her chest. "I will write to you often."

"You be sure to do that. I've loved you like a daughter, and I'll keep my eye on you like a daughter, too." She touched Elsa's cheek, smiling with genuine love and pride.

They embraced again.

"Now run along." Josephine hurried Elsa toward the door. "You've got a big life ahead of you."

Later, as she pressed her face against the rain-soaked train window, Elsa felt a numbness of emotion. The train crossed the East River, and she looked south at the smoke stacks of the factories puffing up into the driving rain. It was the first time she'd left Manhattan Island in the seven years she'd lived there. She knew she would return, but it would be as a much different person.

Why did she feel sentimental leaving a life that had been so harsh? It was only for the people she was leaving behind. But her sister had moved on, and her best friend was dead. Her mother and Josephine, the only two people she really would miss seeing, were happier because she had this chance. She owed it to them, as much as she owed it to herself, to make the most of this opportunity.

With one last glance back at the gray buildings of

Manhattan, she turned her head and her thoughts forward. All the hopes she'd cherished through her childhood, all her hard work, had brought her to this moment. There had been times when she'd almost succumbed to the weight and monotony of despair . . . when she'd almost given up her dreams.

Yet here she was—a survivor of everything America had thrown at her. She had grown strong from it and knew she could endure whatever new challenges this country would surely throw her way.

# PART II

## APRIL, 1912

# CHAPTER EIGHT
# LINDENHURST

Elsa stepped out of the train station into the town of Lindenhurst, forty miles east of New York City on Long Island. The clouds had broken, and now the day was warm. Still, a steady drip from the earlier rain fell from the tree branches and from the eaves of the station house. Water on the pavement and railway tracks evaporated quickly, sending steam into the fresh spring air.

Elsa breathed in deeply. She was disoriented but not afraid. She already liked this place.

She reexamined the letter Pastor Reus had given her: *John Graham, Esq., 410 Hyde Street, Lindenhurst, New York. At residence, inquire for Chris.*

The local station attendant told her to walk south and she would reach the street, which ran parallel to the water. She picked up her bag and started, glad for the opportunity to take a walk.

The warm, wet air entered her lungs with a pungency she could practically taste. The smell of new tree growth and fresh-cut grass mixed with the aroma of the nearby sea. The colors all around were bright and varied—from the greens of the trees to the shades of red brick houses and the multicolored tulips that mingled with yellow daffodils in the yards.

All the houses she passed on the sidewalk were clean and sparkling with prosperity. Even the nannies pushing the strollers of future masters looked wealthy to her. In her gray muslin dress—her nicest—Elsa began to feel self-conscious and afraid. What was she doing in a place like this? They wouldn't want *her* here.

But there was no turning back now. She had come too far, come too close to her dream. She choked back her fear of rejection and pressed on and reached Hyde Street.

She had never considered going into a house like these. Although they were middle-class residences, to her eyes they looked like palaces! Each one had a spacious yard. Some had extensive grounds.

The red brick house at 410 was three stories tall. It was similar to the others on the block. She wondered how many rooms there were and how many people lived in it. A short hedge lined the front lawn while a taller hedge hid the backyard from sight. A newly built wood garage housed the family's automobile.

Steadying her nerves, she walked up the path to the front steps. She took the massive knocker in her hand and dropped it against the door with a loud thud.

A few anxious moments passed. She nervously worked her lower lip between her teeth, rubbing her sweating palms against each other. The door opened. A middle-aged serving man stood before her. She stammered, forcing her eyes to meet his.

"Uh, sir . . . I am here to see a man named Chris."

"That's me." His friendly tone quickly dispelled the worst of her anxiety. "What can I do for you?"

"My name is Elsa Schuller. I am here regarding the German translation job."

His forehead crunched momentarily in question, which terrified Elsa. But then his face dawned with memory. "Oh, yes. You'd be the new maid."

He turned and motioned for her to follow him into the house. Elsa exhaled with relief.

"Mr. Graham wanted a maid who could translate his

German nonsense," Chris said. "That's why we have been without a maid now for three weeks. You can't imagine how relieved I am to see you. As if I could keep this house in order all by myself."

He had taken Elsa's bag and led toward the main staircase. Elsa tried to look around quickly at the rooms they passed. It was all so overwhelming.

"Are you the only servant?" she asked, following him up the great stairs.

"No. There are two of us now. Me and you."

She smiled. "I suppose the Grahams will want to speak with me first before they hire me."

"Baloney. I'm hiring you right now. As I see it, they've all blamed me for the shortcomings around here. But I wasn't the one who went off and got married." He shook his head, his chubby face reflecting his disapproval of the former maid's nuptials. "I'm glad you came along. I had suggested plenty of girls to hire, but he insisted she must also be able to translate for him. It's not like there isn't enough work here for a maid alone. You will be a busy girl."

Whatever Mr. Graham's reason for combining the tasks of maid and translator, Elsa was glad. She knew how to work hard.

Chris led past the first landing up to the top floor of the house. Even to Elsa's inexperienced eyes, these looked like the servants' quarters. All the furnishings on the first and second floors had been ornate and brightly polished. Here, things were plain and white yet still clean.

"This will be your room." Chris opened a door near the end of the hall and setting down her bag.

She smiled with delight. The west-facing window let in natural afternoon light. The bed looked soft and luscious. There was a sink in the corner and a dresser against the wall.

Chris politely gave her a moment to look around.

She could learn to feel at home here. Picking up her single bag, she opened the closet door. She shook her head with a little laugh. If even this, her nicest dress, didn't meet with approval here, what use did she possibly have for a closet? She set the bag down and removed only Josephine's Bible, which she set reverently on the table beside the bed.

Stepping to the window, she looked down into the backyard. A brick patio extended from the back of the house, enveloping a small fountain. A white table and matching chairs sat on the brick. White flowerpots filled with pink-and-purple gardenias lined the outside of the patio. After about ten yards the brick transitioned to grass, which stretched all the way to the back hedge.

She ran her finger along the base of the glass—no dirt, no bugs, not even a speck of dust. And this was the condition of a house that had been without a maid for three weeks! She could keep this room, this house, and even herself as clean as she wanted. In the life she had known, cleanliness was a luxury for which there was seldom time.

"My room's right across from you," said Chris. "My daughter Katherine has a small room attached to mine." He paused for just a moment. "It's a big house, as you can see . . . you'll think it's far *too* big once you start cleaning it. The three of us have this top floor all to ourselves. Though Mr. Graham has filled a few of the rooms up with all his boxes of documents and his books."

Elsa smiled. So there were books in the house!

"Do you have any experience in serving?" Chris asked as he led her back downstairs.

"No. I always worked in a clothing factory."

"Oh, you can sew. That's good."

Elsa almost burst into laughter. If he only knew.

"You can learn the rest. I'll help you."

He stopped and looked at her inquisitively.

"What is it?"

"Do you have any other frocks?"

"Yes. But this is my nicest one."

"Hmph. We'll have to do something about that. But it can wait until tomorrow. Come, I'll show you the kitchen. The Grahams take dinner at seven."

She followed, feeling suddenly ashamed about her dress. Soon she felt another presence behind them. She turned. A girl of about ten, wearing a blue dress, had begun to follow them. She had tightly curled brown hair.

"You must be Katherine." Elsa smiled.

The girl nodded, as she darted away.

"She's shy at first," said Chris. "But she'll be your friend soon enough."

Elsa hoped so. She felt like such a misfit here and hoped they would like her -- not only Chris and his daughter, but also the Grahams.

"Where are the masters now?"

Chris laughed. "The masters! Where did you learn to talk like that? Mr. Graham and Mrs. Graham will do just fine when addressing them. And Miss Dafne, of course."

She was going to ask who Miss Dafne was, but as they reached the first landing, the front door swung open below. An energetic woman blew in. Tall, athletic, and beautiful, she moved with a grace that gave elegance to her haste. Chris quickly descended to take her wide-brimmed hat.

"Mrs. Graham," said Chris, "this is our new maid, Elsa. She speaks, reads, and writes in German as well as English."

Mrs. Graham paused and looked at her. Elsa curtseyed, a maneuver she and Sonja had jokingly performed to one another. Nobody laughed, so she assumed she'd done it properly.

"Wonderful," Mrs. Graham said after a moment. "Welcome to our home." She hurried off, the skirts of her long dress flowing behind her.

Chris took Elsa to the kitchen, then left, assuming she could take care of herself. Finally alone, Elsa allowed herself a big smile.

This was the opportunity she had worked for, all those nights studying to read and write, sometimes sleeping only two or three hours before getting up for another grueling day at the factory. She felt happy and relieved. What would have become of her if she had come all this way and not been given this job?

But she *did* have the job, and what a wonderful job it would be. She stood there in the kitchen hardly believing it wasn't a dream. She had never even stepped into a house like this before, and now she was living in one. Yet as new and unfamiliar as this place was, she already was beginning to feel at home. The house was large and posh, but not imposing. The people she had met so far were kind. She welcomed the chance to learn her role in the Graham household, even as she feared making some error.

Elsa began to feel the pressure of her responsibilities right away. First and foremost, she had to make dinner for the family that night. The stress of this realization came upon her gradually, finally striking her with its full, worrisome force. Although she knew how to cook, she doubted her skills were enough for this task. Rich people like the Grahams would surely expect something more involved than the simple meals she had made for her family. She doubted she had much margin for error.

She looked around the kitchen as her palms began to sweat for the second time that day. In the little kitchen at Andretti's, they only kept enough food to make one or two meals at a time. They hadn't owned a refrigerator, so advance storage of food was impossible. In the Grahams' kitchen, there was enough food to feed the family plus the servants for weeks. Elsa couldn't guess whether something specific was intended for tonight's meal. Who had done the shopping up until then? Would that also be her responsibility? She would have asked Chris, but he had just driven off in the automobile.

After her examination of the refrigerator, she opened the

freezer. There was meat in it, but it was unusable. It was like the meat that froze out in the shed during the winters in Germany, or the meat that had likewise frozen on their kitchen counter during some of the worst winter nights in New York. This kind of meat had to be thawed over the fire before being cut and cooked. How strange to own a machine that provided this inconvenience in April. Elsa decided then and there that she did not approve of freezers.

Ignoring the frozen things for now, there was still plenty with which she could make a meal. She could have made ten meals. That was the problem. She wanted some instruction. What if she used something she wasn't supposed to? All her life she had been accustomed to clear instructions and commands. Now she was on her own. She sat down at the table, at a loss how to start.

It was completely overwhelming.

A strange patter approached the kitchen. It sounded like steps, but unlike the fall of any shoes Elsa had known. She started and looked toward the door just as a teenage girl entered the room. Elsa lurched to her feet.

"Well, here she is!" said the girl, whose cropped blonde hair was slicked down against her head.

Elsa curtseyed. "Miss Dafne?"

"Yeah, I'm the one." Her eyes quickly scanned Elsa from head to foot, then back up again. "So what are we sitting at the kitchen table for?"

Elsa was terrified. "I'm making dinner," she stammered, barely above a whisper.

"I see."

Elsa had never met anyone before or after as quick at understanding an implication as Dafne Graham.

"So let me guess," said Dafne, "you don't know what we expect from you, and you're afraid if you do it wrong, you'll get axed, yeah?"

Elsa nodded. She had never heard the word "axed"

referring to anything other than trees, but the context made the meaning perfectly clear.

Dafne laughed. It was a friendly laugh, not making light of Elsa's plight, but suggesting that it was unworthy of so much stress.

"Okay, darling, let's see what we've got."

Dafne strode toward the refrigerator, hurling her short jacket with perfect aim over the back of one of the chairs. She opened the door of the cooler, leaning in with one hand on her raised hip. It was in this posture that Elsa noticed the floppy galoshes on her feet, which she had presumably worn that day because of the morning rain. This accounted for the odd sound of her approach.

"The first thing you need to learn around here—what's your name?"

"Elsa Schuller."

"Elsa." Dafne turned back from the refrigerator and beamed at her. She quickly resumed her inspection.

"The first thing you need to learn, Elsa, is that you're in charge around here. I suppose you've been working for other folks all your little young life. But now you're the boss. This is your house."

Throughout her speech, Dafne plucked things out of the refrigerator and piled them on the counter.

"There you go. Some beef, some veggies ... the bread's over there. What self-respecting serving girl couldn't make a feast out of this?"

Elsa finally smiled. Dafne's personality startled her, but she had begun to relax in her presence. She knew Dafne wasn't an enemy.

She took the meat and vegetables over to the counter, placed them on a cutting board and began her work.

Dafne sat at the table, leaning back in her chair with her galoshes on the table. She questioned Elsa about her former life—both in New York and in Germany—deducing whatever

Elsa didn't say from the short answers she gave.

Dafne's appearance shocked Elsa. She had never seen this hairstyle before—short and slicked to one side. Dafne's dress fell straight from her shoulders to her calf. Only a tiny line designated her natural waist. The sleeves fit her upper arms snugly, leaving the lower three-quarters of her arms bare. At sixteen, Dafne didn't have noticeable curves—not that anyone would have noticed in her straight dress. Her makeup was light and barely noticeable.

Elsa's eyes kept returning to the galoshes, elevated on the table. They must have been worn all day as some bizarre fashion statement, even when the rain was gone. It was very odd.

Dafne's appearance defied the old feminine ideals that even Elsa knew. How different her attire was from the flowing gown and wide hat in which Mrs. Graham had appeared that morning. Dafne seemed to be a modern girl in every way she could manage.

"Do you go to school?" Elsa asked, finally daring to pose a question to her young mistress.

"Yeah. I guess it's a good thing to do. I don't suppose you got to go to school?"

"For a little while in Germany. But not here in America."

"But you've learned English perfectly. You must write it, too, if my father hired you. To do that without school . . . you must be a clever gal."

Again she surprised Elsa with her deductions about her former life. Dafne seemed to know everything about her without her telling.

"I have tried to learn whenever I had a chance."

"That's neat. I'm so bored with school." Dafne yawned.

Elsa wasn't sure whether the yawn had been intentional to illustrate Dafne's point, or whether it was inspired by the mention of school. Either way, the young lady seemed to be suddenly both tired and bored.

"You got it now," she said, standing up slowly. "I need a nap."

Daphne walked toward the door. Her genuine smile warmed Elsa to her core.

"I'm going to like having you here," Dafne said. "You'll do just fine."

She winked, then galoshed her way upstairs.


To Elsa's relief, the first dinner in the Graham house was uneventful. Nobody commented on the cooking except Dafne, who complimented it repeatedly and sent Elsa encouraging looks throughout the meal. She felt the family was satisfied with her first effort at domestic service.

Mr. Graham had come home just before the meal. Elsa still hadn't been properly introduced to the man for whom she would be doing the majority of her work. Her first impression of him, at the dinner table, was positive. She liked the whole family already.

After dinner, Dafne had a friend to the house who supposedly wanted to meet Elsa. Nervously she answered the summons to Dafne's bedroom, where Jeanette Streppy waited on the edge of the bed.

"Oh, she *is* cute!" said Jeanette.

Elsa curtseyed for the third time that day, having become rather confident in the maneuver.

"Elsa's been working in a factory in lower Manhattan," said Dafne, flinging her arm around her servant and compelling her to enter the room farther than she was comfortable with.

"She never went to school, but she reads and writes in both English and German. She can do anything. Your only problem," she turned from Jeanette to Elsa, "is that you're too afraid of doing something wrong. Our last maid ran this house."

She turned to Jeanette again. "She bossed Mommy and

Daddy around like you wouldn't believe. I think she hated me, because whenever she told me to do something I'd just stamp my foot and say no! I'm glad she's gone." Turning back to Elsa, "Remember, you're the factory boss now."

Elsa couldn't help but smile.

"I can't see you in a factory," said Dafne before turning back to Jeanette. "She's been following orders instead of giving them, but that'll change soon." She looked back at Elsa. "Sit down, dear. Jeanette wants to ask you about Germany."

"Germany?" protested Jeanette as Dafne slid a chair up behind Elsa. She was glad she wasn't required to sit on the bed.

Dafne continued her narrative while standing. "Didn't I tell you? She came over from Europe when she was twelve in a big, crowded ship like you hear about, with people freezing their toes off and catching horrible diseases. Then she lived in one of those tenements in the city that the socialists and reformers and my mother are always complaining about, with bugs and sewage and more disease . . ."

Elsa didn't recall telling Dafne anything about her voyage or apartment in the city.

". . . then she worked all day in a sweat shop, making clothes for practically no pay, yet she learned to speak, read, and write English better than I do!" Dafne looked back at Elsa. "I don't know how you did it."

Jeanette didn't ask Elsa about Germany. Dafne *told* Jeanette about Germany, occasionally requiring a sentence or two from Elsa, from which she would construct a fantastic tale of Elsa's life. Amazingly, Dafne's stories were never far from the truth, even if they were more elaborate.

The longer she stayed in their presence, the more Elsa felt like one of them, rather than inferior in social standing. Yet once she recognized this feeling, she resisted it. She had to remember her place. She looked for an opportunity to slip away.

Suddenly Dafne demanded that Jeanette play billiards with her. They dashed down the hall to the room with the billiard table. Elsa hadn't seen this room on her tour with Chris, who had skipped the entire second floor.

Elsa thought this would be a good moment to make her escape, but Dafne made her stay and watch as she thrashed Jeanette in a game of pool.

Next, Dafne insisted that Elsa learn the game. Elsa vehemently protested, knowing there was still work to be done in the kitchen, but Dafne was unmoved. She authoritatively thrust the stick into Elsa's hand. After several inept attempts, Elsa finally sunk a ball. She hopped in place with pleasure before she could stop herself. She was then required to play a game with Jeanette.

"My brother Glenn came home today," Jeanette told Dafne before striking a ball.

"Really?" Dafne didn't sound very interested. "Came home from where?"

"Harvard, you silly!"

"Oh, is he graduating?"

"No. He still has another year. He'll be home for two weeks. He'll be at the dance at the grange tomorrow and knows all the new dances. You're coming, of course?"

"Nobody told me there was a dance." Now Dafne's interest was piqued. "Who else'll be there?"

"The usual crowd," said Jeanette as she hit the cue ball again. Elsa's turn had been quick and uneventful. After watching the satisfying plop of the ball into the pocket, Jeanette turned back to her friend. "Yes, that means Will Sweeney, too."

Dafne smiled.

Jeanette floated around the table to take another shot. "There's a hot little band from New York that's coming to play, so it should be a good show."

By now Dafne was nearly giddy in anticipation of the party.

Jeanette missed her shot, and Elsa prepared for her own. But she never got to take it. Mrs. Graham appeared at the top of the stairs and summoned her to follow. Elsa straightened quickly, fearing she had been caught doing something very wrong. It didn't matter that Dafne had forced her to play. She expected to get fired.

With growing dread, she handed the pool cue to Jeanette and followed Mrs. Graham down the stairs, chiding herself again and again for having been caught playing a game. Mrs. Graham led her to Mr. Graham's study—one of the first-floor rooms in which Elsa hadn't yet gone. He sat in a big chair behind a desk. Elsa curtseyed.

"What's your name, girl?"

"Elsa Schuller."

"What part of Germany are you from?"

"*Niedersachsen*, sir."

He motioned for Elsa to sit and for his wife to leave. As soon as she was seated, Elsa began to feel more relaxed. At least she wasn't getting fired this very moment.

Mr. Graham's study looked notably older than the rest of the Grahams' modern home. Although the actual structure of the room was the same, the antique desk and chairs, walls of old books and two corrugated-metal candlesticks on the desk gave the office an ancient feel. Although there was an electric light in the center of the ceiling, Mr. Graham clearly preferred to work by candlelight.

"I have seen samplings of your translation work," said Mr. Graham, "so I trust you are equal to the task. But I would like to see you translate a brief of mine tonight so I can observe your work for myself."

As her fear subsided, Elsa took a moment to observe Mr. Graham. He seemed to be a serious but gentle man. His brown hair was a light enough shade that Elsa did not immediately notice where it was streaked with gray.

He handed a three-page document to Elsa. Rather than sitting back down, he stood by the side of his desk.

"I received this yesterday from a client in Bremen. My

work is in import/export law. I doubt you follow politics or economics, but I will tell you that over the past two years, trade between the United States and Germany has increased while also becoming tense. Germany is growing stronger in Europe, and some in this country do not think we should keep trading with them. There is even talk of war breaking out in Europe. Because of this, the German exporters need a good lawyer. I'm not German myself, but I fail to see the threat posed by German commerce. I understand some German, but not well enough for what my work has come to demand. That's why I need you."

Through this speech, Elsa had been glancing over the brief. Now she looked up at Mr. Graham with a new and terrible fear. The document was written in German, yet she could hardly make any sense of it. Had she already come to know English that much better than her native language?

"I am sorry sir, but there are words in this document I do not understand."

Rather than being upset, Mr. Graham smiled. "Don't be worried. This brief, like all the documents you will translate for me, are full of legal terms that I wouldn't have expected you to come across before."

He stepped to one of the bookshelves, brought down a heavy, leather-bound book and handed it to Elsa.

"Here is a dictionary of German legal terms, along with their English and Latin equivalents. Once you know the basics, the conjugations and tenses will come naturally to you. Consider this office your own. Pens, paper and all the supplies you will need are in that cabinet." He pointed. "Any time I'm not in here working, help yourself to any of these books. I trust you will learn quickly."

Elsa took the brief, the book, paper, pen and ink, and headed to her room to begin studying.

She felt so relieved. Not only was her new master a kind man. He had also given her access to a wealth of new knowledge.

She was excited to get started on the German brief.

Back in her room, Elsa left her light on late, working through Mr. Graham's brief and studying the legal dictionary. Not familiar with electric light, she wondered whether she ought to be careful not to leave the light on too long. At Andretti's they had to pay in advance for their ration of gas to light the lamps. Did electricity work in a similar way?

The task was tedious, but not as difficult as she expected. The dictionary gave clear examples for the words and concepts she saw in the legal brief. After two hours she was satisfied with her translation. She knew that the words and grammar were accurate. Mr. Graham could read it and see whether she had also gotten the concepts right. After her first interview with him, she felt he would be patient with her if there were things she still needed to learn.

She turned off the light with a happy sigh, leaning back onto her soft bed. She couldn't believe it had only been that morning when she took the train out of Manhattan in the rain. Her whole life and world had changed in one day.

Elsa felt proud. Yes, she had been fortunate to land this position, but it was exactly what she had worked for all these years. So many people had told her she couldn't, or shouldn't. But she always believed she would. She had done it for herself, yes, but she also felt she did it for all the girls who would never find their way out of the sweatshops. She did it for her mother, who long ago prepared her to make her way without waiting for a man. She was a career woman now. It was a title she had earned and of which she could be proud.

# CHAPTER NINE
# DAFNE GRAHAM

"Elsa, how quickly can you finish your work tonight?"

Dafne had come charging into the kitchen, barefoot, her body wrapped in a robe and her hair a wet, tangled mess.

Elsa smiled. "Well, I suppose your dinner will be over at eight, then maybe an hour to clean everything, unless your father gives me another translation."

"Nonsense. You're coming to the dance with me."

Elsa started to say something, but Dafne cut her off. "No, no, no! You are not getting out of it." She shook the wet mess on top of her head. "I'll eat with you and Chris and Kat at six. Leave the rest for Mommy and Daddy. They can handle it themselves."

"But what about all the dishes? I have to clean up, too"

"Do it tomorrow. Just toss everything in the sink." Dafne was already walking out the kitchen door. "Don't worry about a thing, I'll clear it for you with Mommy."

Elsa stood alone in the kitchen as the door banged behind Dafne. She didn't know whether to laugh or to cry.

She really didn't want to go to a party. Her new life in this house was all the stimulation she needed. If she was lax in her duties, she worried that it would no longer be as pleasant. But Dafne was obviously not going to be argued with on this matter. Dafne was one of her new masters, too, so Elsa was obliged to obey.

She wished Dafne wouldn't treat her so informally. Dafne

seemed to have decided that Elsa was her equal. But Elsa believed that she was not Dafne's equal. She had embraced her role in the serving class. This itself was a large step up from the labor class she had just left. Much as she was growing to love Dafne and welcome her friendship, she felt their class difference had to be maintained. She shouldn't be shooting billiards with her and her friends, or going to dances with them.

But since in this case she had no choice, Elsa began to look forward to the party just a little.

Dafne's plans came together perfectly, as Elsa should have known they would. While her parents were still eating their dinner, Chris drove Dafne and Elsa across town in the family automobile. Mrs. Graham had acquiesced in allowing her to take Elsa to the dance but wouldn't go so far as to let Dafne drive the car herself.

Elsa felt a rush of excitement. She had never been in an automobile before. She also felt good and even a little pretty in her new clothes.

Chris had come back from town that morning and presented her with a box filled with several neatly folded white blouses and two dark skirts. It felt like Christmas or a birthday. At least that was what she imagined the holidays felt like; her family had always been too poor to exchange such extravagant gifts. Everything fit her perfectly. She asked Chris how he knew her sizes so well, but he said the credit all went to Dafne.

She glanced across the seat toward Dafne. Her straight, blue satin dress was covered by a man's tan overcoat. She had a fedora on her head.

"How do I look?" She grinned at Elsa.

Elsa kept her mouth shut, at a loss how to answer. Dafne giggled.

"I know, you think I look ridiculous, don't you? You can tell me."

"It . . . is not a style I have seen before."

"It feels like it might rain. I should have worn my galoshes."

Now Elsa knew Dafne was trying to shock her. She burst out laughing, surprising herself. Dafne laughed too, as she clutched Elsa's hand.

"I know you hate my style as much as my mother does. But aren't my shoes pretty?"

She leaned closer to Elsa and wiggled her feet in their blue, high-heeled shoes.

"Yes, they are lovely." Elsa could certainly agree to that.

"Oh, darling, I'm going to simply *love* having you around!

"The drive across town to the grange was short. Chris gave Elsa a note with the Grahams' phone number written on it, then drove away. They walked through the entrance, which opened onto a small lobby, then through another set of doors into a large, open space. Twelve round tables with chairs were set up on the closer half of the wood floor; the rest had been left open for dancing. An eight-piece ragtime band played from atop a stage set into the far wall. The coatroom sat just off the entryway, but Dafne marched into the ballroom still wearing her coat and hat. Most eyes turned toward her. Satisfied with her entrance, she hurled the masculine attire over Elsa's arm. Elsa was not naïve about the fact that she was as big a part of Dafne's strategized entrance as her shocking outer garments.

Elsa waited a moment for Dafne to locate her table and her friend Jeanette. She took her coat and hat back to the antechamber, wondering what else servants were supposed to do at a dance.

Dafne sat down next to Jeanette and her brother, Glenn. She did not look directly at Will but could tell that he had noticed her entrance. Also sitting at their table was Mr. Harris, a middle-aged man who always came to these sorts of parties, even though he was one of the oldest ones there.

"Isn't my new servant cute?" Dafne bragged. It was grand to have one's own maid!

She began to tell Elsa's story. The others at the table listened dutifully. But Jeanette, who had heard it all already, scowled at her. Dafne stopped talking, feeling embarrassed. She always wanted to be the life of the party, the center of conversation, but didn't think she was very good at it. As the conversation turned to other people, she allowed herself a smile across the table at Will.

She was skilled at understanding people's motives. When people gave her attention unwillingly, she knew and it embarrassed her. With Will Sweeney, she still wasn't sure. That was how she knew she had a crush—her judgment was clouded.

Will wasn't the first boy she had liked, but this crush was the first that she thought might actually amount to something. After all, several girls her age already had boyfriends. It was time for her to have a boy. Her parents didn't agree. They said she had to wait until after her debut before she dated. But Dafne had always been bold. Almost seventeen was plenty old enough.

She couldn't envision what the actual result of her intended involvement with Will would be. She wanted to kiss him, but what would happen after that? Would she be expected to marry him? She didn't like him *that* much.

"Will, aren't you going to the city next weekend to look at colleges?" Dafne asked, feeling so jealous. He was only a year older than her but that seemed like a lot.

"Yes," said Will. "I hope I get into Columbia."

"That's a good choice," said Glenn Streppy.

A tall brunette approached their table. Dafne immediately recognized Thelma Blaine in her scarlet gown.

"Welcome home, Glenn," she said warmly, bending over his seat to hug his shoulders before sitting in the empty chair next to him. Her full, dark hair was pulled on top of her head.

"Miss Blaine, how you've changed," said Glenn.

"Two years can do a lot for a woman."

Dafne had to agree. Miss Blaine was only a couple of years older, but could have easily passed for a woman in her early twenties. She looked stunning. Dafne caught Will's eye drifting toward the table's new beauty. It also seemed that Thelma kept looking over at *her*. Dafne felt nervous. She chattered at Will, desperately trying to hold his attention.

"Come and dance with me, Glenn," Thelma said.

The two rose and began the One Step to the music.

With them gone, Dafne found it much easier to maintain Will's attention, leaving Jeanette to reluctantly converse with Mr. Harris.

The band was comprised of a piano, a trumpet, two clarinets, a trombone, a violin, a banjo, and a drum set. Dafne had not heard music this good in Lindenhurst in a long time. If only she could spend more time in New York!

Jeanette became much more excited about the company of Mr. Harris when he pulled a flask of whiskey from his coat pocket. She held her cup of club soda under the table for him to spike. Dafne, observing the proceedings, bit her lip nervously, then grinned and slid her cup over as well.

As she watched the dancers, Dafne's mind wandered, first to New York City, where Will would be going next weekend, then to Boston. She should ask Glenn about his experiences at Harvard. Oh, to be out in the world, as these young men were! How long would she remain trapped in sleepy little Lindenhurst?

Glenn and Thelma returned to the table. Although she participated in the conversation, Dafne's mind was now elsewhere.

She wanted so many things for her life but didn't know best how to plan for them. She had one more year of school, after which she expected to carve out her place in society. Hopefully that place would be in the city, not out here on

Long Island. She knew her parents' expectations for her but didn't worry about them much. Ultimately, as long as she chose a respectable man, her parents would be pleased. It wasn't like her mother had been any less of a rebel in her youth.

Her mother had been the toast of Richmond, Virginia, in her cotillion days. At the time of her debut she could have chosen from a dozen or more willing bachelors. But she shocked everyone by marrying John Graham, a law student at Columbia, and moving to New York. Her husband's quick success had justified her brashness. Dafne knew her mother fancied herself to be a fully modern woman, taking on the suffragist cause with all her boundless energy. Despite all this, she expected the same traditional destiny for her daughter that had been expected of her. She eagerly anticipated Dafne's debut next year, failing to see how drastically her daughter's dreams and passions differed from her own.

Dafne wished she were past it all—past school, and past the false pretense of a social debut. She had already been going to dances for over a year! Then she could go to New York and dine in the beautiful hotels on Madison Avenue. Although she didn't want to marry for some time yet, she sensed that to fully enjoy the society life she desired, she would probably need a man.

"Miss Graham, would you care to dance?"

Her eyes jolted up and met Glenn's. He had stood and now extended his hand. She smiled and took it. Although she had been waiting and hoping for Will to ask her, she needed to dance, and felt special in the way Glenn asked. Jeanette had said her brother was good at the new ragtime dances. She took his hand and stood up.

Glenn, who had appeared shy and even slightly awkward at the table, was in his element on the dance floor, executing the steps with confidence. Dafne thoroughly enjoyed dancing with him.

After the song ended, the bandleader paused. He put his hand to his forehead and looked out over the crowd of young people.

"Where are your chaperones?" he asked loudly to hearty laughter. "Where are your parents? No chaperones? No parents?" he continued. "Well then, lads and lasses, I believe it's time for the turkey trot contest!"

The girls squealed with delight. Dafne hopped and clapped before turning eagerly toward Glenn. She was glad to be with the best dancer, but didn't like seeing that Will and Thelma were dancing together.

The one step may have been the most fashionable of the ragtime dances, but the turkey trot was the most notorious. It had recently been banned by the Vatican, as well as by most American Protestant organizations, which, predictably, had caused the dance's popularity to soar.

Dafne and Jeanette had practiced it together but had only been able to dance it in public two or three times. At most of the dances in Lindenhurst, some older attendee was sure to stop any turkey trotting. Tonight, they had no such problems. Glenn took Dafne in his arms and began to hop to the quick music.

Of the twenty or so couples who participated in the turkey trot, Glenn and Dafne stood out dramatically from the rest. While most of them hopped awkwardly first on one leg, then on the other, Glenn glided through the motions. Dafne felt light as air, hardly noticing whether her feet touched the floor.

They were the unanimous champions and stood with the bandleader while all the others applauded. He handed Glenn a silly tin trophy of a turkey mounted atop a small platform. Glenn laughed heartily. He handed the trophy to Dafne—who beamed with delight—then offered her his arm and led her back to their table.

Back in the car, Dafne leaned her head on Elsa's shoulder as Chris drove them home."

"Did you have fun?" Dafne asked her servant.

"I did." Elsa smiled. "I loved watching the dancing. Especially when you won the contest. That young man was very good."

"That was Jeanette's brother from Harvard."

"He appeared to be quite a gentleman."

Dafne giggled at Elsa's description, but she was right. Glenn carried himself as a thorough gentleman, unlike some others at the local dance. Her mind had been so focused on Will that she'd failed to notice it.

"You certainly seemed to have a lot of fun," said Elsa.

"Of course I did!"

As soon as the words were out of Dafne's mouth, she realized that there was no *of course* about it. She always looked forward to these dances, but didn't always enjoy them. She felt self-conscious about how young she looked and about her limited knowledge of adult subjects.

But tonight had been different. Will's eyes had certainly been more for Thelma than for her. Yet instead of ending up crying alone in the powder room as she so often did at these dances, she enjoyed herself.

# CHAPTER TEN
# A FORBIDDEN ADVENTURE

Dafne had hoped to see Glenn Streppy again but didn't expect him to answer the door.

"Oh, hello," she said.

"Hi." He smiled. "Miss Graham. What a pleasure."

Dafne was pleased by his initial reaction at seeing her. Her mind immediately returned to the dance and how much fun she'd had dancing with him.

"May I come in?"

He quickly moved to the side of the door, looking embarrassed for having unconsciously blocked her entry.

"Is Jeanette home?" She turned her head over her shoulder toward him as she entered. It was still fairly early on Saturday, a week after the dance at the grange.

"I believe she's bathing," he said. "You're welcome to sit down."

His manner seemed apologetic. She remembered how awkward he was at the party until he began to dance, but she found it endearing.

He was a handsome man, despite the apparent lack of confidence. He stood slightly under average height but was still taller than Dafne. His dirty-blond hair had natural waves. His shirt and vest were comfortably filled out, but he was by no means overweight. Dafne thought he dressed well. It was no wonder—given that he'd lived near Boston for three years.

He closed the door as she sat on the edge of the couch,

propping her elbows upon her knees.

"I was going to make tea," he said. "Would you like some?"

"Yeah, great!"

He disappeared into the kitchen as Dafne chuckled. She wondered where the Streppys' servant girl was, that Glenn would prepare tea himself.

She had always liked the Streppys' house. It was built in the same style as hers but to a smaller scale, having only two stories. The front door opened into an antechamber separate from the main sitting room, where she now waited. Dafne thought this house was cozy, while Jeanette thought it was cramped. Conversely, Dafne considered her own house vast, while Jeanette claimed it was luxurious. They had bickered on the subject many times.

Glenn returned and set the tea tray on a small table. It looked like he had taken a moment to quickly comb his hair. He lifted the table with the tray on top and moved it effortlessly in front of the couch. Dafne was impressed. She couldn't have moved that table without spilling a few drops of milk or water.

She took the cup he poured and sipped at it, immediately starting away as she burned her tongue. She set her cup down and reached for a piece of toast while it cooled.

"Will you tell me about Harvard?" It was the question she wished she had asked at the party.

His smile verged on laughter.

She laughed for him. "I reckon that's what everyone asks you."

"It's all right. What else are we to talk about?"

"Any number of things. I never have trouble finding things to talk about."

"Then I should talk to you more often."

"But I want you to talk to *me*. You're the one who's been to college."

This time he did laugh. "I'm afraid I didn't make Harvard

as exciting as some have."

"But to a girl who's stuck in Lindenhurst, the very idea of Boston is thrilling."

"You'll get your chance, too. How old are you?"

"Seventeen," she stretched.

"See. I'm twenty. It's not such a long time."

"I can't go to college, though."

"But you will do other things."

"Like what?" She picked up her cup of tea, which had now cooled to an acceptable temperature for sipping.

"You will soon be spending more time in New York, I'm sure." He paused for a second. "You know Thelma Blaine?"

"Yes." Dafne sat up rigidly.

"Well, she went to New York just yesterday."

"What!" Dafne momentarily lost her composure. "How the dickens did she get away with that?"

She took a large glug of tea. While the tea was at an ample sipping temperature, it wasn't suitable for glugging as Daphne felt her throat begin to burn from the hot liquid.

"She went with a fellow going to look at colleges for next year. He was at our table last weekend at the dance, though I don't know him personally. Swanson . . . Swaner . . . something like that."

"Sweeney." Dafne scowled viciously.

"Yes, Sweeney. That's him. It's nothing, really. The Blaines have family in the city. But it just goes to show you how close Lindenhurst really is to the rest of the country. You could go to New York yourself."

"Somehow I don't think so."

Glenn could obviously tell how much his casual gossip had upset her. It seemed to confuse him as he quickly ate two pieces of toast. Oh well, let him wonder.

"Jeanette must be ready by now. I'll go upstairs." Dafne picked up her cup with a thought of draining the remaining tea. Remembering her scorched throat, she set it back on the tray and rose. "Thank you for the tea."

Jeanette wasn't finished with her toilette. When she returned to her bedroom, Dafne was stretched out on her bed, sobbing. Jeanette stood precariously above her. She wasn't used to being cried to.

"How could he?" Dafne moaned.

Jeanette bit her finger. "What did he do? Who are you talking about?"

"Will, silly! He ran off to New York with Thelma. It's like they're laughing at me."

"What a pig! I thought he liked you."

"It's hard for me to compete with Thelma."

"Well, if he's that fickle, he doesn't deserve you."

"I don't want a boy who deserves me. I want a boy who'll take me to New York!"

"What a scandal this could be, though," Jeanette's voice was suddenly excited. "Think about it, Daf!"

Dafne sat up on the bed to listen.

"Do you suppose they got rooms in the same hotel? If they're caught together at night their names will go in the paper!"

For a moment Dafne was excited too, but then she shook her head. "They wouldn't be so careless, and Will isn't that bold even if he did fancy sleeping with her. Your brother said she has family in the city, so she's probably staying with them."

Jeanette nodded.

"I bet he kissed her, though." Dafne grimaced.

"Thelma will probably blow him off in the end," Jeanette said. "Then maybe he'll want you again."

Dafne wiped her eyes. "I don't like him anymore—especially if he kissed her. Eww! What we need is to meet some new boys."

"Where are we going to meet new boys? We know every boy in Lindenhurst."

Dafne thought for a moment, then squealed and grabbed Jeanette's arms. "Let's go to Coney Island!"

Jeanette gasped. "My mother forbade me from going there again."

"We won't tell anyone. We can go right now and be back in time for dinner. It's only an hour and a half on the train."

Jeanette hesitated, but that was enough encouragement for Dafne. "Come on, get ready. I'm calling Elsa so she can bring my things and meet us at the train station."

Jeanette whirled into high gear. Dafne dashed for the telephone. In half an hour the three girls were on the train heading west on a forbidden adventure.

Elsa didn't have time to consider the implications of Dafne's call until it was too late for her to do anything about it. Only once they were on the train did Dafne tell her explicitly that the trip was a secret.

"Darling, I couldn't tell you before, or you wouldn't have come!" Dafne smiled.

Elsa remained dismayed.

"Don't worry, you won't get in trouble. You're my servant, too, and you have to do what I tell you. Besides, our parents will never know."

Elsa had heard of Coney Island when she lived in the city. Some of the girls at the shirtwaist factory talked about going there on Sundays. Now she knew that parents on Long Island felt the same way as parents in the city about the notorious peninsula of fun. It was supposedly no place for nice young ladies. Elsa didn't like the idea of going to a place with such a raunchy reputation.

As they got closer, Dafne began to plan their activities like a regular veteran of the amusement park. She and Jeanette had each been only once before, but Dafne had heard all the latest from her classmates so she felt well prepared to organize their adventure.

A layer of morning clouds had burned off by the time the

train reached Brooklyn. At Coney Island, the sky was clear. The boardwalk shone in the late morning sun. The ocean sparkled, blue and inviting. Colorful flags flapped in the wind above painted rides and booths. There was mechanical music coming from several parts of the park. The giant Ferris wheel towered above everything.

Despite all Dafne's plans, Jeanette insisted that they go on the Ferris wheel first. Dafne disagreed, and they engaged in a heated argument as soon as they stepped off the train. Elsa had never seen friends argue that way before and wondered whether this was the end of Dafne and Jeanette. But after a few moments Dafne acquiesced, and peace was restored. Elsa was beginning to learn how normal these types of arguments were for them.

As they approached the Ferris wheel, Dafne smirked. It seemed she might win after all. The line extended all the way back around the steeplechase ride and the hotdog stand.

"This will take us all day," said Dafne. "Come on, let's go shoot darts at the balloons."

Jeanette, having won the argument, wasn't to be let down now. She quickly devised a plan. She spotted three boys together near the front of the line and pointed them out to Dafne.

They sauntered over. At first Elsa held back, but Dafne forced her to come along.

"Fellas, thanks for holding our place," said Jeanette as she approached. Dafne was right behind her with a smile and a wink for the boy she had selected. After a moment of hesitation, the boys were in on the plan and had let the girls into line.

In order to maintain their guise for the suspicious people behind, no names were asked or exchanged. Dafne and Jeanette skillfully drove the conversation as if the six young people had been friends for years.

The boys looked close in age to Dafne and Jeanette, a few years younger than Elsa. It was easy to see they were schoolboys, not working boys, although their accents gave them away as not being from the upper rungs of Brooklyn society. They all wore wool tweed caps that were a little too big, though that was the style. The boy who acted like the leader of their little group had a necktie sloppily tucked into his vest. He had been quick to pick up on the girls' plan and now looked to be making some plans of his own. The second boy, on whom Dafne was focusing, seemed shy but was the most handsome of the three. As Jeanette talked to the leader, Elsa felt she was expected to make some sort of conversation, or at least make eye contact, with the third boy. Naturally, they had left the fat one with red cheeks for her.

She didn't mind. She thought she would like this one best—a misfit in this game of flirtation, like herself. Despite her continued apprehension, Elsa was actually enjoying the adventure and smiled at the boy in spite of herself.

Reaching the front of the line, the girls expected to be on their way. But the boys had other ideas.

"Them's big cars on this wheel," said the boys' leader. "We can all fit on, nice and cozy-like."

Unable to protest after they had let them in line, the girls boarded the Ferris-wheel car but got cozy with one another on one side while the three boys jostled and shoved into the other side.

Conversation during the ride was painfully awkward. But at least they finally managed to exchange names. The leader was Tommy. Nate was the shy one. And the chubby one they called Turnip. Try as the girls did, Tommy and Nate—not to mention Turnip himself—refused to reveal his real name.

Elsa tried to distract herself by looking out at the view, but the height was terrifying. She wished Dafne had let her sit in the middle like she'd wanted to. When the car revolved back toward the base she expected it to stop, but up they went again for another terrible rotation. By the third time around Elsa finally began to relax and look out at the view. The sparkling ocean extended out to the jetty of the Rockaway Peninsula. Far past her right shoulder she could see the Jersey shore stretching south. It really was incredibly beautiful. She was actually disappointed when their ride finally ended.

The boys hurried to get off the car first with the intention of helping the girls off. The move was less for the sake of chivalry than for the prospect of getting to touch a female hand. But as Tommy and Nate exited, the weight imbalance dropped the girls' side precariously. Jeanette shrieked as their legs kicked ungracefully in the air. The ride operator steadied the car just before poor Turnip would have fallen into their laps.

As if nothing had happened, Tommy doffed his cap and offered Jeanette his hand. Dafne smiled sweetly at Nate to make him do the same for her. Then Tommy returned, usurping Turnip to assist Elsa out of the car.

"You gals want a hot dog and a cola?" asked Tommy.

"Why, sure!" they answered in unison.

The six of them spent the entire day together. They rode more rides. Tommy threw darts at balloons and won a stuffed bear, which he gave to Jeanette. They saw a freak show featuring a blue-faced man, a bearded lady and "The Strongest Man in the World," who lifted a thousand-pound weight. They ate more food that gave Elsa a stomachache. But it was some of the most fun she'd had in all her life.

Before any of them realized it, the afternoon sun was getting low in the sky.

"Oh, gosh, we gotta go!" said Dafne, realizing that they only just had enough time to get back for their family dinners.

Tommy, Nate, and Turnip walked them to the train station. The girls already had their return tickets, but the train was just pulling out when they got there. They would have to wait another fifteen minutes.

As Elsa looked around she realized that Jeanette and Tommy had disappeared. At first worried, she glanced at Dafne and saw her smiling. She understood. Tommy had probably taken Jeanette behind the station to kiss her. She saw Dafne slipping her arm inside Nate's, perhaps hoping he would get the same idea. Elsa took a half step away from Turnip.

Jeanette ran up just as the next train pulled in. Tommy walked behind her with a smug expression.

Handshakes were the extent of their intimate good-byes as the girls boarded the train.

"Well, did he kiss you?" asked Dafne once they were settled in their seats.

"I'm not telling."

"He did! Did you enjoy it?"

Jeanette couldn't help herself. "Yeah, he was sweet."

"Aww. I would've liked it if Nate had kissed me." After a moment, she added softly, "I'd really like to be kissed . . . by someone." She had already confided to Elsa that she had never been kissed.

"Would you have let Turnip kiss you, if he had tried?" Jeanette asked Elsa.

"Certainly not!"

Jeanette and Dafne both laughed.

"Don't worry, dear," said Dafne, "we'll get you kissed soon enough."

The train moved slowly through the suburbs of Brooklyn. Would they have made it in time had they caught the first train? Elsa rather doubted it. But on this train, she quickly knew they would be late and their cover would be blown. The dinner hour came and went. The train continued to be painfully slow.

Elsa admitted she had told Chris she was going to the train station that morning. She didn't know at the time it was a secret. By now he had probably told their parents. Jeanette and Dafne tried to devise an excuse that didn't involve Coney Island. The train didn't reach Lindenhurst until almost nine o'clock.

Mrs. Graham and Mrs. Streppy were at the station themselves, stoic and angry. Stepping off a Brooklyn train, their arms loaded with trinkets and stuffed animals, no excuses could be made. They were busted. Dafne and Jeanette were immediately grounded. There would be no dancing, no boys and no fun for at least two weeks.

Elsa was terrified. Surely now she would get fired. But Mrs. Graham didn't speak a word to her about it, either that night or ever again.

Back home, Chris offered her supper in the kitchen, but her stomach still hurt from the hot dogs. So did Dafne's, so she didn't mind going to bed without supper.

Alone at last in her room, Elsa prepared for bed. But just as she put on her nightgown, Dafne burst into her room and sat on her bed, smiling and laughing. Elsa was taken aback, but Dafne grabbed her and hugged her tightly, then sat up with her legs crossed on Elsa's bed.

"Oh, wasn't that fun!"

"Yes, it was. But was it worth it?"

"Oh, 'course! Mommy will forget she grounded me in a day or two."

"But what about me? Now I will get axed for sure." Elsa surprised herself by how quickly she had adopted some of Dafne's slang words.

Dafne laughed. "You're adorable, darling. You're not in trouble at all. Just say I made you do it. That's true, right?"

"Well, yes, I suppose."

"Exactly! You wanted no part of it. I made you go. Mommy knows that."

Elsa smiled. She realized in that moment that as long as she kept Dafne happy, her place in the house was entirely secure. It made her feel good to have such an ally and friend. But she wanted to please Mr. and Mrs. Graham, too.

Dafne was so innocent, almost even naïve, but Elsa found her to be like a breath of fresh air. The things Elsa had faced in her life had been serious and heavy. It was refreshing to have a friend whose worries were about which boy looked at her and why. There was so much Dafne could teach Elsa about this new world she was in, but Elsa might end up teaching Dafne a thing or two as well.

Dafne slipped back to her room down the servants' stair. Elsa was still too wound up to sleep. She had so much on her mind, for it really had been quite an adventure.

She sat at her small desk and turned on the lamp. It had become clear that nobody minded how late her lamp shone. She took out a sheet of paper and pen, and began to write in German.

*Dear Mother,*

*I am sorry it has taken me so long to write a first real letter to you. My first note announcing my arrival hardly counts. I have been kept exceedingly busy. It has been . . . in a word, Wunderbar!*

*My employers, the Grahams, are good people. Mr. Graham has been a patient teacher as I learn the craft of legal translation. I worry less about my frequent errors. He knows how hard I try, and I do think I improve a little each day.*

*Dafne is my employers' daughter. Though, I sometimes wonder if I am Dafne's servant more than Mr. and Mrs. Graham's. She requires me to accompany her on all her adventures. But more than a mistress, Dafne has become a friend. She includes me as if I were her equal. Although I have sometimes to remind her of propriety, I am honored by her friendship. She is a remarkable young woman.*

*I do hope you are well, and that your work is manageable. I wish I could come visit you one day . . . as well as Sonja and Christof. Dafne always talks about wanting to come to the city. Perhaps she will bring me along and make this wish come true.*

*Your loving daughter,*
*Elsa*

She blew the ink dry and folded the page. She would ask for an envelope and postage tomorrow. She had almost told her mother about her specific adventures with Dafne—the dance party and trip to Coney Island. But since Nina couldn't read, Elsa suspected she would take the letter to Pastor Reus to read it to her. The minister who had known Elsa since her childhood would be horrified to learn that she had grown up to consort with strange boys at Coney Island and go to dance halls that permitted turkey trots and tangos!

She smiled.

# CHAPTER ELEVEN
# SUMMER DAYS

Elsa followed Dafne into yet another shop in Lindenhurst's modest downtown area.

"This is the last store, I promise."

Elsa had been with the Grahams for almost three months. This morning, in mid-June, the humidity wasn't yet heavy, but the air promised that the heat of summer wasn't far off. She waited near the door for Dafne's quick and fruitless pass through the racks of clothes.

Coming out of the shop, they almost collided with Glenn Streppy.

"Why Mr. Streppy," said Dafne. "Since when have you been back? And shame on you for not calling!"

"Only since yesterday." He removed his straw hat and nodded.

"Okay, you're forgiven." She beamed.

After nodding at Dafne, Elsa found her eyes connected with the gentleman's as he looked and nodded at her. She was surprised and felt a small flutter in her chest. She was accustomed to being invisible around strangers of the upper class.

"What brings you ladies to town this fine morning?"

He even referred to *her* as one of the ladies.

"An errand of total futility!" Dafne said. "The Summer Days festival is this weekend. We're having a party at our house after the parade, and I need a new dress. I don't know why I thought I could find one here. We've just given up."

"I'll walk you both home."

"Lovely."

They started back. Glenn and Dafne walked side by side with Elsa following a step behind.

"I'm glad to see you again," said Dafne. "I felt I was kind of rude that day when I had tea with you, and then I haven't seen you since."

"I don't remember you being impolite."

"You still never told me about Harvard."

"What is there to tell? I'm not as exciting a man as you might think. While my fellows were amusing themselves with dissipation, drunkenness, and atheism, I mostly spent my time with my books."

Elsa thought this sounded extremely exciting.

"You still have another year to 'lose yourself,'" Dafne encouraged.

Glenn laughed. "I suppose I do."

Dafne sighed with longing. "Oh, to have been out in the world as you both have."

It shocked Elsa to hear her experiences being considered enviable.

"What field are you studying?" Dafne asked him.

"I'm working toward a business degree."

"I won't lie; that does sound rather dull."

Glenn smiled. "Many of my colleagues at Harvard feel the same way. These days, it's more popular to study philosophy, psychology, or other theoretical fields, and imagine yourself changing the world. This stems from a collegiate that mostly does not need to work. If a young man can count on having plenty of money for the rest of his life, why spend college years studying something practical like business or law?"

"I see. Now forgive me if this question is crass, but what makes you different? You have no pressing need to start a career?"

"Not financially. But I *want* to work."

Dafne had no immediate response. Elsa felt she understood Glenn perfectly.

"Where will you go after college?" Dafne asked.

"Probably to New York, or I'll stay in Boston at first. I do want to establish a career. But eventually I'd like to come back here."

"But that's incredible! Why ever would you want to live here when you could be in New York?"

"When I'm away at college I miss the simplicity of Lindenhurst. It's refreshing to go to a dance where the turkey trot is still scandalous."

Dafne grinned.

"Or a town where nearly grown girls are punished for going to Coney Island."

"Hey!"

They all laughed.

"I still don't get it," Dafne said at length.

"If you leave and come back, you'll learn to love this place."

"Maybe."

Glenn glanced toward Elsa. In their momentary meeting of eyes, they communicated their mutual love for Lindenhurst.

They walked for a few minutes in silence. The day was beginning to heat up. Elsa was now walking beside the other two. She hadn't even realized it until Dafne took Glenn's arm and surged a step ahead. Dafne always treated her more like a friend than a servant, and it was Elsa who made sure to retain their stations, so this surprised her. Had she seen Elsa and Glenn's moment of understanding and felt jealous? The thought almost made Elsa laugh.

"Next week is the first of summer," said Dafne. "I can't wait."

"Yes," he said. "I had forgotten about the Summer Days festival."

"You are coming, aren't you?" she said, more as a command than a question. "We sent your family an invitation, but if you just returned, perhaps your mother forgot to tell you. We'll have a band playing in the yard, with dancing, of course. It's just a concrete slab, but we can make it work. I know you like to dance. I hear they're even going to have fireworks this year, though we probably won't be able to see them from our yard."

Glenn smiled.

"Yes, I'll come."

They had reached Hyde Street.

"Here we are," said Dafne. "Won't you come in?"

"No, thank you," Glenn demurred, "I should not impose on your family unannounced."

"Okay. Thank you for the company. It was swell talking with you."

Glenn doffed his cap and bowed again, first toward Dafne, then toward Elsa.

"Until Saturday, then."

"Yes, until Saturday."

Back inside, Elsa checked in briefly with Mrs. Graham, then excused herself to her bedroom. There was no housework that could not wait an hour or two. Sometimes she needed to take a moment to herself to reflect on how much her life had changed in this short time—as well as on the things that would never change.

Walking home, when Dafne surged ahead with Glenn, served as a reminder to Elsa of who she really was.

Dafne had repeatedly told Elsa she was more a friend to her than a servant. Elsa loved her for it, but worked to maintain her place. It was not only more proper but also safer. The last thing she wanted was to risk her position by becoming too close to Dafne. Even her friendship to Dafne— real as it was—had an element of service to it.

Dafne herself didn't realize how desperately she needed the attention and friendship Elsa gave her. Elsa quickly noticed, because it was a need so foreign to her prior world.

Her life hadn't provided many opportunities for friendship, and none for attention. That these things were so vital to Dafne seemed strange to her. Yet Elsa had grown up with a sister, while Dafne was an only child.

Whatever the cause for Dafne's needs, Elsa was happy to give her devotion. She had grown to care deeply for her young mistress. Dafne considered her a friend because she knew Elsa's affection was genuine. It made them a perfect pair, each craving what the other needed most to give.

But Dafne craved attention from others, too. Elsa had realized that the night of the dance at the grange. So today, when Glenn showed them equal attention, Dafne felt jealous. It reminded Elsa that she needed to remain careful. Her friendship with Dafne was real, but friendship across classes was always tenuous.

Minutes before eight o'clock, Dafne stepped out to the deck above the yard and surveyed her handiwork.

Everything looked just about ready. The ragtime band was setting up on the lawn. This local band was nothing compared to the band from New York that had played at the grange, but they would do just fine. Dafne had heard them dozens of times and knew all their tunes.

Direct sunlight had just left the yard, turning the hot day into a pleasant evening. Chris and Elsa had transformed the yard into a beautiful summer garden. Chris walked the perimeter, lighting the temporary lampposts they had installed. Additional electric lights had been strung across the magnolias and hydrangeas. Six square tables had been set up, three at each side of the yard. Each table had two crystal buckets, one filled with flowers, the other with ice and champagne. Guests had already begun to arrive.

No one but Jeanette and Elsa would ever know that the Grahams' Summer Days party was entirely Dafne's idea. It had been a somber spring in New York and Long Island. It seemed everyone knew someone who had died on the Titanic, so nobody was in the mood for revelry.

Dafne felt it was now time to get on with life. She was dying for a party. A few weeks back she had decided to take matters into her own hands. She subtly planted the idea in her parents' heads until they thought they'd come up with it on their own. Tonight was the culmination of her grand scheme.

Yesterday Elsa and Chris had gone to the train station to pick up six crates off the New York train. Dafne had gotten a good laugh watching in the kitchen as Elsa opened the cold crates, her eyes widening to see the small sandwiches and individual sweets, fully prepared and ready to be put on a plate. Such was the marvel of refrigerated train cars.

With the food pre-prepared, Dafne had tried to get Elsa to come to the festival and parade that morning. Elsa had refused, insisting there was much work still to be done. Preparing for a party was no simple thing. While Elsa worked frantically in the kitchen, Dafne had tried to talk her into coming with her, even as Jeanette and Glenn waited in the sitting room. That was when Chris stepped in to insist that Elsa remain at the house. Dafne knew if she became more stubborn they would go to Mrs. Graham, and she would be overruled. She gave up and left for downtown with only Jeanette and Glenn. The day had still been fun, but it would have been better with Elsa. Her servant missing the festival was the price Dafne paid to have her party.

Standing above the yard, Dafne knew she looked lovely. Her soft lavender gown enhanced the sun-kissed color of her cheeks. A daisy perched in her hair. This wasn't a new dress, sadly, but she doubted anyone here tonight other than Jeanette and her parents had seen her in it. Her mother had objected to this dress originally. It left her upper back and most of her shoulders uncovered. Looking at herself earlier in her bathroom mirror, she thought her breasts filled out the bodice of the dress a little bit better than the last time she'd worn it. At least she wanted that to be true.

She felt both proud and shy, standing there with a smile as eyes floated up toward her from the garden. Much as she wanted to be a woman, not a child, it was a complicated desire, and an even more complicated process.

She determined to mask all her apprehensions tonight. She stood as tall as she could, excited for what the night might bring.

Jeanette stepped to Dafne's side. The Streppy family had just arrived.

"Aren't I a genius?" boasted Dafne.

"Who are all these men?"

"Mostly sons of my father's clients." Dafne didn't need to ask which "men" Jeanette referred to. There were four handsome young men milling around among the mostly older crowd below. "I think they've just come back from college like your brother."

"I wonder if he knows them."

"I was thinking the same thing."

Together they found and latched on to Glenn, hoping he would provide them with the social advantage they were seeking. But Glenn, while pleasant company, was hardly one to rely on for introductions.

Glenn had dressed more casually than the majority of the men, but Dafne thought he looked particularly handsome in a gray suit and long blue tie. The Grahams had dubbed this a casual summer party, but most of the gentlemen wore their evening uniform out of habit. Glenn's attire set him apart. Yet Dafne could tell by the way he fidgeted that he felt self-conscious because of his choice. He probably wished he'd worn a tuxedo.

Jeanette decided to press her brother. "Do you see any of your college fellows here?"

"No. None of these chaps went to Harvard. But I

recognize a few of them from high school. There's Jim Rutherford over there with the crooked tie. He was a football star back then. He went to Princeton, but I don't think he plays anymore."

They proceeded to the table where the football player stood with his second glass of champagne and third egg sandwich. Before the thing was swallowed, Jim had informed them all that he did *indeed* play football for Princeton. Another young man joined the group and "accidentally" revealed that Jim had only been on the practice team.

Scowling, Jim introduced them to Mr. Carter, who had been with him at Princeton. The football player further informed them that, as he would be returning to Princeton for his senior year, they would soon hear his name in connection with the football team.

Mr. Carter wasn't nearly as impressive physically as Jim Rutherford, but his manners were better. At least his tie was straight, and his speech wasn't garbled by a mouthful of egg sandwich. He had a crafty expression and twinkling eye. Having graduated from Princeton, he was preparing to apprentice in his father's shipping business in Brooklyn. It was through this business that his family knew the Grahams.

Jeanette was interested less in one or the other of the two men as in the combined attention of them both. Dafne was already bored by them. She liked Glenn better than the others. They left the table.

Now a couple rather than a threesome, Dafne thought it appropriate to take Glenn's arm. They shared the task of introductions as they mingled through the growing crowd. It seemed that any person who didn't know one would be in the other's circle of acquaintance, making them convenient partners for the festivities.

Soon they danced.

Glenn was so graceful on the dance floor. Just like when they won the turkey-trot contest, he floated with her across the patio, his feet hardly seeming to touch the stone. There would be no turkey trots tonight, obviously. But he danced the waltz and one step with equal grace. He wasn't shy about them being the only couple dancing in front of the band, even though his usual personality was loath to draw attention. She was growing more and more interested in this man.

They danced three songs. Other people were dancing by then. Jeanette's eyes rolled back and forth as she endured a plodding dance with the football player.

Although Glenn seemed more natural conversing with people her mother's age than her own, Dafne chose to retain her position on his arm. There were many more people of that age group at the party than their own. That, Dafne now realized, had been the one flaw in her plan.

"Let's take a walk," she said. "I want some fresh air. Maybe we'll be able to see the fireworks."

He consented easily. Dafne wondered whether he was enjoying the feeling of her bare arm draped inside his own.

Hyde Street continued from the Grahams' house a half mile until it reached the beach. They didn't speak through the walk. Dafne, usually boisterous, didn't mind the silence at all.

Reaching the end of the street, Dafne released his arm and walked out to the edge of the sand. She wanted to kick off her heels and sprint out into the foam. If she didn't like this dress so much, she might have done it.

"I used to come here when I was a little girl and watch the ships sail past toward New York. I wonder if I watched the ship Elsa came on." She spun around. "Have you been to Europe?"

Glenn hesitated, surprised by the seemingly random question. In Dafne's mind the connection was clear.

"No," she answered for him. "I don't suppose you would have." She looked back toward the sea. "I want to go to Europe. Vienna, I think. Everybody's scared of Europe now. Do you think there will be a war, Glenn?"

"I don't know."

"If there is, I'll go anyway. It would be exciting."

She stood gazing at the starlit surf until a loud bang sounded behind them. She squealed and ran back to Glenn's side as both turned toward the town.

"They *did* get fireworks! Oh, how exciting." The multicolored explosions burst, one after another, low over downtown. Dafne watched, gradually wrapping her bare arms around each other.

The short show finished. A breeze had come up over the sea.

"Are you cold?" Glenn asked.

"Yes." She felt his warm coat close around her shoulders. "Thank you."

"I'll find us a taxi."

He took her hand and led her back to the street. Although they had held hands before while dancing, feeling his hand take hers now, alone on the street at night, felt entirely different and gave her body a tingle.

Because it was a celebratory night in the town, Glenn found a car without much difficulty.

As soon as they were settled into the cab, Dafne leaned toward Glenn and kissed him. She pulled back and smiled at him, inviting him to kiss her back. He did. She wrapped her arms around the back of his neck, savoring the feeling of being kissed for the first time in her life. Even if she had to initiate it, she was happy. She told herself he had really initiated it back when he took her hand.

She didn't know why Glenn Streppy so suddenly came to interest her. She didn't know why she felt compelled to kiss him. But it was good; it was time she had a man.

More than half the guests had left by the time they returned to the party. The orchestra was on their final set. Nobody seemed to notice their disappearance and reentrance except for Jeanette, who looked disapprovingly at Dafne, still wrapped in Glenn's gray suit coat.

# PART III

MARCH, 1916

# CHAPTER TWELVE
# THREAT OF WAR

America had grown tense, gazing across the Atlantic as Europe floundered in the greatest war the world had ever known. As the years dragged on, neutrality was ever harder to maintain.

*How long would it be before American men had to join the deadly fray?* Not only was it a question for the political halls in Washington, London, Paris and Berlin. The impact of the question had reached every corner of the country, even the Grahams' tearoom in quaint Lindenhurst.

"But why should it be our problem?" said Mrs. Graham to her guests, more as a declaration than a question. "Europe has been fighting itself for centuries. There's no reason for American boys to die."

"Have we even decided what side we're on yet?" asked Mrs. Streppy.

"Mother, we clearly could not support Germany's aggression!"

The women in the room all looked at Glenn, surprised by his passion. Even Elsa looked up from her serving. Mr. Graham glanced up cautiously from his cup of tea.

"Germany is bleeding the life out of France, our ally," Glenn continued. "They sunk that ship last year, a civilian ship sailing from New York. It's pure aggression. I don't understand how in good conscience we can *keep* from joining the war."

"But Germany has been our ally as well," said Mrs. Graham. "The German people must be suffering terribly, too."

Elsa wondered if she was thinking of her husband's clients. Elsa had seen and translated some briefs. Her heart broke at rumors of starvation in her homeland.

"The war is on French soil," said Glenn. "The action hasn't come to Germany yet. And did you hear what the German troops did when they marched through Belgium? Atrocious!"

Elsa slid between the couches to inspect the status of the six teacups. She was glad her presence continued to be required. The conversation interested her greatly.

"If we're going to fight we had better get on with it," said the sixth tea guest, Mrs. Reynolds. "All anybody talks about now is this war. No domestic politics get done anymore. I thought we would have the vote by the end of this year, but now it won't even be considered until next year at the soonest."

Mrs. Graham gave Mrs. Reynolds a nod of approval. Elsa glanced at Glenn's mother, who was leaning back in her chair with folded arms. Politics could be a contentious point at the Grahams' house. Elsa knew that Mrs. Streppy didn't think women should have the vote.

Glenn brought the conversation quickly back to the war.

"I agree with Mrs. Reynolds," he said. "The longer we wait, the more French and English will die. There's no sense sitting comfortably over our tea while Europe slaughters itself! We have the force to decide this war if President Wilson chooses."

"I just don't see why our boys need to die when it's not our problem," said Dafne, speaking for the first time.

"But darling, it *is* our problem! Not only morally but also politically. It became our problem after the German U-boats sank the Lusitania. This new submarine warfare is ruthless!"

Elsa glanced at Mr. Graham and briefly caught his eye.

She wondered how much he knew about these underwater ships. His business primarily consisted of German shipping interests. Things were never as simple as they seemed—she certainly knew that. After all, she was a German herself!

"Furthermore, the Kaiser has allied with Mexico," Glenn said. "They are devising a plan to attack us from the south."

Nobody seemed very alarmed by this latest threat.

"Tell us, Glenn," said Mr. Graham. "How have you heard all these developments about the war? I didn't see anything about Mexico in the papers."

Glenn, so confident a moment before, suddenly grew unsure of himself. "Well, I talked to a military man who was in town this week."

Dafne glared suspiciously at him. "What kind of military man?"

"I suppose you would call him a recruiter."

The conversation stopped. Even the clatter and slurping of teacups paused for a moment as all eyes fixed on Glenn. Elsa stood motionless beside the table.

"I'm thinking about enlisting in the army."

"Glenn, do you realize what you're saying?" asked his mother.

"Entirely. If we join the war, all us young men will be drafted anyway. There would be months and months of training. By the time the army was ready it might be too late. But if I enlist now I might have a chance to do some good."

"Would you have to go away to one of those bases in the South?"

"No. There is a training camp in Brooklyn. So I wouldn't need to go far."

"Until you go to France," said Dafne. She had been sitting silently beside him, her eyes burning with ever-increasing rage.

Suddenly Dafne lurched to her feet.

"How could you?" she screamed. "I'm your fiancée! Don't I deserve to be thought of before you throw your life away?"

"Darling, I—"

"Don't darling me! I don't care if you go off to France and get killed!"

She spun on her heels and ran upstairs.

An uncomfortable silence hovered over the gathering. Finally, Mr. Graham rose and came across the room.

"I'm proud of you, son," he said. Glenn stood hesitantly and shook Mr. Graham's offered hand. "It's a brave thing to consider, and we'll all be proud if you do enlist. Even Dafne, once she has time to think it over."

"Thank you, sir."

The three ladies nodded and muttered in agreement. This *European* war suddenly seemed much closer to home.

Elsa looked at Mrs. Graham, who nodded. Elsa followed Dafne upstairs. Mrs. Graham served the remainder of the tea herself.

Elsa found Dafne crying on her bed. She sat beside her and rubbed her back.

Dafne didn't look up from the pillow. She knew the feel of the hand on her. "Will he really have to go to Europe?"

"I don't know. He didn't say it was certain yet."

"Oh, rubbish." Dafne turned her face to speak over the pillow. "He told everyone like that because he was afraid to tell me alone. He's decided. Maybe he's bored with me. Do you think he's tired of me?"

"No."

"Why does he have to be such a man?" She sniffled and smudged her mascara vigorously on the pillow. "Maybe he doesn't want to marry me anymore. We were already thinking about waiting until the war was over. Now I reckon we'll *have* to wait. Do you think I should marry him?"

Elsa laughed lightly. "It is a little late to ask me now. You already told him you would."

"But you wouldn't say what you thought back then, either."

"It was your decision."

"Oh, golly, Elsa! Why can't you ever have an opinion? I have far too many of my own. You can borrow some."

Elsa smiled. "Do you still love him?"

"I do. It's just that, you know . . . I'm still here. I'm going to be twenty-one soon, and I've still never left this town for more than a couple days at a time. Now I'm engaged to a man who wants to stay here and add more children to Lindenhurst. Poor dears! They'll be just like me." She cried again.

Elsa brought both hands to Dafne's shoulders to soothe her. Those shoulders weren't as bony as when Elsa first met her mistress. These four years had been good to Dafne. She was still a slender girl but had put on weight in exactly the right places. Her cheeks had grown full and playful. Her shoulders were soft and smooth. As Dafne had discovered her feminine sensuality, she gradually moved on from the boyish fashions of her teen years. Elsa wondered whether she realized what a beauty she had become.

"It all happened so quickly." Dafne rolled onto her back while holding Elsa's comforting hand on her stomach. Although she was talking about her relationship with Glenn, Elsa thought how she could have been talking about her development into a woman.

"I kissed him before I even thought if I should. Then a few years go by and we're engaged. It's not that I have regrets. I love him dearly. It's just . . . oh, I don't know. I wish I'd had the chance to do more before this all happened. Both with him and on my own."

"I know." Elsa smiled at her mistress.

"I wonder if we hadn't gotten so settled all of a sudden, if maybe I could have discovered and experienced more things . . . I've never even kissed anyone else."

"Didn't you hear him, though? If he goes to a base in Brooklyn, perhaps you can go to the city to be near him."

"Yeah, I thought of that. But it's sort of too late now. I

don't think I could have the fun in New York that I might have a year or two ago."

"Don't be silly. Of course you can."

"Oh, thank you, dear." She half rose and hugged her servant. "You always encourage me. I'll take you along to New York. I couldn't live without you."

"But your parents need me here. Your father's work—"

"Nonsense. Don't you see what's happening? My father's German clients are all disappearing. Besides, you're *my* servant. I'm keeping you. And I always get what I want." She frowned for a moment. "Except from Glenn."

Dafne laid her face back onto the pillow. Elsa rose and looked out the window. She saw Glenn pacing alone on the street outside.

"Go on down," Dafne said. "The tea's probably over. No need for me to keep you."

Elsa left her but instead of returning to clean the tearoom, she went down the back stair and met Glenn at the side of the house. He stopped with his hands clasped behind his back. His coat was open and pulled unflatteringly away from his vest.

"How is she?"

"She will be all right." She paused. "You should have told her differently."

"I know." He rearranged the bottom of his shirt, which had begun to poke out from between his vest and trousers. "I meant to talk to her about it, but I never had the chance. Every time I tried, she started talking about something else. Then I just sort of blurted it out without thinking."

"I know you did not mean to hurt her. But it *was* insensitive." He said nothing. Elsa wondered whether she had been too direct for her station. "You did decide to enlist."

He nodded.

"When did you decide?"

"In there." He inclined his head toward the house.

"I thought so."

"*You* understand why I need to do this, don't you?"

"Yes. I do."

Glenn started walking again as Elsa fell in beside him. "I think you understand Dafne and me better than we understand each other."

"That is true. Sometimes you miss the most obvious things about each other. For example, the reason why neither of you is content. It makes sense to me."

"Why aren't we?"

"Dafne wants to get away from Lindenhurst. You love it here but need to feel purposeful. That is why you are joining the army, is it not?"

"That's exactly right."

"I understand you because I have worked my whole life. I would not know what to do with myself without work. I can see how restless you are. Dafne has never worked, so she does not understand."

As they spoke, Elsa thought of the various business attempts Glenn had made in the three years since he graduated from Harvard. None had gained traction, and Dafne always thought him silly for trying. Elsa remembered, when she'd first met him, that he'd said he would probably need to spend some time in New York or Boston in order to start a career. But that was easier said than done when he loved Lindenhurst, loved a girl here, and had a good life. The three of them—herself together with Dafne and Glenn—had had such good times through these years. But it would be foolish to think it could last forever.

"You're very wise, Elsa. I envy the need for labor you've had. When nothing forces me to do something with my life, it's hard to initiate anything."

Elsa had a brief recollection of all the horrors she had endured at the Triangle Shirtwaist Factory: the foreman's molestation, risk of frostbite each winter, the tragic, terrifying fire. Her present situation was wonderful, but she had gone through hell to earn it. Glenn hadn't yet gone through his trial.

"How can I make Dafne understand?" Glenn asked.

"Just talk to her. Do not let her think you are running away from her."

"You're right." He turned back toward the house. Elsa almost reached for his arm, but stopped herself before she touched him. She had grown so comfortable with him that she sometimes had to remind herself of her position.

"Not now," she said. "Give her time. Go home and call her tomorrow. I think you will be able to explain yourself better."

He nodded.

"This may be a good thing for the two of you. Dafne can come to New York to be close to you. Then you will each have what you always wanted."

They both smiled.

"You are a blessing to both of us, Elsa."

"I do what I can. Your world is still something quite foreign to me."

They stood for a moment, awkwardly smiling at each other.

"I should go in and rejoin my mother," he said at length.

"Good day, Mr. Streppy."


Dafne plopped ungracefully to the sand. She didn't care whether the grains got stuck in her dress. She was tired of this one. However, her shoes waited for her on the grass just off the beach.

Everything was moving so fast. It had only been a couple weeks since Glenn dropped the bombshell of his enlistment. His base was in the city, so naturally she was going too. Now her things were already being packed.

This spot on the beach always reminded her of the night she decided to fall in love with Glenn. That choice had turned out better than she could have imagined. She knew she wasn't the easiest person to get along with, but Glenn was always patient with her. He put up with her impulses. He let her monopolize their conversations. She couldn't imagine what she would do without him.

Yet she had to wonder how these four years might have passed had Glenn not come into her life. Would she have found her way to New York? Or would she have been stuck in Lindenhurst regardless?

She didn't regret her choice; she only regretted the things she'd missed. And if she would have missed them anyway, then she might as well miss them while enjoying romance with a wonderful man. She couldn't complain about her life— between Glenn and Elsa, she had the best people to love. Still, she felt discontented.

Glenn had taken her to the city several times, but the trips hadn't met her expectations. He was timid and didn't know anyone; she was a small-town girl. They had no inroad into society. She knew she could work her way in if she had the chance, but it would take longer than a weekend. Dafne could never relax when she and Glenn went to New York together. She didn't *belong*, and it made her feel nervous. Once they took Elsa along and that helped. It seemed as if they needed the final member of their threesome to maintain the right chemistry. She laughed to think how shy those two were, and what unlikely friends they would be without her.

Perhaps Elsa was right—Glenn's enlistment could be just the chance she needed. Now that her anger had subsided and she really thought about it, this might be the best thing Glenn ever did for her. Without such a drastic step, she would have been destined to grow old in Lindenhurst. As long as the war ended in time and he didn't actually have to go fight in Europe, it would be a good thing.

Dafne stood and scampered to the edge of the water. Pulling up her skirt, she kicked her bare feet into the foam. Although the spring day felt warm, the water was icy.

The three years since Glenn finished college had been so

much fun. She, Glenn and Elsa had been together almost nonstop. Whether shooting billiards at her house, dancing at the grange, or sunning at the beach in the summertime, their fun and adventures never seemed to end. It seemed like it could last forever. Dafne still wanted to believe it could.

Whatever passion she may have had for Glenn, it had passed. Honestly, it had never been very passionate. She remembered how Jeanette used to describe the rush of being kissed by a boy. Dafne never really felt that rush. But she still enjoyed it and wished he would do more than his impeccable sense of propriety allowed. She wanted Glenn to find her irresistible.

But she put up with his lack of adventurism for all the other things she gained by being with him. How she loved the times she spent with Glenn and Elsa. She had to marry Glenn to preserve this wonderful time. She saw no reason why it couldn't last, no matter what anyone said.

She feared the future because of how it might change her memories. She even feared New York. All her life she had wanted to be there. Now, on the verge of realizing her dream, all she wanted was to keep the happiness she had gained here.

Yet on the other hand, what an opportunity this was! If they could bring the magic of their friendship to the city, how much more wonderful it would be. It frightened her, but as long as they had each other she believed they would be happy.

She kicked at a clot of foam that floated toward her toes. It exploded on her foot and splashed all over the bottom of her skirt. She squealed and jumped out of the water. She sat back down on the sand and shook her head.

"I knew it!" She always got her dress wet eventually.

Elsa felt wistful as she gave Mr. Graham what was effectively a tour of his own office. In recent years she had spent more time here than he had. But tomorrow she would move to New

York City with his daughter. Her sadness was twofold: She wasn't eager to return to the city of her childhood after the wonderful life she'd found here. Also, she regretted leaving the service of this man, who had given her such an opportunity to further her education and start a career. Yet she understood how her usefulness to him was waning.

"Every translation I did for you is filed here." She opened drawers of the file cabinet along the wall behind his desk. "They are alphabetical by case name; both the German to English, and the English to German are in the same files."

He watched her absentmindedly.

"Elsa."

"Yes, sir."

"When you are in the city, it would be smart not to tell people you are German."

She nodded, not needing to ask why, and also, in a flash, understanding what the fate of her translations would be. He didn't have the heart to tell her that he would burn all her hard work as soon as she was gone. These years of records of his involvement with the German shipping industry had to be destroyed. He couldn't risk having someone comb through his files and find a distant connection with the inventors or financiers of the U-boats.

"In your position," Mr. Graham continued, "you do not need to use your last name very often. "But you still might consider changing it. When we go to war . . . and we will . . . things may become difficult for your countrymen here."

Elsa nodded again. Just as things would get difficult for her and her family, so they would for him. What a shame that an American patriot like Mr. Graham was already under suspicion because of his work with Germans long before anyone had thought of going to war with Germany.

"Thank you." Elsa understood there was no need to continue her summary. "Thank you for giving me this opportunity. I am sorry to see it end, but this is probably best."

"Yes, it is. I'm glad you're going with Dafne."

She left the office for the final time. In the morning she would leave this house and this town—also perhaps for the final time. She hoped not. These four years in the Graham household had been more than the culmination of a dream.

The day Dafne and Glenn announced their engagement was the happiest day of Elsa's life. Up until then, Elsa had always felt concern about her future. In that moment, she stopped worrying—the engagement had seemed to assure her of a secure future serving the people she loved. The ambition that had driven her childhood could finally rest. What joy could compare to serving Dafne and Glenn in their marriage?

Now, for the first time since the engagement, she began to wonder. She had expected to serve Mr. Graham for many years, yet now it was over.

Today reminded her that things never could last forever. Truly, she would not want them to. Happiness had just temporarily allowed her to forget that she did still have dreams and ambitions. There was so much of the world still for her to learn, even if security had to be risked. It would not be the first time.

She still hoped she could serve Dafne and Glenn for the rest of her life. The last few years had been wonderful. The coming years could be just as beautiful. But there was no guarantee. Life never gave guarantees, especially for one in her station. As far away in her past as the clothing factory seemed, she remained only a small step away from being plunged back to it.

Walking upstairs, she heard the gramophone spinning as Dafne and Glenn danced together in the billiard room.

*"We were sailing along, on Moonlight Bay,"* hummed both voices together with the music.

Elsa tried to slip into the room to watch unseen. It always made her happy to watch Dafne and Glenn dance together. Dafne saw her and extended her arm away from her fiancé, brightly smiling and inviting Elsa toward them. She walked over. Dafne slipped her arm around Elsa's back, rocking with her until she was dancing, too. Dafne laid her head on Elsa's shoulder, still humming the tune of *Moonlight Bay*. Elsa could hardly help being aware of the brush of Glenn's arm against her other side.

"How I love you both," Dafne cooed as the song ended. "As long as we three are together we will always be happy. Nothing ever needs to change." She flitted away in her cornflower blue dress and put the needle back at the beginning of the record. "One more time, then you can give Jeanette her record back." The song started again.

Dafne plopped into a chair, draping her legs over the padded arm. "I don't think I will miss Lindenhurst at all, since we are all going to New York together."

"You'll miss it more than you think," Glenn said.

"Nonsense." She closed her eyes and hummed with the music. "Dance with Elsa."

Elsa, who had remained standing in the middle of the floor beside Glenn, immediately started to back away toward the wall. Dafne lurched out of her seat and pushed her back toward Glenn, who was just as hesitant as Elsa. She grabbed him too, and thrust them together. Dafne forcefully shaped Elsa's arms into a proper dancing posture around Glenn, and then she commanded Elsa to relax.

Glenn began to walk to the beats of the music. He was easy to follow. After a moment Elsa forgot herself and really did start to relax.

"Don't look at your feet," said Glenn gently. "If you think about when to step, you will be late. You can feel the rhythm through me."

Elsa tried to follow his instructions. Dafne followed them, encouraging and repeatedly lifting Elsa's drooping chin.

Elsa was glad when the song ended, only then realizing how much fun it had been. She stood back properly against the wall, even though she felt giddy inside. She had never been in that sort of physical contact with a man before. It was inappropriate to have enjoyed it so much.

Dafne smiled and patted her shoulder. Elsa could tell that Dafne understood exactly how she felt. Her face grew red.

"There will be a lot more fun for you in New York," said Dafne. "Just you wait and see."

# CHAPTER THIRTEEN
# LOST IN MANHATTAN

The train trip was stressful for all.

Dafne found herself snapping at her companions several times. She couldn't help it. Soon Elsa and Glenn had both clammed up, afraid to say anything. But as soon as the train pulled into Penn Station, Dafne's mood transformed.

Hailing a cab, she knew exactly where they were and where they needed to go. She'd dreamed of being here for so long that she had mentally walked every street. She directed the cabby to the east side of the park and to their new apartment, on 71st Street between Lexington and Park Avenues.

Dafne adored the apartment at once. The building was a modern, three-story brownstone. The stairs rose from the sidewalk to their entryway. A lower staircase descended from street level to an apartment below. The first level of their new home contained the living room, dining room, and kitchen. The living room was fairly small but had all the furniture Dafne had requested. She planned to entertain often.

A staircase of carpeted marble took them up to the bedrooms—a small one for Elsa and a large master suite with a patio for Dafne. Each had its own bathroom. The patio looked out onto the courtyard that separated the buildings on 71st from those on 70th. To the right could be seen a small glimpse of Park Avenue and the trees of Central Park beyond.

Dafne gasped when she saw her new bedroom.

"Oh, Glenn, thank you, thank you!" She squeezed him tightly. "I love you so much."

"Your father arranged everything, you know."

"Yes, but you made it possible." She kissed him quickly, and then resumed her examination of the apartment.

Suddenly, she turned back toward him and frowned. "I'm still mad at you, though."

Glenn had arranged to stay at the Carlton Hotel for the remaining two weeks before he reported for training at Fort Hamilton in Brooklyn.

Dafne already had a full slate of plans for those two weeks. She needed Glenn to introduce her to Manhattan society before he left for the base. Naturally, it was *she* who would press herself upon the fashionable crowd at the Carlton, the Biltmore, and the Plaza Hotel. By the second night, she knew her plan would work.

It was during those first weeks in New York City that Dafne discovered she was beautiful. The revelation enthralled her.

On the last afternoon before Glenn left for base, Dafne sat with Glenn and Elsa on a bench at the south end of Central Park. She looked across at the Plaza Hotel, enjoying the warmth of the late sun against her neck.

"Oh, Glenn, isn't it perfect? I do enjoy being people of leisure."

Glenn and Elsa both looked at her with reproach.

"How stupid of me." She was the only person of leisure among them. "But it is still so perfect. Don't you love it here, Elsa?"

"Yes."

"No, you don't, you liar. But you will soon, I promise."

Elsa couldn't fool her. Dafne turned to Glenn. "I wish you could stay with us. But that isn't why you came to New York, is it?"

"No, dear. But I will miss being with you."

"You're sweet." She kissed him. "We'll still have the

weekends, though."

A cloud suddenly passed over Dafne's face. She realized that her new joy was hers alone. Neither Glenn nor Elsa could possibly enjoy this time as much as she. She felt ashamed of her selfishness and obliviousness to the trials of the two people she most loved.

All Elsa wanted was to serve her, and all Glenn wanted was to love her. That would be enough for them, as long as it would also be enough to make her happy. Was her very selfishness a necessary component in their joint happiness? She wished she could give more to each of them, but if she bottled her joy as a gift, it would slip away.

Walking home in the twilight hour, Dafne felt as though everything sped up around them. The carriages and cars darted through the streets in a vibrant cacophony. People on the walkways wove like ants, creating an unbroken line in each direction with utter efficiency except when the lines met by mistake, usually at a street corner, in a moment of confusion. The various classes mingled without a second thought. Gentlemen in high-collared suits and silk hats passed women in torn, shoddy coats and colored bonnets left over from the last century. Seldom did a passerby notice or acknowledge another.

Dafne, too, felt antlike in her anonymity. She clung to Glenn as she took up her minuscule spot in the path of human insects. She heard shouting and laughing, and words of no particular language from the passersby. It made her feel small and slow as she edged through the whirl of noise and confusion.

Soon she was in a taxi. The car's speed slowed down the rush around her as she pressed her face to the glass. She slid her hand into Glenn's and brought her head down onto his shoulder, though her eyes still gazed outside. She was lost in Manhattan, but happy to have lost herself. It was the home she had always dreamed of.

* * * * *

Boot camp at Fort Hamilton presented Glenn with the greatest challenge of his young life.

Much as he had wanted to work, he'd never experienced the daily rigor of even a simple profession. The demands of the military were far more extreme. The day would come when the United States would draft an army from all social levels. Training would then be easier for the higher classes. But Glenn had joined a volunteer army, and the commanders wanted their men tough. He was singled out early on by his companions and superiors who eagerly watched for the "swell" to break.

His latrine duty was frequent. He was a favorite boot-shiner and bed-maker for the officers. Each rainy day seemed reason enough for him to be ordered on a two-mile march.

But Glenn's determination grew with each blow to his pride. By the first leave, following the third week of training, he felt he was beginning to win the respect of the commanders and his fellows.

He checked in for his two-night furlough at the Carlton Hotel, changed to a civilian suit, bought a bouquet from a flower girl on the street, and made his way to Dafne's apartment.

She wasn't at home.

Frustrated, he leaned against the doorjamb. It was four o'clock on Friday. She hadn't been expecting him until later that evening. Even Elsa was away.

He remembered that Dafne enjoyed the tea dances at the Biltmore. He walked to Fifth Avenue and hailed a cab to the hotel. The tea dance wasn't lively, however, and there was no sign of Dafne. He sat down in the lounge and ordered tea.

Once he had his cup and sandwich, he looked around the room. It embarrassed him to see how out of place he was. The evening was young, but he was the only tea drinker. All the other gentlemen had either a highball or a rocker in their hand. Many had shed their coats and loosened their ties. It looked more like a country club than a tearoom. Glenn ignored the gaiety around him until a young man abruptly sat down beside him.

"Hello," said the newcomer.

Glenn looked up, undecided whether to be annoyed or relieved to have company. "Good afternoon."

"Awaiting a lady?" The man nodded toward the bouquet Glenn had set on the table. "That would explain your good behavior."

It took Glenn a moment to understand that he meant his tea. He chuckled. "I'm not much of a drinker. I had hoped to call on my fiancée, but she wasn't at her apartment. I'm only back from Fort Hamilton for the weekend."

The man's eyes gleamed. "We have a hero among us! By Jim, I'm proud of you boys. Can hardly wait to go to war, eh?"

Glenn smiled.

"I say, I'm glad to make your acquaintance. I'm from Brooklyn myself. You must give me a call when you have a free night at base."

"Thank you. I will."

"Brian Halifax." He extended his arm across the table toward Glenn. "But everyone just calls me Hal."

"Glenn Streppy. A pleasure."

Hal was a slender, athletic man. He had neat chestnut hair and sparkling blue eyes that darted quickly from his drink to Glenn, then around the room. The best word Glenn could think of to describe his demeanor was *quickness*. Whether in the motion of his eyes, the movements of his body, or the connections of his words, speed was in everything he did. He seemed uncomfortable in his chair, for he was constantly squirming in his seat. Yet he wasn't in a hurry. Glenn felt that Hal was completely present with him in their conversation.

"Well, then, my friend," said Hal, "let me buy you a drink

while you wait for love."

"Thank you, but I prefer tea."

"That's right. You are a well-behaved sort. Well, we need more men like you." Hal said as downed his highball.

"Have you considered a military career?" asked Glenn.

"I'm no hero. But if we go over there, they'll surely send me when the time comes. No need to waste time in training now."

Glenn nodded. He understood this viewpoint, even if it wasn't his own.

"If you will excuse me, Mr. Halifax," said Glenn, "I should try phoning my fiancée."

"I will only excuse you if you will drop the 'Mister!' Remember, it's Hal."

Glenn laughed as he rose. "Very well."

He walked into the hotel office and picked up the phone to dial. Elsa answered.

"No, Miss Graham is not home but should be shortly. I must have been at the market when you came by. So sorry to have missed you . . . We had not been expecting you until later. She has invited some guests over tonight. I hope you will come. She will be delighted to see you."

Glenn said he would, but felt disappointed to have to share Dafne with a party. He returned to Hal. "Apparently she's entertaining tonight. I had hoped to see her alone."

Hal placed a comforting hand on his shoulder from across the table. "Cheer up, buddy. She probably wants to celebrate your triumphal return!"

"I suppose you're right. Say, why don't you come along? She's sure to have a few attractive young ladies there."

Hal's blue eyes sparkled. "Well, I . . . why not?"

"That's the spirit!" Glenn began to rise again from his seat.

"No hurry, bud." Hal applied a slight pressure with the hand that had remained on Glenn's shoulder. "Finish your tea, let me order another highball, and then tell me all about the hardships of military life. A party never suffers for gents showing up too late."

Almost two hours had passed before the new friends finally arrived at the 71st Street apartment. The small front room was already crowded with a half dozen guests. Dafne beamed at her fiancé's arrival, clearly thrilled that he had brought a handsome friend. Her soft pink dress played well against the glow of early summer on her cheeks and neck.

Glenn could tell she was happy to see him, but her greeting was subdued. She kissed him quickly on the cheek and momentarily embraced him.

"I've missed you, darling," she said.

Glenn presented her to Hal, whose eyes had grown wide, taking in her beauty. Dafne floated away, glancing back over her shoulder. He knew she purposely made sure they both saw how her dress fully exposed her beautiful back.

Hal clapped Glenn vigorously on the shoulder. "Good work, bud! She's a tiger!"

Several more people walked in on the heels of the two gentlemen, further crowding the small room. Glenn was surprised to see Thelma Blaine, now Thelma Sanderson. He remembered Dafne's jealousy years ago—a detail he'd learned from his sister rather than from Dafne herself. But time had rendered those feelings obsolete. Dafne had grown into a famous beauty; Thelma had married, borne two children, and developed a mature femininity. While still beautiful, Thelma lacked the freshness Dafne had discovered in herself. Dafne explained that she had encountered Thelma shortly after Glenn left for base. They had quickly built a new friendship.

Glenn had never felt comfortable at parties. He felt especially uncomfortable now. He was glad to have his new friend with him. It helped to pass the time. Yet all he really wanted was time alone with Dafne. His eyes followed her through the room. Each smile and each sparkle of her eyes entranced him. He felt a flutter of attraction whenever she subtly folded her shoulders in and laughed. But she was the hostess tonight. Her flirtations were for the room, not for him.

Eventually people started to leave. Hal left with the last of the guests, but not before writing down his Brooklyn address and phone number for Glenn.

Once everyone was gone, Dafne grew tired. Glenn sat with her for a few minutes as Elsa cleaned up, but it was late and Dafne seemed like she would fall asleep on the couch. As Glenn wrote down his room number at the Carlton, Elsa came out of the kitchen and took the note from him. He and Elsa smiled at each other; no words needed to convey their understanding. Glenn left, knowing Elsa would remind Dafne to call him at the hotel the next morning.

Elsa listened to the door click shut behind Glenn, then resumed cleaning up from the party. It wouldn't take her long. She had been quietly cleaning up after the guests even while they lingered. She continued her task as Dafne relaxed on the couch.

Except for these nighttime soirees, Elsa had mostly been left alone in their new apartment. As she'd arranged everything into a comfortable abode, she grew to feel it was *her* home. She remembered Dafne had once told her she would learn to think this way. Finally, she was the mistress of the house.

Elsa knew from the start that she would be lonely here. Dafne hardly spent any time in the apartment. At the Grahams' house in Lindenhurst, Chris and Katherine were always there, even when the masters were away. New York City reminded her of the big lonely rooms on Ellis Island, where people pressed in from every direction, yet they were only bodies, not personalities. Their presence only increased the loneliness. Here there were people everywhere—she couldn't walk down a sidewalk without brushing by dozens of people, and in the market she had to hold her basket in front of her in order to cut through the crowd. When Dafne entertained, these anonymous people came in and out of the apartment. Seldom did anyone speak to or even seem to notice her.

In the early days, before Glenn left for base, Dafne and Glenn had taken her with them to Central Park, Washington Square, and even to Broadway. Elsa enjoyed it for the companionship, but the new sights didn't fascinate her as they did Dafne. She had lived here before and knew the dark underside of the city. She suspected that Dafne, like many before and after her, loved the *idea* of New York City more than New York City itself. How long would it be before Dafne realized this as well?

Now that Glenn was gone, Dafne had new friends with whom she did these things. It was no longer appropriate to bring Elsa along. So Elsa spent her time alone. Her duties had thus far kept her too busy to visit her mother or her sister, but she planned to make time to see both as soon as possible.

By the time she had finished cleaning, Dafne was sound asleep on the couch. Elsa took the final half-empty champagne flute from the table beside her, debating whether to wake her mistress. For the sake of her crumpling dress, Elsa decided she should. She knelt down beside her and gently rubbed Dafne's arm. The debutante half woke, smiling sweetly. Elsa smiled, too, wishing Glenn could have seen this genuine tenderness on his fiancée's lips.

"Come, Miss Graham." Elsa helped Dafne to her feet, then wrapped her arm around her bare back and walked upstairs. Dafne's head rested on Elsa's shoulder. They came into Dafne's bedroom. Elsa switched on the light, which had been tinted soft, per Dafne's instructions.

"Help me with my dress, dear. I'm so tired."

Elsa froze for a moment. She had helped Dafne with her clothes before, but not since she had begun to wear *these* sorts of dresses. She recovered herself, but not before Dafne saw her hesitation and smiled. Elsa slipped the weightless dress up over Dafne's head. She hung it up while her mistress waited for her. Elsa unhooked Dafne's short girdle and garter belt, modestly trying to avert her eyes from Dafne's bare breasts.

Despite Dafne's tiredness and the alcohol she had drunk, Elsa knew she was watching her, perhaps even testing her, but she didn't understand why.

She quickly found Dafne's nightgown, but before putting it on, Dafne sat on her bed and made Elsa pull off her silk stockings. Once Dafne was safely covered in her nightgown, Elsa finally looked her in the eyes. She realized that this had not been a test but an invitation. The moment she realized it, the moment had passed.

"Thank you," Dafne said sweetly, climbing into bed. "Good night."

# CHAPTER FOURTEEN
## HAL

Despite the late party, Glenn awoke early. Military habits, even after only a few weeks, had changed his body clock. The phone rang earlier than he expected, but it was Hal, not Dafne.

"I'm passing by right now on my way to the Boylston Club for breakfast," he said. "Come down."

Glenn was already dressed, and breakfast did sound good.

Outside the hotel, Hal leaned against a post in his shirtsleeves, puffing on a cigarette.

"Good morning!" Hal clapped Glenn on the back. "Let's go, I'm starving.

The Boylston Club was only a few blocks from the Carlton.

"Here you will find the sorts of men I associate with," Hal said. "Shallow chaps blessed with easy money and carefree days."

Glenn laughed. He usually disliked the boisterous atmosphere at gentlemen's clubs but anticipated that it wouldn't be rowdy yet at this hour.

"You know, buddy," said Hal immediately after they had ordered their meal, "you and I are not so different. We both have money we didn't earn; you went to Harvard, I went to Columbia. Yet I've known you a whole day and I don't understand you anymore than I could understand a horse. Why you've chosen to join the army of your free will is a complete mystery to me."

Glenn smiled. He had certainly doubted his decision during these early weeks. Hal's attitude toward it actually helped him to remember his reasons for joining.

"I want to feel that my life has some worth." It was the most common explanation he used. Hal had not been the first to ask.

"Of course you do. So do I. But how is turning your life over to Mr. Wilson going to give it worth?"

"I believe it can."

"Do you have any idea how idiotic that sounds? You're going to be miserable, and at the end of it all you might die! Sure, I'm not making much worth of my life right now, but at least I'm having a hell of a good time."

Glenn smiled. He glanced around the room, which was noisier than he had expected at breakfast. There were about a dozen other men there. On the walls, there hung mementos of sporting successes, mostly golf and horse racing.

"Tell me, then," he said, "what would give life value?"

Hal shrugged.

"I'm not the one trying to validate myself, so I don't know the answer."

"If I were an artist, would you say that had value?"

"Only if you were a very special artist."

"What about a statesman?"

"Certainly not!"

"A clergyman?"

"Maybe, but I'm inclined to say no."

Glenn laughed. After a second Hal laughed too.

"Maybe you don't try to find value in life because you don't even believe in it," said Glenn.

"*Au contraire!* My life has value to me. I make the most of each day and enjoy it fully. I have nothing to complain about. So I'm content."

"I don't know why I can't live that way."

"'Cause you're a do-gooder son of a gun! Look at you— you have everything. Look at that girl of yours. If I were you I'd marry her as quickly as possible and then never leave the

house. But you have to go on your moral quest for meaning."
He broke off. "Ho, waiter!"

Their breakfasts and a pot of coffee were placed on the
table. After a few mouthfuls, when Hal spoke again, it was
with more thoughtfulness than Glenn had yet heard from him.

"Another thing I don't understand: you make yourself out
to be such a moralist . . . a good Christian, I suppose. And yet
you are eager to fight in *this* war? It doesn't make sense."

Glenn was confounded. "It's a moral war!"

Hal snorted. "This war is less moral than I am!"

"You don't support us entering it?"

"Actually I do, because I have few morals. I just wish
people like you could admit what's at stake. Germany is
fighting against England and France for control of Europe.
Good old Wilson down in Washington is working for a peace
that will increase America's power. But inevitably he'll send
you and maybe me over to gain power by force."

"That's not the reason we'll join. Germany's aggression
has to be stopped! Have you read about the atrocities they're
committing in France and Belgium?"

"Oh, please! That's just war. France wanted the war as
badly as Germany did. They waited for Germany to make the
first move because they knew it would bring England in. Why
do you think public opinion here turned as soon as the
German U-boats hit the water? Because it disrupts American
trade routes. The politics are all based on commercialism and
power. Personally I'd love to see American power grow, so
I'm all for it. But don't tell me it's a moral war. If you can't see
that then you're a blind soldier."

Glenn sat, dumbfounded. Of course the war was moral
from the Allied side. He refused to believe what Hal said. He
picked at his breakfast, struggling to regain his appetite.

"What does that girl of yours think about your moral
quest for suffering and hard labor?" asked Hal after a minute.
"I bet she ain't so thrilled with it."

"She likes that it has brought us to the city."

"No doubt. She's a small-town flower who's never had the chance to bloom. But mark my words, her charm will either fade or come between you. New York City is not the right place for you, Glenn. I barely know you, but it's obvious. On base you can forget you're in the city, but once this war is over, you'll want to be back in your sleepy village on Long Island."

Glenn nodded. On this point, he knew Hal was right.

"So if your girl loves it here as much as you say, what will you do? Will you stay in a place you don't like just to please her?"

Glenn said nothing. Dafne was a lot like Hal, wanting to enjoy her life to the fullest and live in the moment. Often he wished he could be more like them, but that kind of life wouldn't make him happy. He needed to work. That was why the army suited him. Yes, it was difficult, but now that he was committed, he couldn't quit. For a man like him who had no urgency to earn an income, joining the army had been the surest way to jolt him out of the leisure that dissatisfied him so much.

After breakfast, Glenn returned to his hotel, expecting a message from Dafne, but she hadn't yet called. He waited in his room for another hour before she finally called, having slept into the early afternoon after her party. By the time she was dressed and ready they only had a short time together before going to see a play in midtown. Returning to base on Sunday, Glenn felt his visit had been very short. He wouldn't be able to leave again for two more weeks. He resumed his training, frustrated but newly motivated by his work.


Dafne had looked forward all week to Glenn's next visit. Hal would be joining him on the Brooklyn train, and they all three planned to go to the opera on Saturday. It would be her first time at the Metropolitan Opera House on Broadway and 40th.

Hal accompanied Glenn uptown on Saturday morning

but made his visit at Dafne's apartment brief.

"I'll mosey on down to the 'Bilt and let you lovebirds get reacquainted," he said. "Remember, dinner promptly at six. We can't be late for the opera."

"I can't wait," said Dafne.

"Neither can I. This new Strauss is supposed to be really something!"

Dafne and Glenn stood with their hands clasped until the door closed behind him.

"Glenn, Glenn!" Dafne tossed her arms around his neck. "Oh, I have so much to tell you." She led him to the sofa and launched into the tales of her new life in New York. There was gossip of new friends, reviews of musicals on Broadway, and a description of her new favorite pastime—motion pictures.

"Everybody's been so nice to me. I haven't been lonely at all. Thelma has introduced me to all her friends. I've been invited to teas and parties almost every night." She paused suddenly. "You don't care, do you?"

"Of course I do."

"I know." She smiled, squeezing him in her arms again. "But you don't care where I've been or who I've seen. The names don't mean anything to you."

"Not really. But I like the way you tell me about it."

"I wish you could be here all the time. When you finish your romp in the army and we get married, we should live right here."

"Wouldn't you prefer a big place down in the Forties?"

Her face crinkled in brief consideration. "No." She quickly waved her head from side to side. "I like my little apartment just the way it is."

Glenn said nothing, content to bask in her glow. She liked glowing for him.

Elsa soon had lunch ready. Excited as Dafne was about their evening plans, she had looked forward to this afternoon alone with Glenn too.

After lunch, Dafne threw herself onto the couch. Glenn sat on the opposite side from her. Giving him a glance of reproof, she rearranged her body to lay her head on his lap. His hand stroked her hair a few times before resting timidly on his own leg. Dafne sighed.

After cleaning up from lunch, Elsa had slipped discreetly upstairs. Dafne noticed and wondered whether Glenn had, too.

"I love you, Glenn."

"I love you, too."

She reached for his hand and placed it back on her head.

"Why are you afraid to touch me?"

He shifted uneasily. "What do you mean?"

"I feel like all you ever do is kiss me." She tilted her face to smile at him. "I like it when you kiss me. You could do more, though. I wouldn't push you away." She relaxed her head and hugged his bent knee. "This is nice."

"Soon, darling," he said. "Soon there will be much more we can do together."

She sighed again. He often referred to their married life this way. His excuses tired her. She respected him for his Christian morals, even as she hoped to make him break them. She would be a good wife, but longed to live a little more now.

Did he *want* to touch her? Did he *want* to make love to her? Was she attractive to him? She desperately wanted to think so, but he gave her no indication that he did. He often told her she was beautiful, but if he really thought so, how could he so easily keep his hands off her? Here she was practically offering her whole body to him, yet she had to twist her head just to make him start rubbing her hair again!

These were the moments she craved, yet when they came, they left her unsatisfied. It was easier to fill their time with activities.

How would he respond if she took his hand right now and placed it on her breast? Would it arouse him for more, or would he be repulsed? She wanted to do it but couldn't risk it.

The thought first made her smile, but then a wave of insecurity came over her.

She took so much time making herself beautiful. She was the toast of New York City, but her efforts seemed to have no effect on him. Did he think her ugly? She had put on a few pounds since the beginning of their relationship. Had he ceased to find her attractive yet didn't dare to say so? If he truly thought her beautiful, he should be longing to tear off her clothes and cover her body with his hands and lips. Was it too much to ask that he lust for her?

Even Elsa couldn't look at her that night when she asked her servant to undress her, unsure herself what she desired. All she really wanted was to feel loved. Was that so much to ask?

She closed her eyes tightly, trying not to cry.

She might have, except that Glenn's hand finally moved from her head and rested on her shoulder. It was a small gesture, but enough to ease her insecurity.

Elsa had allowed herself to doze off when she heard the apartment door crash open. She hurried downstairs as Dafne, Glenn and Hal came in.

"Oh, Elsa, it was wonderful!" Dafne shouted. "I wish you could have seen it. Remind me to buy a record of *Der Rosenkavalier* once it's published."

Hal walked straight past Elsa into the kitchen. She glanced disapprovingly as he invaded her domain. He opened a cupboard and pulled out a bottle of whiskey.

"Where did that come from?" asked Dafne with delight.

"I stashed it this morning."

"Well, aren't you spunky!"

He looked at Elsa. "Come on now, girl, be a sport and fetch me some glasses and ice."

She stood a few obstinate seconds, staring at him with ire, then reluctantly obeyed.

"I don't know, Hal," said Glenn. "It is rather late, and Dafne and I don't drink much."

"That's why I need to loosen you up."

"Don't worry, dear," said Dafne. "A drink or two won't hurt you."

Elsa watched Glenn's face ease into consent. She understood. He didn't want to get in the way of Dafne's fun.

Hal balanced his rocker on the edge of Dafne's gramophone while he stacked records inside. As the music began he picked his glass back up and began a silly dance with his drink. Glenn and Dafne both laughed at him. He paused and looked at Dafne.

"Are you going to dance with me, or should I continue with my glass?"

"Oh, your glass, to be sure."

He gazed affectionately at the glass, then with a sudden dramatic inspiration, took on a strange manner which made no sense to Elsa, but which Glenn would tell her the next day, mimicked the comical Baron from the opera they had just seen.

"Beautiful *Mariandel*," he sang to his glass, "although you are not what you seem, I love you just the same."

He twirled and hummed the song from the opera, which clashed mercilessly with the ragtime records.

"Do shut up, or I'll *have* to dance with you!"

"Too late. I'm happy with my sweet *Mariandel*."

"Oh, shut up!" Dafne exploded with laughter.

Elsa watched from the kitchen as Hal poured each another drink.

She could feel the room growing louder and more out of control. Hal's ridiculous speeches and Dafne's laughter dominated the sounds, but even Glenn's voice had begun to rise. She had seen Dafne get drunk and giggly before and didn't really mind. It wasn't her place. But she didn't want to see Glenn like this. She had come to know him as a controlled and steady man. She liked him that way. Though he was obviously not excited about this scene, he had succumbed to the pressure from his fiancée and friend. She understood it would have been hard for him to resist, but she wished she didn't have to watch it.

Hal bounced up to her with a small glass he had just poured. He thrust it toward her while Dafne giggled behind him. Elsa left her hands folded in front of her and scowled at him.

"Tell your girl she needs to have a drink with the gentleman."

"Go on, Elsa," Dafne said. "It'll be fun!"

Elsa, like Glenn, usually had difficulty saying no when things were demanded of her. But this wasn't one of those times. Hal's drunkenness made him look weak and ridiculous to her. She stood staring back at him, rigid and angry until he couldn't help but look away.

"Look what you do to me, darling, now I'll have to drink them both."

Elsa hated to be called darling by *him*.

Hal turned back into the room with a glass in each hand. He began to dance again as Dafne joined him. However, he was incapable of dancing with two glasses and a girl. One of the glasses crashed triumphantly to the floor. But the dance went on.

Sighing, Elsa turned away and walked upstairs. She would clean it up tomorrow, in peace and quiet.

# CHAPTER FIFTEEN
# TIME SPEEDS ON

Elsa had nearly restored the apartment to normal when Glenn arrived the next morning. She squinted slightly as she opened the door, letting in the light and heat of the summer morning.

"I'm sorry about last night," he said as he entered.

"It was not your fault." She closed the door but opened the curtains, wanting to preserve the sunshine.

"Still, I feel responsible. I'm ashamed of myself."

"You were rather silly and careless. But nobody was harmed."

"I was not myself. I don't like that. I won't do it again." He sat on the couch with his cap resting on a knee as Elsa resumed the last of the mopping.

"You do not need to make any promises to me," she said, then added with a smile, "I am not your mother."

"No, you certainly aren't."

"Perhaps she would want me to look out for you, though." Elsa smiled playfully. "I certainly cannot depend on your friend Mr. Halifax to keep you out of trouble . . . or Dafne, for that matter."

She put the mop away and came back. Standing in front of him, she suddenly felt awkward about the informality of their conversation. "Dafne is still in bed, if you were wondering." She felt she needed to say something about her mistress.

Glenn tried to glance inconspicuously at the clock.

"Half past ten," said Elsa, catching him.

He laughed. "I forget that the schedules of a military man and a young debutante vary greatly."

"I understand. I can never sleep once the sun is up. I imagine you are beginning to feel the same way."

He nodded.

"You don't think much of Hal, do you?"

"I hardly know him." She shifted nervously where she stood.

"I saw the way you looked at him last night."

"I was irritated with him, yes. But I have no right to dislike him."

"And yet you don't like him. Why not?"

"I do not entirely trust him." She wished she hadn't said anything. "I have no reason not to. He is a gentleman, and seems to be sensitive to your relationship with Dafne . . . I will try to like him."

Glenn laughed. "You can dislike him if you want. I find him refreshing because he is so different from me. He never makes plans. He claims to be totally amoral. And yet I trust him because I assume he abides by the masculine code of ethics."

Elsa finally sat down. "What masculine code is this?"

"I'll explain it as best I can: once two men pass the initial bonds of friendship, they become bound to stand up for one another, respect the other's wife or girlfriend, and help each other out in time of need."

"Do all men stand by this?"

"Not necessarily. But they all know it. If a fellow breaks it, he can be sure never to be trusted within that social circle again."

Elsa pondered this glimpse into the intricacies of male society.

"Hal claims to have no morals. Yet within the distinctions of society and honor, he actually does. There are countless other ways in which we are *expected* to behave in society, no matter what our beliefs, religion, or anything else. Only a social deviant can truly be amoral."

Elsa was fascinated by this new way of thinking about people's behaviors. She supposed much of the way she had learned to behave was based on society's expectations rather than her own sense of what was right. How much of it was based on conditioning, and how much on belief, she wasn't sure, but it was interesting to think about.

"Have you seen your mother and sister since you've been in the city?" Glenn asked, interrupting her thoughts.

"I have seen my sister and her husband. Their shop is in Yorkville, not very far away. I walked there last weekend. It was good to see them. They have two little boys and a baby daughter now!" Elsa smiled, thinking how quickly time had flown for Sonja and Christof. "I have not been able to see my mother yet."

"Why not?"

"She still lives and works in the Lower East Side. I would need to take the train, and it would have to be on a weekend when she is off work. There simply has not been time. I do intend to see her soon and feel badly that I have not."

"Surely Dafne would allow you a day to go."

"Oh, yes, she has encouraged it. But Dafne is most busy on the weekends. I do not want to leave her alone."

"Perhaps she would go with you. So would I. It would be wonderful to meet your mother. Why not today?"

"She only works half the day on Saturdays. That was a recent reform for the garment industry."

"Then it's settled. We'll all go."

"Go where?" asked a sleepy voice from up the stairs. Dafne's slippers made an arrhythmic sound on the steps until she came into view. Her hair was still disheveled from sleep. She rubbed her eyes in the brightness of late morning.

"To visit Elsa's old home in the Lower East Side," Glenn said, standing up. Dafne shuffled toward him and fell onto his chest.

"Darling, why are you here so early?"

"It's not early to me."

"My head hurts. Does your head hurt, darling?"

"No."

Dafne titled her face toward Elsa.

"Does *your* head hurt?"

They all laughed.

"So how about it?" Glenn continued. "Are you up for a trip downtown?"

"Today? Oh, I couldn't possibly. I'd never have the strength for the dance tonight. You two go. I'll rest so I can be fresh and beautiful for you later."

Elsa felt awkward that Glenn had pushed so hard for her sake, but was already feeling excited about the prospect of seeing her mother.

"I'm going to get dressed," said Dafne. "I can't let you see me like this."

"I already have."

"Shut up. Let's pretend you didn't." She padded back upstairs.

Elsa also went up to her room to change. In a half hour they were on their way.

Once they were on the downtown elevated train, Elsa suddenly thought how strange it was that she should be traveling alone with a man far above her station. She worried less now than at first about the supposed impropriety of her friendship with Mr. Streppy. Just as Dafne had always done, he treated her as a friend rather than a subordinate. It usually took Elsa to remind them both that she was still a servant. Her mother would surely find it odd.

Elsa and Glenn's friendship had been slow in developing. Both of them were quiet and reserved. The first few months of his romance with Dafne they seldom said more than pleasantries to one another. But Dafne, with her love for each of them, eventually cemented their care for one another. As the years passed, Elsa and Glenn had developed a deep understanding that went far beyond their mutual relationship with Dafne.

She could tell that something was changing in both Dafne and Glenn. It had started some time ago but only became visible since coming to the city. They were both discovering themselves in new ways. Where those discoveries might lead was impossible to predict. Furthermore, the friendship of the three of them had inevitably changed. Glenn wasn't around much, and Dafne didn't need Elsa's friendship the same as before. There were new people for Dafne here, all of whom had exciting things to share with her. Elsa had begun to worry how these changes would eventually affect her.

Elsa gazed out at the city as the train inched along. It amazed her how quickly the whole city had risen since she'd lived here just a few years ago. The train picked up speed and the buildings started flying by. She was reminded of the solitude of this crowded place. She had spent much of her life in solitude and never considered it loneliness . . . until now.

While Dafne had found in Elsa a person she could count on for friendship and support, Elsa had grown to enjoy being a constant friend. Now that Dafne had found new support mechanisms, Elsa no longer had anyone to need her. She missed it.

Soon the train stopped at the Bowery. Elsa had never been to her mother's new apartment, which she shared with another single woman. But she had written the address on many envelopes and was familiar enough with the neighborhood to walk there without trouble. She worried that her mother, not expecting her, wouldn't be home. But she was. Nina and Elsa greeted each other joyously.

Glenn was planning to wait outside, but Elsa wanted him to come in. Nina had read enough of Elsa's letters to know him immediately, and to feel comfortable welcoming him into her humble home. She didn't comment on the strangeness of their traveling together.

Nina had aged in the years since Elsa had seen her. But she was aging happily and looked healthy to Elsa's eyes. It had been a hard life, but she had much to be content with. She had helped better the conditions for the women working in the factories, while both her daughters had good lives. She said she was at peace working in a small clothing factory, earning enough to support herself and save a little. She hoped in a few years to move north to live with Sonja and her growing family.

But when Elsa probed, her mother admitted to being tempted to join the women on an upcoming march for suffrage. Rachel Shapiro had told her that New York seemed ready to grant women the vote, even if nationally the measure failed to pass. Elsa encouraged her mother to go on the march. She liked the sparkle she saw in her eyes when she talked about it.

After they left the apartment, Glenn asked Elsa to show him the places from her past. She hesitated to take up so much of his afternoon, but he insisted. In a taxi they drove by Andretti's tenement building, which despite the progress of much that surrounded it, looked exactly the same as the first winter the Schullers had spent there. They directed the taxi past St. Mark's Lutheran Church. Elsa declined Glenn's suggestion that they step inside. She knew Pastor Reus had retired, and there were no other memories to revisit. The Triangle Shirtwaist Factory had been razed after the fire. Josephine, following her daughter's death and Elsa's departure, had moved to Queens to live with relatives willing to take the old widow in. The taxi returned them to the Bowery train station.

Glenn dozed off briefly on the train trip back uptown. Elsa sat across from him as sunlight sliced through the windows on the west side of the train.

*What a good man!* she thought, looking at him. His sleeping face maximized the gentleness of his features, which he sometimes tried to hide behind his masculinity. Elsa hadn't known many men, but she understood how special Glenn was. To take this time just for her, on one of only three days he had for leave, was a demonstration of his true character. She had grown to deeply care for this man who would marry her mistress. How she hoped the conflict in Europe would end soon so there would be no need for him to go to war.

Glenn and Hal lumbered into the clubhouse of the Dyker Golf Club. It had been a long game, made longer by Hal's insistence to stay behind a trio of female golfers. Glenn had continually suggested playing through, but Hal wouldn't hear of it. So after each hole they stood by the next tee as Hal flirted with the young ladies. Despite the delay, Glenn thoroughly enjoyed the spectacle.

They sat down heavily at a table. The waiter brought Hal a highball and Glenn a club soda.

"I don't believe you haven't golfed in three years," said Hal. "By Jim, you're terrific at it!"

Glenn laughed. "I had fewer distractions."

"Hogwash! You would have beat me handily even if it weren't for the female rumps ahead of us."

Hal took a big sip through his straw. "But seriously, bud, there are more important things in life than golf. You made me do the work of three men out there! I know you're engaged, but it wouldn't kill you to flirt a little. Those were some luscious dames!"

Glenn laughed. "I may be good at golf, but I've never been any good at flirting. I'm glad I don't have to try."

"How did you get Dafne, then?"

"It was very sudden. I certainly never flirted with her."

Hal shook his head. They sat at a small table across a corner from each other. Hal looked straight ahead, while Glenn watched him. Hal's eyes darted around the room, though his head was still. By the time he finished his drink and started another, a cloud had gathered in his expression. Finally he turned toward his friend.

"We're getting old, Glenn." He sounded suddenly panicked.

"No, we're not, you idiot."

"But we are! I'm twenty-six. Before long I'll be too old to flirt anymore. I'll have to do something—least of all I'll have to marry—to stay in society's good graces."

"So marry. How bad can it be? New things will motivate you. When you are older, life will gain more significance on its own, especially if you have a family."

"That's easy for you to say. You're the one who's challenging life to be significant."

"Yet you repeatedly express astonishment at my choice to join the army."

"Yes, because the army destroys what life a young man has left. I feel when my youth is over I may as well die."

Hal looked very depressed. It worried Glenn. Was Hal's usual joviality merely a disguise?

"Why burden the time I have left as a young man planning for when I'm old and worthless?" Hal said.

"Do you really think you will one day see yourself as old and worthless? When you are older you'll still be the same man. You will be wiser for the experiences you've had."

"You talk as if you've been there. You're younger than me."

"Barely."

"But you have more to live for than I do."

"Do you mean Dafne?"

"Yes. But as lonely as old age would be without a family, I can't imagine giving up my freedom and marrying now."

"You hate to plan, don't you?"

"I don't see the point. It would just depress me. What could I plan that would beat what I have right now?"

"You're more a realist than an atheist."

"I'm not an atheist," said Hal. "I'm agnostic. Whether there's a God or not, I just don't care. The reason you're Christian is because you need something tangible to expect for your future. You plan for the afterlife just like you plan for next week or next year. But I don't want to think about that at all. I can't even imagine life beyond the age of thirty!"

Glenn pondered this for a moment. He hoped this wasn't really the reason for his belief in Christianity. He didn't have the time to think it through right then.

"It's your world, isn't it?" said Glenn.

"It's yours, too. Or anybody's who'll take it."

"You're a selfish sort."

"So are you. It's just that I exercise my selfishness in pleasure, you in morality and self-worth. But you only do it to feel good about yourself, just like I do."

Glenn couldn't have disagreed with Hal more. Their philosophies were completely opposed. He said nothing, not wanting to enter an argument that would have no winners. Hal grew somber again.

"I should go," said Glenn at last.

"That's right, you leave tomorrow. How long will you be in the field?"

"Thirty days."

"That's a long time."

"Training is beginning to get serious. So, I think, is our course toward war."

They both rose.

"Say, if you're in Manhattan while I'm gone," said Glenn, "I'd appreciate it if you popped in on Dafne once or twice. I doubt she'll be lonely, but I'd feel better knowing one of my chaps was checking in on her."

"Sure, buddy. I'd be happy to pay her a call."

"Thanks."

"Hey now, don't work too hard up there. You're already getting thinner."

Glenn smiled. "You may not recognize me after this adventure!"

They laughed together and shook hands. Glenn left. Hal ordered another drink and settled back into his seat, looking more depressed than ever.

# CHAPTER SIXTEEN
# WINDS OF CHANGE

Glenn leaned his cheek against the window of the eastbound train. The glass actually felt cold, signifying the change in season so quickly after the oppressive heat that had marked his time in the field. The maple leaves of the forest they passed were already beginning to turn from green to gold.

This month upstate had been the most rigorous phase of his training thus far. A realistic war-scenario had been built in the hot farmland southeast of Buffalo, complete with trenches and scorched landscape. The experience had been physically brutal, but still afforded him time for reflection. He'd desperately needed this break from the city, though he hadn't realized it beforehand. There had been no distractions up there, not even any phones the soldiers were allowed to use.

He thought a lot about Dafne during his time away. He could feel that they were growing apart. This time had helped him to see how they were both more fulfilled now than ever before. He felt purposeful in his work, while she had found happiness in New York society. What did it mean to their relationship that they had found these satisfactions while apart?

He and Dafne were no longer each other's first priority as they had been in Lindenhurst. Their relationship had never been quite the same since the shock of his announcement to enlist in the army. He now realized how badly he'd hurt her that day. Dafne may have forgiven him for his insensitivity, but how could she fail to have lost a portion of trust that could never be regained? He understood now that the nature of his enlistment had not only hurt her but also forced her to wonder about the depth of his commitment to her.

Glenn didn't regret his decision to join the army. His military career was the best thing for him, just as Manhattan was the best place for Dafne. For each, individually, this made sense. But for their relationship, the logic unraveled.

Would he give up the army for Dafne? If it were that simple, yes. But the army represented something he had found in himself that she hadn't yet shown an ability to understand. Giving it up wouldn't change who he was, nor would it change who she was.

He determined to do what he could to fix their relationship before it desperately *needed* fixing. He couldn't let them grow further apart. Dafne needed all the love he had to give. He decided to go straight into Manhattan and apologize for his insensitivity last spring. He would do whatever it took to make things right.

It was late afternoon when the train reached Grand Central Station. He disembarked and took a taxi up to Dafne's apartment. Predictably, since it was a Saturday, she wasn't home. Elsa thought she was at a tea dance with Mr. Halifax, but she didn't know where. Glenn assumed they were at the Biltmore. Hal always stayed there when he was in town.

Despite his eagerness to make things right with Dafne, he was happy to see Elsa and realized that he had missed her almost as much as he had his fiancée. She'd prepared a simple dinner for herself, and he was delighted to share it with her.

"If I had known you were coming I would have made something nicer."

"After the food they fed me at camp, this is practically a banquet."

Elsa smiled at him across their corn salad and split sandwich.

Glenn stayed longer than he realized, talking to Elsa. By

the time he left the apartment and made it to the Biltmore it was nine o'clock. The host informed him that the dance was over. There was no sign of Dafne in either the restaurant or the bar. Twice now he had come to visit Dafne unannounced, and twice she had eluded him. He needed to be better about letting her know when he was coming.

While deliberating over whether to get a room or to just go back to the base in Brooklyn, he decided to inquire about Hal.

Yes, the clerk told him, Mr. Halifax was staying in the hotel. The clerk, who knew Glenn to be Hal's friend, even told him that he was in room 140 but added that he had requested not to be disturbed.

"Why," Glenn asked. "Is he ill? It's still so early."

"No, he is quite well." The clerk leaned forward. "There was a young lady with him."

At first this announcement didn't rattle Glenn. Hal always stayed at the Biltmore because he knew he could trust them to be discreet about such things. Glenn was surprised they had told him.

It wasn't in Glenn's nature to mistrust; after all, Elsa hadn't even been sure of Dafne's whereabouts. Yet something didn't feel right to him. He looked down, then back up at the clerk as if to ask the question that was gradually dawning on him. A horror of possibility began to race through his brain.

In a sudden frenzy, he ran up the stairs and down the hall to 140. There he stopped.

What was he thinking? Hal was his friend, and Dafne would soon be his wife. Neither of them would betray him, least of all together. He felt ashamed to even suspect what he might find behind this door. What if Hal were with another woman, and he rudely disturbed them? How could he live with the shame?

He waited for several long moments. The light of the electric bulb played on the three metal digits on the white door.

With his mind in indecision, he hesitantly tried the door. It was locked.

That it was locked enraged him. With a burst of recklessness he stepped back, then kicked down the door. He ran through the living room and stopped cold in the entrance to the bedroom.

The only feeling he recognized was sadness. No longer the fear, nor the anger; only sadness. Sadness to see Dafne scrambling to cover her nakedness as tears built in her terrified eyes. Sadness to see his friend quickly pull on his trousers, then stand tall beside the bed, stoically masking his shame.

There was nothing to say to them—no questions to be asked, no answers needed. Everything was clear. In an instant he understood and couldn't believe he'd failed to see it coming. He blamed himself, not for stupidly asking Hal to look in on Dafne while he was gone, but for failing to be a better man for her. If he had taken better care of her heart, she wouldn't have needed this.

Dafne sat shaking on the edge of the bed with a sheet clutched tightly around her. Her mouth and eyes sagged with the weight of guilt and despair. Her lips tried to move, as if trying to cry out to him, but she couldn't make a sound. Glenn's sadness deepened into a terrible grief.

Hal stood motionless, his eyes fixed on Glenn as if Glenn would pull out his military pistol and shoot him dead against the wall. He probably wouldn't have moved if Glenn had. But Glenn wasn't thinking about Hal. He was only the instrument by which Dafne satisfied her neglected desire. Glenn didn't hate him or even miss him. He felt suddenly like he had never known him.

Glenn felt terribly ashamed. It was all his fault. He was the one who should have covered his face in his hands, not these two. He slowly turned and walked back out the door he had broken.

\* \* \* \* \*

Dafne cried in Elsa's arms for almost an hour before she could control herself enough to tell her servant what happened. When she finally did, Elsa pushed her away and stood up indignantly beside Dafne's bed. She wanted to hit her mistress.

"I didn't mean to do it. Please don't hate me," Dafne pled. "*You* at least have to forgive me!"

Elsa had to do no such thing! It would take a long time for her to forgive Dafne for this.

"It wasn't entirely my fault. I drank more than I'm used to. We were talking, and I was depressed. I've been lonely with Glenn away. I have people all around me, and of course, I have you and I love you. But it's not the same. I started to cry, and then he kissed me."

"How could you let him kiss you?"

"Have you ever been kissed right here?" Dafne pointed to the area between the bottom of her right ear and the edge of her hairline. "If anyone ever kisses you there, then tell me how well you could resist him."

Elsa was not convinced but had no experience with which to argue.

Dafne's face fell into a hideous pout. "Glenn never kissed me there." She leaned back onto her pillow and resumed crying.

Elsa stood rubbing her palms together. She didn't know what to do or even what to think. The full weight of the disaster was just beginning to become clear to her.

"What are you going to do?" she finally asked.

"I don't know. What *can* I do?"

"Which of them do you love?"

"Glenn, of course. But I can't beg him to take me back."

"Why not?"

"I can't crawl back to him."

Elsa thought she should have to. As she looked at her mistress, Dafne seemed pathetic to her. She couldn't bear to see her that way. She turned away. "I'm going to bed."

Once in the privacy of her own room, Elsa wept bitterly.

Her dream of serving Mr. and Mrs. Glenn Streppy until the day she died, which only an hour ago had seemed a certainty, was fading fast. Her premonitions since moving back to New York were coming true.

She never wanted to see Dafne again. But even if she didn't feel friendliness toward her, there was far more between them than friendship. The practical implications to herself quickly grew clear to Elsa.

All the time since she'd first left this city played on her memory. Was everything now lost? Indeed, this whole life she had gained for herself was at stake and hung perilously on Dafne and Glenn's splintered happiness. She was foolish to have expected it to last forever. None of the Grahams had ever been there to arrange a situation for her. It was her job to do that for them. If the need was gone, or they grew tired of her, she would be right back in the employment lines at Hopkins & Co, with nothing to show for all she had been through since her first day in America.

That was why she couldn't say everything to Dafne tonight that she wanted to. In recent years she had served Dafne as a friend, not as a servant. She *did* love her mistress. Their friendship might now be permanently scarred; it was too soon for her to know. But she was still Dafne's maid and could ill afford to lose the position. Thus she would support and stand by her mistress through whatever decisions she made.

Oh, but she would miss Glenn! She missed him already. *He* was the one she wanted to stand by to comfort in his sorrow.


In the weeks and months that followed, Glenn devoted himself to his training with new rigor. He seldom left the base. If he did take a leave, he went to visit his family in Lindenhurst. He didn't go into Manhattan at all. The officers noticed his effort along with his intelligence and sharpening skills. Before the Christmas leave he was made a Lieutenant and put on track to become Captain. It was clear that America's entry into the Great War was inevitable. Skillful officers would be in high demand if there were a draft.

His devotion to the military, however, couldn't make up for his piercing regret. Deep down he understood that his and Dafne's failure had nothing to do with the army; it only expedited the inevitable. Still he blamed his enlistment, needing something other than himself.

Hal had come to the base a few days after, but Glenn refused to see him. Dafne had telephoned for him twice, but he hadn't returned her calls. He didn't know why. He still loved her and longed for her. But he didn't know what he wanted. He was confused by it all. If he agreed to see her, he couldn't say what would happen. Would she ask forgiveness? He had forgiven her before he even left the Biltmore that night. He forgave her without ever having condemned her for her betrayal. Would she ask him to give her another chance? How would he be able to refuse?

But that wasn't what he expected to happen if he agreed to see her. He doubted he had the strength not to beg *her* to take *him* back. Glenn had never considered himself a proud man. But this once he felt the need to hang onto whatever pride he had left. Otherwise, even if they reconciled, she would never respect him, and he would never trust her.

Now she was being announced outside the fort. The sentry stood in the doorway to his barracks asking whether she should be admitted. Glenn said no.

It killed Glenn to reject her this way, but he knew what Dafne really wanted. She hadn't come to reconcile. She had come to ask forgiveness so she could move on. He tried to talk himself out of this realization—how could he truly know her motives? Yet somehow, he *did* know and it broke his heart. He wasn't strong enough to see her under those circumstances without making a fool of himself.

He leaned his head down onto his knees as he sat on his low mattress. Several times his hands wiped perspiration from his brow.

She was so close. Probably only a hundred yards away. He could imagine her scent. It wasn't the smell of her perfumes that played in the senses of his imagination, but the smell of *her*, which was there when she wore no fragrances, and cut through even when she did. The essence was so uniquely hers. He had never thought of it in all those years they'd spent together. Now he knew he would never forget it.

He longed to go out to her. Even if he couldn't hold her in his arms, just to sense her essence would be wonderful. Yet it would weaken his resolve, making it harder to move on.

There were new passions now. He had become a good soldier. Soon he would go to war. When the order from Washington finally came, he wanted to be on the first ship to France! Why wait? He had joined the army to help win a war.

Even if he could win back Dafne, what would keep her from cheating again, especially after he left for the war? There were two fights in front of him, and he only had the strength for one. Better to fight for the cause he believed in, rather than the one he was coming to doubt had ever really been true.

As Dafne left Fort Hamilton, denied the chance to see Glenn, she felt her heart harden toward him.

Two months had passed. At first she'd truly wanted reconciliation. She had run from the Biltmore that night without letting Hal get her a cab. She jumped on the first uptown bus, needing to be away from him, feeling disgusted by him. When she got back to her apartment she locked the door just in case he had followed her. The very next day she tried to call Glenn. If he had offered to take her back she would have stayed with him. Much as she had come to understand the flaws in their relationship, she missed him and wanted another chance to prove her love for him.

But as the weeks passed she became confused. His refusal to return her calls hurt her. She didn't know whether she wanted him back or not. All she wanted was amends.

Now, however, she was finished. She had come all this way, and he wouldn't even see her. She knew she had wronged him, but felt she deserved an audience. At least she had made an effort, while he'd made none. Now she knew their relationship was truly over, and would *stay* over.

She walked back to the train station where Elsa waited for her.

"He wouldn't see you?" asked Elsa, reading the meaning of her stone-cold expression.

"No. I'm not trying anymore."

They turned together and went in to wait for the train.

"I know you hated me for what I did. But you have to agree I made an effort to reconcile, while he has not."

"Yes. I am proud of you for trying."

They sat down on the plush, red train seats. Dafne emitted a long sigh.

"I feel just like I did when he announced his enlistment at that horrible tea party last spring—completely rejected and embarrassed. He has shown that he can't forgive my mistake. I don't care anymore. I don't want to be with him now." She paused. "That he won't forgive me actually lessens my regret for what I did. I'm so mad I could spit!"

Elsa said nothing.

Dafne slid her arm inside her servant's and leaned her head down onto her shoulder. "Oh, darling, what use have I for a man when I have you? I love you better than anybody."

She was so glad to have reconciled with Elsa. Her servant may not have forgiven her. But the fact that she had made an attempt to contact Glenn while avoiding Hal restored her somewhat to Elsa's good graces. It felt so good to feel Elsa against her now as the train began its churn back into Manhattan.

She failed to think through the practical necessity of Elsa's loyalty. She still thought of Elsa as more of a friend than a servant and refused to contemplate how permanently their dynamic had changed.

In reality, Dafne *had* seen Hal a few times. Although she hadn't let him contact her directly, he was making a point to remain in her social circles. She couldn't avoid him completely. Although she didn't want to spend time with him, she assured him that she bore him no ill feelings. It was just too fresh for her.

With questionable hindsight, Dafne talked herself into believing that she and Hal wouldn't have gone all the way that night. Glenn had interrupted them naked, on the verge of making love. Yet he *had* interrupted them. Perhaps she'd had no power or inclination to resist Hal that night. But the fact was, she remained a virgin. This allowed her to still think of Hal as a gentleman.

Walking back into the quiet apartment that afternoon, Dafne felt the acute loneliness of being single. Her social calendar was quiet. Yes, there were places she could have gone that night, but not by invitation, and that made it different. With Glenn away she had used her status as an engaged woman to further her social standing. Even now she hadn't told many people of her broken engagement—was it even officially broken? But gradually everyone was finding out. It was becoming necessary to face her new reality.

She wanted nothing more than the life she had enjoyed here but while Glenn was away. She recognized the selfishness of that happiness. In it she'd given him next to nothing, while using only his name to create her comfortable world. He was probably better off without her.

She no longer even had a logical reason to stay in the city, though she couldn't imagine leaving. Once she told her parents she was no longer with Glenn, would they expect her to come home? She knew the apartment was expensive and that her father's business was suffering. Perhaps they knew already, and it was only a matter of time.

By appearances nothing had changed. She and Elsa still lived in the same cozy apartment on 71st Street. She spent her days the same way, saw the same friends, hosted the same parties. But nothing was as it should have been. Despite not telling anyone what had happened, everyone seemed to know. The women no longer doted on her, nor did the gentlemen hold her in the same respect.

At first it angered her that people looked at her differently. She stopped inviting certain people to her parties. But she couldn't find replacements, so her circle simply grew smaller. Now she couldn't think of whom to call.

Thelma Sanderson was her truest friend through that time. Thelma was the one person Dafne felt comfortable telling all the details to. Thelma didn't judge her for her indiscretions. She always heard her with an open mind. It comforted Dafne to be with her. Dafne had used to think she could tell Elsa everything, but Elsa had no sexual experience, and Elsa had her own emotions to deal with.

She knew how Elsa felt about Glenn. She told herself her servant was in love with him. Silly as it sounded, she needed to convince herself of a reason why she could never be as close to Elsa as before.

The next time Hal called, she was feeling especially lonely. She had spent most of the morning crying. Before she knew it, she had asked him to come over. The timing was good, because Elsa was visiting her sister. When Hal arrived Dafne fell into his arms. His kiss comforted her but made her feel ashamed.

She had never learned to be a grown woman without a man. She wasn't strong enough to learn now.

# CHAPTER SEVENTEEN
# COURAGE & COWARDICE

Elsa never would have been this bold if not for the new circumstances.

She felt differently about everything now that Mr. Halifax was back in Dafne's life. She was still committed to serving Dafne to the best of her ability. But this commitment was more for her own security than for Dafne herself.

Dafne was off somewhere today with Mr. Halifax; she probably wouldn't notice. Still, it made Elsa terribly nervous to leave for so long without telling her mistress. Her plan was to tell Dafne she had visited her mother in the Lower East Side. It was on her way after all. She had attempted to, but Nina wasn't home. Now she would be compelled to lie when she returned to Dafne. She didn't like to lie.

She hadn't seen Glenn since the day he shared her simple meal at the apartment. So much had changed for them all since then. She missed their simple familiarity. Without him around, she had no one with whom to share her thoughts. Dafne always told her she could talk to her—that they were best friends—but it wasn't really true. Dafne needed a listener and a comforter; Elsa was good at that. But Dafne was seldom silent for long enough to coax out Elsa's thoughts. With Glenn, it had become natural for her to express herself. Sometimes it was only in a shared glance that they conveyed deep understanding with one another. Only now that he was gone did Elsa realize how Glenn had been her best friend since Beth died. Without his relationship to Dafne, Elsa and Glenn had no paradigm in which to remain friends.

Except that she missed him.

After the broken engagement and Elsa's resolution to serve her mistress faithfully, she had expected Glenn to fade into a pleasant memory. It was disappointing to have a friend snatched out of her life, but she'd faced disappointments before. She still had a lot to be thankful for in her situation.

But it was different now. She was always kind and courteous to Mr. Halifax when he was around. But she couldn't help resenting his and Dafne's relationship. She had no loyalty to him and much less loyalty now to Dafne. Would she want to remain Dafne's maid if she married Mr. Halifax? If their relationship continued, she wondered whether it would be best to look for a new position.

These feelings helped encourage her to take the bold step that today had her on a Brooklyn-bound train. Over recent weeks she had thought more and more about seeking Glenn out, then finally convinced herself to do it. Yet her hands shook as she stepped off at the Fort Hamilton station. The fact that she had kept her action from Dafne made her reconsider, yet again, what she was about to do.

What would it be like to see Glenn? Would he be different? A few months ago she had been completely comfortable with him. Nothing should have changed. Yet *everything* had changed.

Elsa stood indecisively outside the sentry's view for over half an hour. She was afraid to announce herself. At first it relaxed her to stand there, warm in her coat and boots on the brisk February afternoon. Traces of last week's snowfall could still be seen in the shadows on the sides of the street. As the minutes passed she almost lost all courage to go forward. What would she say to Glenn? What common ground had they to stand on now?

Would he even see her after refusing to see Dafne a month ago?

Finally she forced herself forward and had the sentry announce her.

Glenn appeared at the gate minutes later. She thought his eyes looked weary. The sparkle that her visit gave them was lost on her.

"Let's walk," he said. "I would rather not bring you inside the base."

She didn't mind at all. After the years she had spent on this city's streets, a wintry afternoon in South Brooklyn didn't intimidate her. The movement of walking helped her to relax.

"I am glad you agreed to see me."

"Did you doubt it, only because I wouldn't see Dafne?"

"No. I knew you would. I am still glad."

They walked on in silence. Soon the residential streets gave way to the edge of Dyker Beach Park. As soon as the houses were gone Elsa felt the cold winter wind on her cheeks. They continued along the side of the park.

"How are you?" she finally asked.

"Well enough. I've been working very hard."

"I am glad. Does it make you happy?"

"Happy . . . perhaps that's not the right word. But it satisfies me. Look." He pointed out an emblem on his coat. It meant nothing to Elsa, but she smiled when she saw his pride. "I'm a lieutenant."

"Congratulations."

Elsa felt incredibly awkward. Their conversation used to come so easily. Now when they most needed it, neither could muster more than a word or two at a time. Neither even looked at the other as they walked. Yet it felt good simply to be there beside him . . . to see his gentle face.

"Thank you for coming to see me. It cannot have been easy to get away."

"I needed to see you." She looked over at him. He looked

back at her. She smiled.

"Did you tell Dafne you were coming?"

"No."

"Is she with Hal?"

"Why do you need to know that?"

"You're right. I should not ask. It's hard to think of them together."

"I know."

The conversation stalled again, with each of their thoughts stuck on their least favorite subject.

Elsa felt there was so much more she wanted to say, but the impropriety of this walk began to pound at all her personal insecurities. She struggled to remember that this was just Glenn, one of her dearest friends.

"I should return to the train station." She had lost her courage. "I have never been away for this long before."

He nodded. "I'll walk you there."

At the next street, Glenn stopped to turn left, back toward the residences and away from the park. Elsa had been looking at her feet and walked a few steps past him before realizing he had stopped. When she came back he lifted his arm for her. Feeling a flutter in her chest, she slipped her arm into his and let him escort her back to the station. She had never walked on a man's arm before. It felt wonderfully feminine to do so.

"Thank you," he said at the station as her train approached. "It means so much to me that you came."

She smiled at him. She wanted to embrace him. Not for herself, but for him. She knew that he desperately needed a hug. Perhaps if she had been used to receiving hugs when she needed them, she would have given him one now. But she hadn't been hugged very often, least of all when she most needed it. So she didn't hug him now. It would have been very inappropriate.

Elsa cried on the train. Seeing Glenn left her heart breaking for the times they had lost. Despite their awkwardness today, she felt how real her friendship with Glenn was, yet foresaw no outlet for that friendship to continue.

Fort Hamilton was ready. In his anxious anticipation, Glenn managed to ignore his heartbreak.

President Woodrow Wilson had severed all diplomatic ties with Germany following its expansion of submarine warfare. Several American merchant ships had been targeted and sunk by German U-boats. The United States could no longer maintain its neutrality in Europe's war. Despite an antiwar filibuster to block a vote in Congress, President Wilson used an executive order to arm and place navy personnel on US merchant ships to protect them against German aggression.

British intelligence intercepted a German telegram to Mexican President Venustiano Carranza promising restoration of the lands Mexico had lost to the United States if Mexico would attack from the south, diverting US military power. Whether the telegram was truly German in origin or constructed by the British to sway popular sentiment in the United States could never be fully determined, but President Wilson was finally leaning toward war.

In Washington, debates raged, even as sentiment across the country began to turn firmly against Germany. Former President Theodore Roosevelt openly called Wilson a coward for waiting so long to act and accused the antiwar activists of treason. Congress issued a decree that no one could express criticism of the president during wartime.

Glenn devoured every word of these developments in the papers, eager for the war to come. Along with so many others, he was so sick of delays that he could no longer reasonably assess the issues at stake. President Wilson's idealism annoyed him. The President wanted both peace and victory, and couldn't seem to understand the conflict therein. For three years he had been moving the pieces on his chessboard toward a stalemate unacceptable to either side. How could Germany, France, or England accept failure after losing a generation of men?

But America, who would *not* sacrifice a generation, played for its own economic and political future. By 1917, it became clear that a German victory would severely weaken the United States. Germany knew this as well and hoped to cripple England and France before the United States could mobilize. Germany was also confident the Americans would never arrive.

"We can assure you," swore the German naval commander to the Kaiser, "that not a single ship with American troops will reach this side of the Atlantic. To stop them we have the U-boats; that, indeed, is why we have the U-boats!"

The soldiers at Fort Hamilton tried not to worry about the danger they would face in transit. They knew they would be the first to sail when the order came. As soon as they reached French soil—if they reached it—they would be ready and eager to fight.

Glenn had hardly left the base since his estrangement from Dafne. But now that war seemed inevitable, the anticipation made him restless. Finally he accepted one of the frequent invitations to go out with the fellows on a night off.

Captain Cummings and Lieutenant Mueller, together with Glenn, took a cab east along the coast to a small club that Cummings knew about near Coney Island. They shot pool, threw darts and drank beer. Glenn even had a beer, thinking it might do him some good.

Glenn and Mueller completed a game of billiards and sat down next to Captain Cummings. Glenn had won their game easily. He credited his supremacy to the fact that his opponent had just finished his third beer while he was still working on his first. This time they only ordered two more beers. Glenn's second round, which they had insisted on ordering, still sat waiting in front of him.

"Just because you're a soldier now doesn't mean you have to nurse your beer like a girl on the Fourth of July," said Cummings. "We're all in civvies tonight."

Glenn laughed good-heartedly. Here he was trying to loosen up, and these men still thought him a square. He no longer minded being an outsider. He'd learned his lesson with Hal. He didn't enjoy being drunk and wouldn't let himself be pressured into it.

"You're the doggonedest soldier, Glenn," said Cummings. "Always following the rules and the biggest patriot I've ever seen."

"I love my country."

"So do I, but there are other things in life."

Glenn didn't say anything. He finished his beer and obediently took a small sip of the second.

"I'm sorry," Cummings said. "I know there's that business with the girl. The army is probably a good way to keep your mind off it."

"It is. But I think I'm pretty well over her now."

"Easy to say," Mueller said.

"I mean it," Glenn insisted.

In that moment it surprised him that he thought of Elsa. Her recent visit had done more to help him get over Dafne than anything, even while reminding him of how much he missed Elsa as well. Her effort to come so far to see him had warmed his heart.

His companions took drinks from their beers in tandem.

"I know what you need." Mueller pounded his fist on the table. "You need some new women!"

Cummings nodded vigorously. Glenn grew nervous.

"I know of a cabaret just a few blocks from here where we can see all the women we like."

"That sort of thing isn't what I want."

"I insist. I bet you would like a show. If not, we won't tell anybody about it."

Glenn finally consented. Mueller and Cummings finished their fourth beers. Glenn left his second almost full on the table. They walked a short way into a dark side street that seemed hidden from the rest of the neighborhood. Mueller knocked on a red door that popped out from the darkness. When it opened, Glenn peered in. He could see burlesque dancers on the stage, moving in soft, red light. He smelled stale beer and cheap whiskey. He felt disgusted and completely uninterested in entering such an establishment.

Elsa came to his mind again. He remembered how disappointed she had been in him when he allowed Hal and Dafne to pressure him into getting drunk. What would she think of him if he allowed himself to be dragged in here by these two? She would never know, but he liked the virtuous opinion she had of him and wanted to deserve it.

"I'm sorry, chaps," he began backing away from his friends. "I can't go in there. Go ahead. Have fun. Don't worry about me."

He retreated quickly, not wanting to spoil their evening.

It was three miles back to the base, and the night was cold, but he didn't want a cab. The crisp air and brisk walk felt good.

Glenn felt confused. Why could he not enjoy the things other men did—the drinking, carousing, and burlesques? Even Dafne had thought him uptight. At least Elsa understood him.

Was he really a moral man, or simply a man who didn't know how to have fun?

But as he walked he remembered how much fun he used to have in Lindenhurst with Dafne and Elsa. He found his enjoyment in other things than men like Hal did. These days, he had traded fun for purpose and self-worth. With this mindset, he felt that he was better prepared for war than

Cummings and Mueller—and certainly better prepared than Hal, if his draft number came up.

By the time Glenn arrived at the base, an hour had passed since leaving the cabaret. The sentry saw him coming and motioned to him hurriedly. Glenn rushed toward the gate. The sentry handed him the phone. Startled, Glenn took the receiver and listened.

"Glenn, thank God, it's Cummings."

"What's happened?"

"Mueller's been beaten. He's bad. It was all I could do to get him out of that place before they killed him."

"What? Why?"

"How should I know? They said he was German. Called him a Hun and a spy, then started at him. Two men with big sticks. He had no chance to fight back."

"For God's sake, he's an American soldier—an officer!"

"In civvies with a German name."

"How could they?"

"Damn it, Glenn, I don't know. I need your help. Take one of the regiment cars and fetch us. He needs a doctor, bad."

# CHAPTER EIGHTEEN
# EPIPHANY

The words on the front page of the *New York Times* leaped out at Glenn:

*PRESIDENT CALLS FOR WAR DECLARATION!"*

He hurried back into the barracks to read the words of Woodrow Wilson's address to Congress.

> *"With a profound sense of the solemn and even tragic character of the step I am taking,"* read the newspaper, *"I propose that the Congress declare the recent course of the Imperial German Government to be in fact nothing less than war against the government and people of the United States and formally accept the status of belligerence. The present German submarine warfare against commerce is a war against all nations. It is a challenge to all mankind. There is only one choice we are incapable of making: we will not choose the path of submission."*

Glenn's heart beat wildly. He continued to read the transcribed presidential address.

> *"The world must be made safe for democracy. The country must fight for the principles that gave her birth. God helping her, she can do no other. It is a fearful thing to lead this great, peaceful people into the most terrible and disastrous of all wars, civilization itself seeming to be in*

*the balance. But the right is more precious than peace, that a new age might rise from the wreckage of a Europe torn asunder by the evil spirits of imperial plunder and dynastic rivalries, so subject peoples, long suppressed and exploited, might recover the precious independence that Americans had enjoyed since the founding of their nation. So people everywhere might be free at last to speak their minds without the threat of imprisonment, torture or death. "*

*"For this we can fight, but for nothing less noble or less worthy of our traditions. A supreme moment of history has come. The eyes of the people have been opened and they see. The hand of God is laid upon the nations. He will show them favor, I devoutly believe, only if they rise to the clear heights of his own justice and mercy. "*

By the time Glenn reached the conclusion of the President's speech his excitement had waned. He wished Wilson would have stopped after the first few sentences.

Lieutenant Mueller's beating had affected him. Glenn had gone all the way through basic training with this man without knowing he was German. In fact, he was not. It turned out his great-grandfather had come to America from Germany and married an Irish woman. Mueller was only one eighth German. His grandfather had fought in the Civil War; his father in the Spanish American War. Now Mueller would be deprived of fighting for his country by men less American than he. His only fault was his name.

He also thought of Elsa, who was watching her present country march to war against her homeland. How could she reconcile her feelings about this?

Glenn still favored the war. It was what America had to do. But the President's words somehow didn't feel right.

He read the entire newspaper. Tucked away near the back was the dissension from those who had voted against going to war. Congressman Robert La Follette of Wisconsin stated:

> *"The American people will acquiesce on this with the theory that the Congress should have the facts. But in truth the war in Europe is not a war of humanity, but a war of commercialism. I know men like me, who oppose this step, will have their patriotism questioned. But I must ask, is it a gauge of patriotism to vote calamity, debt, death and destruction on our country? Have not those who view it the other way the same right to consideration and respect as those who see relief only through a sea of blood? God forbid that in free America such an unjust discrimination can ever be made."*

Glenn refused to believe that the war to which he offered his life was anything other than a suppression of evil, despite the sobering incident with Mueller. Yet La Follette's point was well made: those who opposed the war weren't less patriotic than those who supported it. La Follette was a patriot. He had proven so. But this, Glenn had decided, was a *just* war.

He put down the paper and leaned back on his cot. The more he thought about it, the more La Follette's words ate at him. America had begun the war truly neutral, continuing to trade with both the Allies and the Central Powers. As Germany gained an advantage in the land war, England took the advantage at sea. As a result of the British blockade, American ships could no longer reach German ports but continued to supply England. The U-boats had changed everything. By the time they appeared, America had staked a huge commercial interest in Germany losing the war.

Despite the economic gain, however, Glenn reminded himself that there were humanitarian reasons. The English blockade hadn't sunk civilian ships. The German U-boats now did this regularly. Furthermore, there was no denying the atrocities of the German army throughout Europe.

Convinced again, Glenn felt better about the cause to which he had devoted his life.

In the days immediately following President Wilson's declaration of war, it became clear that the troops at Fort Hamilton would be the first to sail for Europe. The war was now a gripping reality for Glenn.

His mind gathered up all the memories of the people and places he was leaving behind. Although this brought back memories with Dafne, in these honest moments, he realized he missed Elsa just as much.

Finally, he knew he was over Dafne. He had been hanging onto the pain; now he wanted to let it go. If Elsa could hold just as precious a place in his memory, then Dafne didn't deserve the pedestal he had put her on. He missed the times they had shared, but it had been necessary to move past a comfortable life that couldn't be sustained. It readied him for *this.*

He knew who he was now. Once his military commission was over, he would have learned how to work and how to be strong. This would give him the confidence to enter civilian life in a new capacity. Would Dafne have wanted to be with the man he was becoming? Even if his enlistment had caused their break, he could finally admit that it was worth the price. He was a better man for it.

*But what about Elsa?* Would he ever see *her* again? Her life was with Dafne—as it should be. But he knew she was the one person who might understand this transformation occurring in him.

He missed his conversations with her and their simple understandings. But most of all he missed *her.* He missed her voice, her mannerisms, even her scent just as he had missed those things in Dafne.

Before this, there had been no practical way to imagine keeping her in his life. But the war changed everything. The prospect of death shattered all norms. He desperately wanted to see Elsa again before he sailed.

\* \* \* \* \*

"Who's there?" Dafne shouted from upstairs.

"Just the postman" Elsa knew her voice quavered as she looked at the two envelopes in her hands.

One was from Dafne's parents. The other was addressed to *her*.

She recognized the handwriting without needing to glance at the return address. It was from Glenn. She quickly tore it open and read.

Ever since reading about the war declaration in the papers her heart had reached out across the East River toward Glenn. She knew soon it would reach much farther, for her heart would travel with him to the war. She had dared to see him once. Much as she wanted to, she hadn't expected to go again. Now, in this letter, he was asking her to come.

"Anything good?" Dafne asked, bounding down the stairs in a light summer dress and bonnet.

Elsa quickly stuffed Glenn's note in her skirt pocket.

"A letter from your father, there on the side table." Elsa could never tell a straight lie, but she had gotten more skilled with lies of omission than she liked.

"I'll read it later," Dafne said. "Probably a tedious reminder about finances. Are you ready?"

They left the apartment together and took a cab to midtown. Elsa's fingers kept returning to her pocket and resting on the secret note she had received.

She had always assumed that if she were lucky—or *unlucky*—enough to fall in love, she wouldn't know how to recognize the feeling. In all the plans she had made for her life, love wasn't a circumstance she expected to have to worry about.

She was wrong.

Glenn's note sent her heart into a whirlwind of emotion that she immediately understood. She was in love. Nobody had to teach her how it felt or explain this new sensation that sent tingles through every inch of her body.

She followed Dafne into one shop after another, her mind far away.

"How's this one?" Dafne held up a pink blouse as the store attendant stood by. Elsa thought Dafne looked better in dresses than separates but didn't feel like explaining her opinion.

"It looks lovely."

How long had she been falling? She had never allowed herself to think of Glenn this way before. His note had unleashed a flood of feeling that she'd held back for a long time. Now that it was released, her passion was immediate and irrevocable.

In a little over a week he would be on a ship bound for France—through the terrible graveyard the German U-boats promised to turn the Atlantic into. Early to enlist, he would be among the first fleets to sail, even as most American boys were still waiting to hear whether their numbers were called in the draft.

"Come over here, Elsa," Dafne called from behind a wall of dresses. Then to the attendant, "It's a bit dreary for summer, don't you think?"

He must have known she always checked the mail for Dafne. Still it was risky to send her a note at the apartment. What would Dafne have thought if she'd seen it? What if there had been no second letter today?

How would she manage to get away again to go see him? The first time had been difficult enough. If she told Dafne, what would she say? It didn't matter what Dafne thought because she had to go. More than that, Elsa wanted to go.

Intellectually, she thought she should be sad to be in love. Even if Glenn's note seemed to imply that he had been thinking about her too, there was no hope for such a love. But she didn't feel sad. It was a grand sensation. She savored it.

The joy of love didn't necessarily require hope. The hopes of her life had been for other things, and all those had been rewarded. She wouldn't risk her present situation—for which she had worked so hard—only because she loved a man beyond her station. Still, she enjoyed her love. She repeatedly remembered the two times she had been in physical contact with him—dancing on their last night in Lindenhurst, and in February when he gallantly offered her his arm. Beyond those times, she would content herself with being held by Glenn in her dreams.

"Do you think Hal will like this?"

"I'm sure he will adore *you* in it."

This morning's note was the spark that allowed Elsa to admit something that had been happening in her heart for a long time. Had Glenn not been constantly on her mind since the night of Dafne's affair, when she feared she would never see him again? Was that the first sign, or had it started even earlier? Perhaps that was the time when she failed to understand the sensation of love. All those years she thought she was in love with the *togetherness* of Glenn and Dafne, and the happy life that relationship created for her. Maybe she had been falling in love with Glenn himself all that time.

Her mother had warned her many times against feelings like these. Just because he wanted to see her didn't mean he loved her. She wasn't a woman like Dafne—who drew men's passions. She was a plain and simple girl. A man in Glenn's position could easily get another beauty once he returned from the war.

Dafne made her purchases. Usually Elsa would have given better advice. As the box crossed the counter she worried that Dafne had bought something awful. She hadn't been paying attention and had no idea what was in the box. Elsa didn't know much about fashion, but she knew what looked good on Dafne. Her mistress had grown to rely on her eye.

They left the shop into the summer heat. Many of Dafne's

friends had already left the sweltering city for the summer, but Dafne was afraid if she locked up her apartment for the summer her father wouldn't renew the lease. Everyone was cutting back in anticipation of the war.

As they walked, Elsa wondered whether Dafne once felt this way about Glenn. Did she now feel this way about Mr. Halifax? Elsa doubted it. Both times Dafne had leaped into the relationship with little thought. She knew Dafne well enough to understand that she dated for the way it made her feel more than for the particular man.

Elsa had long felt that Dafne showed *her* more affection than the men in her life. It was one of the things that kept Elsa so loyal to Dafne, though it also confused her. She hadn't been out in the world enough to comprehend the levels of affection some women had for each other. She knew no better than to wonder at that strange night when Dafne made her undress her with a look of invitation in her eyes.

"Do you feel okay, dear?" Dafne asked, slowing her stride.

"Yes. Quite."

"You seem distracted. You sure you're all right?"

Elsa panicked. Could Dafne already know how she felt about Glenn? She had never been able to hide anything from Dafne. How could she possibly hide this?

"You're right," she said. "I'm not quite myself today. It must be the heat."

"Do try to get some rest this evening. I'm going to a dance with Hal. You shouldn't stay up late cleaning a clean apartment like you always do."

Elsa laughed. She was indeed a compulsive cleaner.

"Hal can be tedious to dance with, but he always wants to go. Glenn was a much better dancer."

Elsa was afraid to comment.

"I wonder if anybody will even be there. Everybody's left town. Thelma left this week."

She clutched Elsa's arm and smiled. "Well, once he gets a

couple of drinks in me I'll enjoy myself. Let's get a block of ice and go home to rest."


A few days were enough to solidify Elsa's courage. She told Dafne of her intention to see Glenn before he sailed. Dafne wasn't surprised, nor did she begrudge Elsa for going. Her attitude made Elsa wonder whether her mistress had known her feelings even longer than she'd known them herself.

She was more afraid that Glenn would see the feelings she had for him. How could she hide it—especially now, as he walked toward the jaws of death? Yet even if he did see, it wouldn't be so bad now. Perhaps it would comfort him in the gruesome battles ahead.

Glenn wasn't in the barracks when she arrived at Fort Hamilton. She sat in the gate-chamber for two hours while he finished his drills.

Finally, he entered the room, freshly showered, in his light-green shirtsleeves and dark fatigues. Was it her love, or had he really become more handsome over the last year? His frame had grown strong and lean. His face looked older in the best ways possible. Most of all he looked alive to her. He seemed healed from the pain she'd seen in him in February. She hoped it wasn't only in preparation for a new kind of pain.

She stood and smiled at him. Her heart was aflutter.

He led her outside to a bench in the courtyard. It had been oppressively hot when she boarded the train in Manhattan, but here, closer to the beach, there was a pleasant breeze.

She sat and turned her shoulders toward him. "Are you ready?"

"I feel ready. But how could I possibly be ready for this?" His eyes dropped. "Why does my resolve betray me now just when I need it most?"

She tried to see his eyes in his lowered face, not understanding what he meant.

"The closer it gets, the more confused I grow," he said. "When I joined the army, I was happy because I needed work and purpose. But now that I'm about to enter a real and terrible war, I want to understand it and believe in it, yet I can't." He looked back at her. "Can you see me killing men?"

She shook her head. She didn't want to think of him killing.

"That's what I have been trained to do—kill, repeatedly and efficiently. I want to believe I will be fighting against evil. But I'll just be a weapon in the hands of the men who command me. I have no more will of my own. It's not my job to understand why. But I cannot stop myself from asking."

"I am glad the army has not reduced your ability to think for yourself."

He said nothing for a few minutes. Elsa was content with the silence.

"How do you feel about this war?" he asked at length. "You are German. I imagine that influences your feelings."

She was glad he asked. There had been times in the buildup to this war when she wondered whether he had forgotten her nationality. She knew Dafne had forgotten.

"I am an American now," she said. "As much as you or anyone. But I do hurt for my old country. I do not think I could ever *believe* in a war. Every war flaunts idealism as a way to disguise ambition and distract from the suffering. Those who suffer the most are the ones whose only fault is to be born near the battle line."

Elsa did feel for her people back in Germany. She only vaguely remembered any of her family there. The newspapers were full of the wrongs done by the Germans, but she knew the German people suffered, too.

Would those anti-German sentiments affect her and other Germans here in America? She had worked hard to forge a good life for herself, but that seemed very precarious now. What persecutions lay in wait for her people here? She was beginning to wish she had taken Mr. Graham's advice and changed her name. At least her last name was seldom used in her position. Not so her sister's family—the Steigenhöffers.

"I am sorry," Elsa wondered how much of her thoughts were visible on her face. "I would not plant doubts in your mind simply because I fail to understand politics. All I really care about in this war now is for you to come home safely."

"You understand politics better than you think. I do believe in our cause. But I fear how the war may change our own men. I'm determined not to let it change me."

It horrified Elsa to think of Glenn being a part of this war—fighting against her countrymen. War affected people. Few good men could go to a war like this and come back unchanged. Despite his determination, she feared what might become of Glenn. She would be praying daily for his safety—in mind as much as in body.

They both fell silent. Elsa worked her lower lip between her teeth. Her sweaty fingers wove in and out of one another in her lap.

"I will miss you, Mr. Streppy," she said. "I *have* missed you." She immediately regretted saying it so boldly.

"Really?" he looked eagerly at her.

"I have missed having you around," she tried to backtrack. "We all used to have so much fun together. It will feel so much more extreme once you are on the other side of the world." She knew her face was flushed. She hoped Glenn would credit it to the hot afternoon.

"Oh, Elsa!" He turned his face away from her. She saw that he was flushed, too. "I probably wouldn't say this to you if I weren't going away . . ."

Elsa's heartbeat quickened.

"I realized after you visited me in February . . . I have hardly been missing Dafne at all. I have been missing *you*. The worst thing I lost in losing Dafne was losing my friendship with you."

What could she say?

He looked back at her and opened his mouth to say something more. She waited eagerly, but no more words came. The moment passed.

"You have been a good friend to me," she said. "I hope to continue to be a friend to you." She hated her emphasis on friendship, but it was best . . . for both of them.

A voice called from the bunkers. "Captain Streppy, will you be long?"

"Give me a few minutes, Major."

He turned back to Elsa.

She smiled. "*Captain* Streppy now!"

"I was promoted the day after we declared war. They're desperate for officers to lead all the poor boys who are being drafted now."

They fell silent. The moment of intimacy had passed and couldn't be recovered.

"I will write to you from Europe."

"Really? That will make me glad. Let me know how I can write to you as well. You will need a reminder that someone is thinking of you back home."

"Will you really be thinking of me?"

"I will. I will pray for you every day."

"You don't know how happy it makes me to know that."

Tears dripped from Elsa's eyes. "Please be careful. I cannot bear to think of any harm coming to you."

They sat turned toward each other on the bench. Both resisted the magnetism that worked to pull their bodies together.

In an instant, his arms were around her and their cheeks were pressed together. Her hands held tightly to the back of his shoulders from under his arms while his strong arms locked behind her back. Elsa closed her eyes, lost in the warmth of his embrace. Neither moved. For those fleeting moments, she was content.

She sighed when he pulled away. They both stood.

"I should go," said Elsa.

"Thank you for coming."

"When do you sail?"

"Tomorrow."

She wiped the tears from her eyes. "God bless you . . . Glenn." She had never used his first name before. She had wanted to for a long time. "Come home safely. I will be waiting for you."

"Good-bye, Elsa."

He took and squeezed her hand. As he started away their fingers stretched and held for a last perilous second. He turned, and hurried away to meet his superior officer.

# PART IV

SEPTEMBER, 1917

# CHAPTER NINETEEN
## THE FACE OF SUFFERING

"Don't cry, Dafne. Please."

"Don't tell me not to cry. I have to." She scrunched both of Hal's coat lapels in her hands and buried her wet eyes in his tie.

"I always thought Glenn was silly for joining the army. You weren't so stupid, but it doesn't make any difference." She lifted her eyes. "How can they take you, too?"

"If they hadn't drafted us, they never would have found enough men," Hal said. "But cheer up, sugar."

She dropped her face back to his tie.

"Glenn will clean up the Germans before I ever get there. I'm just going to Carolina to sweat through training and drink nasty moonshine."

She laughed between her sniffles. "I hate the Germans."

"No, you don't. You love our boys, and we just happen to be fighting the Germans." He kissed her. "I have to catch the train."

She drew away from him. "Write me."

"I will."

"Promise!"

"I promise."

"Okay."

She waited for another kiss. Instead he pinched her cheek. "Hang in there."

He bounded down the apartment steps to his taxi. Dafne sulked back inside, fell on the couch, and wept bitterly. Was there any other girl who had lost *two* men to this horrible war?

She sat up in a sudden rage. Going to the kitchen, she poured a finger from the whiskey bottle Hal had left there. She drained it in one very unladylike swig. Then she marched to her record cabinet, took out a Beethoven album, and smashed each record, one by one, on the tile floor. Next, she took a Strauss and crushed it on top of the shards of the first German composer's records.

"What are you doing?" shouted Elsa, rushing down the stairs.

"Getting rid of our German things."

"What good could that possibly do?"

"The Liberty Bond man said it was how we could support our boys."

"Do you know how ridiculous that sounds? I always thought you were so clever. What has become of you?"

Dafne had taken Mozart's "The Magic Flute" out of the record cabinet but hesitated. She began to feel embarrassed.

"That is our favorite opera," Elsa said. "Mozart was not even German, and he died over a hundred years ago."

Dafne's face hardened in determination. She hurled the record set to the floor. Elsa gasped as the beautiful music was destroyed.

"Okay, Miss Graham, show me how much you love your country. Send your German servant away. Better yet, call the police. They can drag me to prison like so many others. I am sure you can think of a pretense. It is not very patriotic of you to employ the enemy."

Dafne's mouth hung agape, even as tears rolled across her lips into her mouth. She had never seen Elsa so angry.

"Oh, Elsa, I'm sorry."

She ran to her servant across the shards of broken records. Elsa slipped away from her attempted embrace. "Get away from me."

She marched up the stairs. Dafne curled up on the couch and wept.

\* \* \* \* \*

The romance and purpose of a soldier's life, which had been Glenn's passion for over a year, disintegrated the moment he landed in France to the sound of German bombs. Two days later, when he joined the small number of American companies that had preceded him in Chaumont, the misery of the war struck a hard blow to his pride and patriotism. All his moral values and priorities had been reduced to one—survival.

The Atlantic crossing had been nerve-wracking for all the men. Nobody put voice to the fear of the German U-boats. But they'd known at any moment they could be killed by the unseen enemy lurking beneath the ocean's surface. However, English radio technology had grown sophisticated enough to detect the submarines. Not a single American military transport ship was hit.

The fear on the ground in France, however, was tangible and graphic.

This war—extolled and debated in so many cabinets, pressrooms, and tearooms back home—wasn't a war of politics, but a war of survival for the suffering and starving people of Europe. Glenn felt not like the messiah that General Pershing made him and the other soldiers out to be, but a perpetuator of the pain—a reinforcement who would make the war last a little longer. Could a battle of misery really be won, or merely be lost less terribly by one side than the other?

For the first few weeks, Glenn and the other Americans waited, billeted in the lonely villages behind the lines, hosted by people too poor to flee the danger. He hardly spoke a word during that time, other than to give or to respond to a military order. He sat alone, tolerating the poor rations and struggling to understand the French culture. The sooner he got to the lines, the better. He felt he could better endure the company of soldiers better than the decaying population in these French towns. The Germans hadn't even reached this far, yet the advance of want had killed more on each side of the front than soldiers ever could.

The status quo of misery amazed Glenn. After the initial German surge, two vast trenches had stabilized the battle lines. In some places the armies faced off as a single row; sometimes they zigzagged across the terrain, now at a distance of a few hundred yards and then coming as close as fifty. Stumps, barbed wire, and bones of those three years dead filled the charred earth of the no-man's-land between the trenches. An advance of a quarter mile was considered a key victory.

The introduction of the machine gun had caused the stalemate. Neither side could gain an advantage. Instead, each poured more men into the trenches to take the places of the dead. If a new trench was built after an advance, the old trench served for the reserve. If in retreat, the new trench became a ready-made grave.

The military strategists who planned this war had been baffled by the modern methods of warfare. These men had been trained in the tradition of the Napoleonic wars. The older ones had seen action in the Franco-Prussian war, or in Crimea. At the first offensive, France sent its finest soldiers forward on horseback with swords drawn, as if advancing for Napoleon himself. The German machine guns ended cavalry warfare forever within the first weeks. Germany, for their part, marched ahead with tightly packed infantry—the old way to invade—only to have entire companies mown down by machine guns or torn apart by the French 75 artillery. Even after trenches stretched from Flanders to Switzerland, generals tried to counter the stalemate with bayonet charges, stubbornly believing that war could be won with sheer bravery.

The glory of conquest, so long a European ideal, had devolved into a sport of annihilation.

In the fall of 1917 the western front was the last place of true contention. Serbia had fallen. Austria-Hungary had fallen. Revolution had put an end to Czarist Russia. The Ottoman Empire was crumbling. The English had placed a viselike grip on the seas all around Europe. The Kaiser had expected the U-boats to end the war in Germany's favor, but England's radio development turned the sea advantage back to Britain. But on the western front, the scene of Germany's first advance, the war raged on. For three years artillery was hurled back and forth, with small forays made into no-man's-land, cleaning out the trenches for younger men.

The civilians of Europe had come to accept a state of total suffering. They put up with the obstinacy of their leaders only because they had grown as accustomed to war as they had once been to peace. How else could the leaders of Germany and France convince their peoples to go on with so little hope of victory?

Glenn quickly forgot what the fight was for. Those lofty phrases of President Wilson and the propaganda publications from home were rendered meaningless. His only hope was that America's entrance in the war would end it quickly. There was no other way to stop the suffering.

The fear he saw in the French people wasn't what he'd expected. It was not a fear of the German army sweeping through and slaughtering them in their sleep. Rather, it was a fear that tomorrow the food would run out, or that next winter they wouldn't be as easily spared from influenza as last year. There was a far more brutal army at work than either the Allies or the Germans . . . and that army had already won the war.

Everyone Glenn had known who lived in privilege thought they knew what suffering was . . . but they'd never seen it. When they did, if nothing else, they realized how far they were from really understanding. Glenn felt he knew Elsa a little better now. She had told him about her youth and the hardship her family suffered. Looking into the eyes of the starving French, he glimpsed something of what she had endured.

Glenn would never forget that first march to the front. Leaving the village where his company had billeted, he felt eager to start. But as he got nearer to the battle line, fear began to enter his bloodstream like a sour poison. He was marching into hell.

The American "doughboys," as the British dubbed them, didn't take well to the idea of burying themselves in the mud of the trenches, yet that was exactly what was expected of the first companies. They were the fresh bodies—the artillery fodder for continuing the carnage. The French and English soldiers, pale and weak, many infected with dysentery, looked warily on the newcomers. They would have preferred for America to send ships filled with fresh clothes, food and medicine, rather than eager Yankees.

The stretch of trench assigned to Glenn's company had been maintained by the French for over a year. It was fortified by wood planks set into the walls and by sandbags above ground. More wood planks covered the bottom of the trench, but it made a sorry floor. Once the first rains started, it was quickly covered in a thin layer of mud that oozed from the sides of the trench. A soldier had to keep his provisions well-guarded each night against the rats. Looking out across no-man's-land, Glenn could see evidence of another trench before a retreat had brought the line to its current position. Several planks stuck out among the barbed wire and bones.

He wrote to Elsa for the first time after arriving at the front, sitting in a bunker dug into the dirt behind the front line and fortified with concrete blocks for a roof, where his company had waited through heavy German shelling the night before. A crude electric light swung over his table.

*Dear Elsa,*

*Neither my training nor my worst nightmare could have prepared me for the horror of trench warfare. I have only been in this squalor three days, yet I feel at my wits' end. Some of those around me have endured this for three years.*

*I have not yet seen a battle, but the artillery barrages are as sinister as any advance. Fortunately, our dugout is well built. It was hit last night and held. Earlier yesterday they signaled a gas attack, and we all wore our masks for an hour before they told us it was a false alarm. Not only is there no progress, but there is hardly even an attempt at progress. Still, men die almost every day. I do not understand it. This is not a fight. It is a mutual execution.*

*But the most painful sight to me was the state of the French towns and countryside we passed through on the trip from the coast. The horror of the war reaches far beyond the battle lines. Innocent people are dying every day from want. This is the true tragedy of the war.*

*Why does God permit such evil to be wrought upon his people? I know now that the Germans across the field are not the evil ones. They are frightened men just like me. The evil is in Berlin, Paris and London not to find the mercy to end this war. Truly, God did give the world to the devil for his own. No man could have imagined such terrible times as these.*

*Oh Elsa, if only I had known I would not have had the courage to enlist. Yet that would only have delayed the inevitable. I have made my choice, and God will give me strength.*

*How I miss our carefree days in Lindenhurst.
Restless as I was, I only remember the joy and
pleasure the three of us shared. Do not resent me for
having been the one to end it. We all should have
known it could not last. Instead of pining for a time
gone by, I hope I can remember those days as the best
time of my life and use my memories to encourage
me through the dark days I have embarked upon.*
     *Pray for me,*

  *Yours, Glenn*

Pray for him, Elsa did. She read the letter again as she sat in
the back of St. Mark's Lutheran Church, long after the
weekday congregation had left. A sacristan dusted the pulpit
and altar rail. A large, empty wood cross rose above the nave.
She had been coming to the Lower East Side more frequently
in recent months. She wanted to spend as much time with her
mother as possible. In lives such as theirs, all time was
precious, and nothing was certain. After moving to
Lindenhurst, Elsa had gone four years without once seeing her
mother or sister. She wanted to use this time when she *could*
see her mother to full advantage.

Her visits to the south end of the island were a good
connection with her past. She never thought she would want
reminders of that life, but time had a way of putting even the
most difficult events of her past into perspective. Being here
was a good reminder of where she had come from . . . and
where she might once again go. She was no longer so naïve as
to assume her position with Dafne would last forever.

Nobody in the church recognized her today. There was a
new pastor, but many of the people were the same. Elsa knew
that her own appearance had changed dramatically. Even if
someone thought they recognized her face, they would talk
themselves out of their memory.

The congregation was smaller now, and despite some familiar faces it was no longer a German parish—hardly any Germans were left in the Lower East Side. There were few Protestants of any nationality. The neighborhood was dominated now by Eastern Europeans who were either Jewish or Catholic. Each year there was a larger Chinese contingent in the neighborhood as well.

Even if St. Mark's *had* still hosted a German majority, the decision to hold services in English was wise. No German Americans wanted to draw attention these days to themselves.

Sitting by herself in the empty church, Elsa prayed both for Glenn's physical safety and for God to protect his spirit. Even if he escaped the war alive, many others would return broken and bitter. She loved Glenn for his pure mind and good heart. To lose those would be the worst tragedy this war could bring to him.

Her eyes fixed on an etching on the altar of the suffering Christ carrying the cross toward his execution. The artist had rendered Jesus's face with uncanny realism. Elsa knew that whoever carved it had suffered. The moment captured a man who knew he was taking the final walk of his life. She had often stared at this etching as a young girl. The expression on his face made her think he was hungry but didn't have the energy to notice.

How often she had experienced that same feeling. This image of the suffering Christ always encouraged her. However much she suffered, she knew that Jesus had suffered worse—not only in hunger and pain but also in rejection and loss. Knowing what he had gone through made her feel good about being a Christian and took away the temptation to blame God for the suffering her family endured.

Now Glenn was living through worse hardships than she ever had. He would know that look in the etched Christ's eyes now. He wouldn't have understood before. She felt closer to him, even from so far away.

She allowed herself a selfish prayer as well. She knew that the price of this war could come calling to her. She wasn't privy to Dafne's communications with her parents, but surely Mr. and Mrs. Graham were reassessing Dafne's expenses. An apartment in the city, along with her own salary, were the type of luxuries people had been asked to sacrifice for the good of the cause. Dafne herself didn't seem concerned, but Elsa didn't want to be unprepared for the possibility of a change.

What would happen to her if Dafne had to return to Lindenhurst? The Grahams wouldn't need her services anymore. If they had a new servant, then that was that. More likely, they were getting on fine with Chris's help. Katherine was old enough to help now as well. Mr. Graham's business had also changed. They would give her a good word to help her find another position, but families weren't hiring servants now like they were a few years ago. Times were changing. She had no assurance of finding similar work.

How wonderful it would be if she *could* go back to Lindenhurst. Her years there had been the best of her life. But those years were finished. Glenn had said as much in his letter. There was no sense in holding onto what could never be expected to last.

Today's reminder of her past wasn't only a memory. It was a haunting possibility for her future. There was always work to be had sewing uniforms. What a sad step backward that would be.

# CHAPTER TWENTY
# BUY A WAR BOND!

Elsa decided to take the train to the Yorkville neighborhood as she returned north. There was time for a visit with her sister's family before returning to Dafne. Christof's uncle, Gerd, was alone at the counter when she walked into the bakery.

"*Tag*, Elsa." He smiled happily at her. "I just took out a fresh batch of *brötchen*, would you like one?"

"*Ja, gerne.*"

He had addressed her in German and she instinctively replied in the same. It felt good to speak it after so long, even though she knew they were not supposed to in these times.

Gerd brought two rolls and a pad of butter and sat with her at the counter. Elsa had smelled the fresh bread as soon as she walked in. She broke into her roll, its thick shell crumbling onto her plate. She spread the butter on the warm soft center. She closed her eyes with the first bite.

"It reminds you of your childhood, *ja?*"

Elsa smiled. Indeed, the taste and smell of the fresh *brötchen* brought back pleasant memories of Germany, before the hard times in New York.

Finishing her snack, Elsa noticed that not a single customer had come into the bakery since she'd arrived. At this time of the afternoon, it should have been busy.

"Where is Christof?"

"He went to buy more flour. As you can see, one can manage the shop just fine."

"Is business slow?" Elsa asked.

"Very slow."

"There are six of you here now. I hope the bakery is managing alright."

"We still have loyal customers. But it is becoming more difficult to support the whole family."

"No wonder. It seems Sonja adds one more mouth to feed each year."

Gerd laughed. "The joy of the children who call me *Opa* makes everything worthwhile."

Elsa smiled. She understood. The children called her *Tante.*

"We have managed to save some money," Gerd said. "That helps us get through the lean times, and I have no doubt all three of the children will be able to go to school. The oldest is almost ready."

"I'm so glad."

"The war has made it harder. The rations made the poor poorer. The community has thinned out. The men have left for the military bases while many of the women have taken factory jobs, sewing uniforms. They say they need two million uniforms, can you imagine?"

Elsa didn't want to think about all the men at war. All the men who had or would die.

"This bakery has been here long enough that I've seen babes in arms grow into teenagers who would stop in for sweet rolls on their way home from school. Some of those boys are having their uniforms sewn now. But many of my regulars haven't been in for some time."

"I noticed you took the German sign down out front."

Gerd nodded. "I still have it in back. Maybe after the war I can put it back up. Still, most of my non-German customers have disappeared. I suppose the taste I taught them for *brötchen* and *bauernbrot* has been sacrificed to their patriotism."

Elsa smiled. The taste of *brötchen* was still on her lips.

The glass door of the bakery opened. A tall, slender man walked in. His suit was too big for his frame, while his overcoat was too short. He held his bowler hat in his hand. Elsa didn't take him for a customer. He looked at the two of them with an odd smile. She realized that they had still been speaking in German when he came in.

"May I help you?" Gerd asked.

The man came forward and laid a black leather folder on the counter. He opened it to reveal a small stack of gilt-edged certificates. He explained the benefits of buying liberty bonds. Elsa listened from the other end of the counter. The salesman was making his proposition to Gerd. After his initial glance upon entering, he didn't seem to notice her presence at all.

"I support what you are doing," said Gerd after the sales proposition. "But my business is struggling. I barely make enough to survive and support my family. I cannot afford war bonds."

"Many are struggling in these times, Mr. Steigenhöffer." The bondsman meticulously drew out the long name. "Yet others have made sacrifices for the war effort. It goes a long way, not only to help our men but also to *demonstrate* one's loyalty to the cause."

The way the bondsman spoke made Elsa uneasy.

"I am sorry, sir," said Gerd. "I wish I could help. I really do. But if I buy a bond today I will not have money to buy flour tomorrow."

"You . . . *do* support the American cause, don't you?" The bondsman leaned forward with his hands on the counter, a suspicious smile on his lips.

Elsa saw Gerd's expression turn angry. "Did you come here to question my loyalty or to sell me bonds? I may have been born in Germany, but I am an American. My family is American. I work to build a good life for them. That is why I came to this country."

The bondsman raised his long arms. "Oh, I believe you,

Mr. Steigenhöffer. But," he leaned back on the counter close to Gerd, "there may be others who are unconvinced of your loyalty. Do you know how many German spies there are in this city? Loyal Americans like you prove their patriotism by buying a liberty bond. You can post it in your window so everyone knows whose side you are on."

"Are you trying to blackmail me? I have no money, and I am a simple man. No sensible person would call me a spy."

A rare customer entered the store. Gerd looked at him, then back at the bondsman.

"I have work to do. I must ask you to leave."

The bondsman turned with a snort, flashing a hateful glance at Gerd, then at Elsa. He put his round hat on his head in a manner that suggested the shop hadn't warranted its removal in the first place.

Elsa was about to go upstairs to see Sonja and the children, but Christof returned just as Gerd finished ringing up the customer's purchase. He slung a sack of fresh rye flour behind the counter. Elsa stayed while Gerd told his nephew about the bondsman.

"Perhaps we should buy a bond for the store," Christof said. "It would be difficult, but we could manage it. We must be careful. I have heard of Germans being beaten, even lynched for no reason. Not here in the city yet, but we should still be careful."

Gerd scowled, but finally nodded his agreement. "Fine. If the salesman returns, we will buy a bond. I hope he does not come back."


Sonja awoke with a start. Something had disturbed her from the street below, but when she became alert, all she could hear was the rain pounding on the roof. Christof and the children slept.

Then the raucous sound returned. She lurched up in bed.

There was a crowd of people at the door to the bakery below. She threw on her robe and started quickly down the stairs. Gerd emerged from his room and called for her to stop. "Let me handle this. Stay with the children and lock the door behind you." Just then there was a loud crash as the glass of the bakery door shattered. Sonja gasped and ran back up. Christof had awakened and sprung from bed. The three children also awoke in confusion.

"No, stay." Sonja grabbed her husband's arm. "Help me with the children."

"Where is Gerd?"

"He told us to stay here and lock the door."

At that moment Gerd screamed in pain.

"Get up, Kaiser lover!" shouted a voice—Christof ran down the stairs, making sure the door to the upper apartment was locked behind him.

Sonja began to cry. The baby wailed while the two older children shivered in terror.

Angry shouts and the sounds of breaking glass continued below. It was followed by the sounds of breaking wood as the counters and cabinets of the bakery were smashed and cracked. Sonja could no longer hear the voices of Christof and Gerd, lost in the shouts of the intruders. If these men set fire to the bakery she and the children would be trapped up here in the apartment, with nowhere to flee.

Suddenly it was over. The only sounds were her whimpering children and the pounding rain outside. Sonja feared the worst. She ran to the door and listened anxiously.

"Sonja," Her husband's voice called out. "Come quickly."

She unlocked the door and hurried down. The shop was dark. All the lamps were shattered. She stepped carefully through the rubble in her slippers. The only illumination came from the streetlamps outside.

She saw her husband kneeling in the center of what had

been their bakery. The faint light illuminated cuts and bruising on his face.

Then she saw Gerd prostrate on the floor.

"Oh, God!"

Horrified, she rushed to his side. Gerd was breathing with difficulty.

"Do not move him," said Christof. "I think they broke his back. See if the phone still works."

Sonja tried their phone behind the counter, but the lines had been cut.

"I will go to the Charles's shop to use their phone."

Sonja ran to their friends' store a block away. Mr. and Mrs. Charles owned a general grocery and similarly lived in an apartment above their store. After making a great racket at their door, Sonja woke Mr. Charles, who finally opened the door. She told him what had happened. She called the police and the neighborhood doctor. Mr. Charles rushed to the bakery to see if he could help.

Sonja struggled to convey the urgency of the incident to the police respondent. When she finished her call she couldn't be sure whether the police would actually come or make any attempt at justice. She didn't know what else she could do.

She returned home accompanied by Mrs. Charles, who had awakened and dressed while she was calling.

By the time they reached the bakery, Gerd was dead.


The police didn't arrive until eight o'clock the next morning.

The doctor had come during the night. Besides setting Christof's broken ribs and bandaging his cuts, there was little he could do. He wrote an official pronouncement of death for Gerd, The doctor left as quickly as he could. He clearly didn't want any involvement in this scene or with this German family.

As dawn came, the light revealed the extent of the

damage. Everything in the bakery was destroyed. Even the walls had been battered with clubs by the intruders. Cracks in the support beams left the very structure of the two-story building in question. Across the front of the building, "HUN STORE" was scrawled in dripping red paint.

By the time the police finally came, Christof was agitated. The mustached officer listened to the account of the incident, jotting down far less in his notebook than Christof had said. A second policeman poked around disinterestedly in the rubble. Sonja watched with her children huddled close.

"What are you going to do?" Christof asked.

The policeman looked at him as if he didn't understand the question.

"Are you going to find the men who did this? A man was murdered! Our store was destroyed."

The policeman kept looking at Christof distractedly. Finally he spoke. "We will try. But you must see how there is nothing simple about this case."

"What do you mean? It is as simple as can be. Four men vandalized our shop. They killed my uncle!"

"The deceased was a known supporter of Germany. I have been informed that he was under federal surveillance. While violence is not the right answer, he should have considered the consequences of his loyalties."

Sonja watched her husband anxiously, hoping he wouldn't lose his cool. Had he forgotten about the incident with the bondsman so quickly?

The policeman looked at him with suspicious eyes. "You called this our store. Am I to understand that you are an owner?"

"Yes. My uncle and I owned it together."

"You are also German?"

"Yes. I am a German American." Christof was losing control of his voice again. "But I support America. I always have. So did my uncle. We never speak to anyone in Germany anymore."

"This bakery was a refuge for German spies. As you are

the owner, I will need to take you in for questioning."

He grabbed Christof by the arm. Sonja cried out. For a second he resisted, then regained his head.

"Stay with the children," he called back at his wife, making a point to continue in English, even though they seldom spoke it with one another.

Sonja ran back up to the apartment in tears. She held her children. She was too upset about her husband's arrest to even grieve the death of the man who had been like a father to her for eight years.

The rain had stopped, but the day was cold and winter would be coming soon. Surely they wouldn't hold Christof long. But she couldn't help replaying the ominous memory of her own mother's realization that she was alone in this city as winter approached. With her children so young and their livelihood destroyed, she didn't know how she would survive if anything happened to Christof.

After a few hours she collected herself and walked to the police station with all three children in tow. They stepped carefully through the rubble of the old bakery. She didn't yet have the will to start cleaning it up. At the station they told her he was being held for disorderly conduct and could see no one until the next day. She went home, distraught and exhausted. Her body finally overpowered her mind, and she managed to sleep part of the night.

Returning to the police station in the morning, again with the children in tow, the officer on duty had no idea that Christof was even there. There was no official record of his arrest.

Sonja started to cry. The officer tried to get her to leave, but she refused and sat down on the bench, still crying. Soon her children started to cry, too. The uncomfortable officer finally started making some phone calls. After an hour his supervisor came to speak with Sonja.

"You are that man's wife?" he asked.

"Yes. And these are our children. Please release him. We cannot survive without him."

"I do not want to bring hardship on any family," the police captain said carefully. "But your husband has behaved suspiciously, and we must be sure of your family's loyalty."

"Please. We are simple people. We are not interested in politics."

The police captain raised his eyebrows. "You are not interested in the American cause?"

"No. Yes. We are. We support America."

"If you purchase a liberty bond, that would be a good way to demonstrate your loyalty."

"Please, sir, our store was destroyed. We have nothing."

"You people should have thought of that before you supported the wrong side."

Sonja didn't know what to say.

The police captain glared at her. "Shall I telephone the liberty bondsman and tell him you want to help the cause?"

"How much do they cost?" Her voice was barely more than a whisper.

"I believe a fifty dollar bond would be sufficient to remove suspicion from your family."

"Fifty dollars!"

The captain shrugged. "If we deport your husband, you have the choice to go with him along with your children. If you are to remain in this country, we need to know you are loyal."

What choice did she have but to pay? They *did* have the money. But if she used it for a war bond, there would be no money to rebuild and restock the bakery. There would be no money for next month's rent. But when faced with deportation to war-ravaged Germany, paying was the only choice. At least here she had some family, even though she would be loath to rely on her mother or sister's charity.

She returned to get their savings and appeared at the station in the evening to meet the bondsman.

Sadly, she passed fifty dollars to the lanky salesman.

"Do you swear loyalty to the United States of America and President Woodrow Wilson?" he asked with a satisfied smile.

"Yes."

"Do you renounce loyalty to Germany and Kaiser Wilhelm?"

"Yes."

The bondsman paused menacingly. "Do you condemn the treason of your relation, Gerd Steigenhöffer?"

Sonja's stomach turned with rage. Quickly she looked down at the hopeful faces of her children, remembering her own fatherless youth. "I condemn it."

"You condemn *him.*"

"I condemn him."

He produced a shiny, gold-trimmed certificate, wrote some terms, signed it, and then indicated for her to sign. He made her shake his cold, clammy hand. "Your country thanks you."

The police captain released Christof. The two elder children ran and hugged his waist. Sonja sighed with relief at seeing him. When he reached her she laid her head briefly against his chest. It was the closest thing to an embrace they could manage within the clutch of three children.

The family walked home in silence. Sonja didn't need to explain everything, least of all their increased poverty. She knew he could hear most of what happened from his cell in the small precinct station.

Again they stepped through the rubble of their former store. They *would* rebuild. Sonja knew that already, even if she didn't know how.

As soon as enough time passed for Sonja and Christof to think straight, they agreed to change their last name. The three children would grow up calling themselves by the name Stone.

# CHAPTER TWENTY-ONE
# O DREAM TOO BITTERSWEET

That night, for the first time, Glenn knew he had killed.

"Jerrys coming! Jerrys coming!"

The shout awoke him moments before grenades started popping. The *rat-tat-tat* of machine-gun fire quickly followed. Glenn lunged for his weapon. The action was down the trench to his right.

The Germans had used a thick midnight fog to climb out of their trench and rush across the gap at the Allies. The men scrambled for their guns and helmets as grenades exploded at their feet. Suddenly the Germans were at the top of the trench. Through a forty-yard stretch they killed every man from their elevated position, then leaped into the trench on top of the bodies.

At each end of the massacre, Allies and Germans shot and hacked at one another in hand-to-hand combat. Men from both armies, intent on their individual survival, pulled planks, sandbags, and mud from the sides of the trench. Soon the passageway was blocked on both sides of the Germans by bodies and rubble.

The Allies regained order. Machine guns from farther down the Allied trench swept no-man's-land, ensuring no more Germans could cross the foggy waste.

Crouching in the trench, Glenn heard artillery buzzing close above him, cutting down the soldiers trying to come in support from the reserve trench. The whizzing buzz of a shell rang in his ears, exploding just behind him. He flattened himself against the trench wall as pieces of dirt rained down on his helmet. The man who had been standing next to him a moment ago lay on the trench floor, screaming from shrapnel wounds.

Some sixty German soldiers were struggled to hold the stretch of trench they had taken. For a time they continued their slaughter, using the blockage as protection to shoot at the advancing Allies from both sides of the trench.

Glenn willed himself forward. A French soldier just ahead of him hurled two unpinned grenades over the blockage. One exploded immediately. The second, though a dud, rolled menacingly for a few moments among the feet of the panic-stricken Germans. French and Americans climbed from their trench and rushed at the German position from both sides. The Germans who had taken the Allied trench were quickly overwhelmed.

With an enemy at a distance, a trench is unapproachable except by surprise or far superior numbers. But with an enemy at hand, the low position and lack of retreat routes make a trench no better than a waiting grave. Once the Allies reached the top in numbers, sweeping down with automatic fire and grenades, the Germans had no chance.

Those who could still stand threw down their guns and raised their arms, but the shooting continued. Taking prisoners was a humanitarian luxury of the early days of the war. The Germans tried to scramble up the dirt. The front wall of the trench caved in. Some made it to the top before dying. A handful made it far enough to twist their feet in the barbed wire stretched in front of the trench only to be cut down by fire from both sides. There these would stay, lacking men brave enough to retrieve the bodies. None from the brash German advance lived out the night.

Even as the battle continued, Glenn was called back with his company to dig a new trench, directly behind the old.

Having stopped the advance, the Allies were unwilling to fall all the way back to the reserve trench. Once the shooting stopped, the dirt was pushed forward to fill the old trench and bury the bodies. They retrieved as many dog tags of the dead that they could, as well as boards and sandbags to support the new trench. But the first priority of each man was his own survival.

Glenn never felt the exhaustion in his arms through the fighting and the digging that followed. If he had been wounded he wouldn't have felt that, either. He fought and worked like a machine, not a man.

Before that night, men had surely fallen to his fire, but they were distant and anonymous. But that night he looked men in the eye before firing at point-blank range. There was no doubt that there was no way to separate from the carnage. In the desperate battle there were no people, no faces. The enemy became a poison intent on his life, with his gun as the antidote. He didn't feel like he had killed men; he had survived a terrible night. He worked frantically through the early-morning hours to hide the bodies in the ground before sunrise revealed their faces.

German fire continued through the night. In the danger of their task, much of their lumber and supplies were left behind in the old, ruined trench. Most of the dead on both sides would be anonymous until the next day's grim roll call.

When it was done, the Allies had retreated ten yards. The new trench was a poor one. Only six feet deep, with its sides mostly made of bare earth, it offered poor protection. But for survival, it would do until it could be improved.

A gray dawn rose on the desolation. Glenn began to process what had happened. He had learned to kill that night. Would it become easier? He hoped he never grew jaded to it, even though as a soldier he had a job to do in this war. He never wanted to forget that those across from him were men just like himself.

The distance between the trenches was now half what it had been. The Germans had gained nominal yardage, but were no closer to breaking through to march on Paris. Nothing had substantively changed, though three hundred men lost their lives.

Twenty yards past the top of the filled-in trench lay the German soldier who had made it the farthest at the end of the struggle. All the others had been pulled into the mass grave, but this one was too far for safety. Many of the men would later wish they had risked their own lives to bury him. His leg was caught in the barbed wire, his body twisted back toward them by the fire from his own side. His helmet had flown off at the end. His blond hair stuck to the stubble of old grass on the field, caked by his own sweat and blood. His eyes were wide open. His expression captured his final terror. As hard as Glenn tried not to look at those eyes, he couldn't keep his gaze away. This man's dead, terrified eyes began to haunt his dreams.

The opposing trenches were now only seventy yards apart. Any gunfire was deadly. Grenades were almost in range for a man with a strong arm. Death poured daily into each trench. Neither side made any more vigorous advances, yet daily survival remained a challenge. The new Allied trench was deepened and properly fortified, but it was poor protection from the shell fire.

The nauseating smell of death mingled with the stale odor of dirty men and dry gunpowder. Glenn lost his will to eat in the days after the battle. It was all he could do to force his rations down to avoid malnutrition.

At first when the rain started he was thankful. It dulled the stench. But as it continued for three days, the men began to cough and shiver. They rotated with the companies in the reserve, but there weren't enough men to give any adequate rest. A new group of Americans arrived which helped a little.

It replaced a week's worth of dead.

On the fourth night, the sky cleared and dropped the first frost onto the ground. The wet dirt caked into dirty ice. The bottom of the trenches didn't freeze, thanks to the continual stomping of boots. But the tops of the boots themselves often froze until they were plunked into warmer mud. Glenn was among the lucky ones whose boots were starting their first winter. Most of the boots that had already seen a winter or two had sprung holes. Once a man's socks were wet, there was no way to dry them. The first frostbite of the season slithered into the trenches like mustard gas, hiding in the low spots, an invisible and sinister killer.

Glenn wanted to curse the American soldier who reminded him of the calendar.

"Tonight's Christmas Eve, boys," he said, inducing a hateful glare from anyone who could understand. Glenn was initially glad those within earshot were mostly French, but the man had no mercy. *"C'est la veille de Noël, hommes!"*

The glare he earned from the French soldiers was far worse, not only for the reminder but also for his horrible pronunciation of their beloved language.

Glenn hardly slept on Christmas night. He was glad for the two hours he had been assigned on watch.

He would have gladly forgotten that it was Christmas, but now he spent his watch remembering beautiful Christmases past with his family. Then there were the four Christmases with Dafne. Yes, Elsa was there, too. The last Christmas they'd spent together was two years ago, in Lindenhurst. That year, Elsa gave him a small book of poems by Christina Rossetti. He managed to smile, remembering her embarrassment, and how she'd nervously pointed out a particular poem that contained a line they had talked about the month before. Dafne had sat nearby, laughing at her.

The happy moment warmed his heart as he looked out across the waste before him. He clutched the barrel of his

upright rifle in the same spot so the metal remained warm
through his gloves. His toes felt very cold, though he was
thankful they were dry.

Elsa's boldness with the gift only struck him in hindsight.
At the time he hadn't thought it through; he'd only felt
grateful. Nor had he realized then how that particular poem
prophesied how he would feel about those times.

Despite his watch, he allowed himself to briefly close his
eyes and remember. Although he tried to recall Christmas in
Lindenhurst, the image that came to him was Elsa on the
bench at Fort Hamilton the day before he sailed. He
remembered how her soft brown eyes had widened in that
moment—fearful for him, conveying love, wet with tears.

He wished he had brought the book with him. Still, the
poem came back to him easily.

*Come to me in the silence of the night;*
*Come in the speaking silence of a dream;*
*Come with soft rounded cheeks and eyes as bright*
*As sunlight on a stream;*
*Come back in tears,*
*O memory, hope, love of finished years.*

*O dream how sweet, too sweet, too bittersweet,*
*Whose wakening should have been in Paradise,*
*Where souls brimful of love abide and meet;*
*Where thirsting longing eyes*
*Watch the slow door*
*That opening, letting in, lets out no more.*

*Yet come to me in dreams, that I may live*
*My very life again though cold in death:*
*Come back to me in dreams, that I may give*
*Pulse for pulse, breath for breath:*
*Speak low, lean low,*
*As long ago, my love, how long ago!*

Glenn leaned his head down till his helmet touched the barrel of his rifle, squeezing his eyelids shut against the onset of tears.

Each man worked so hard to disguise his own emotions that no one noticed how every man cried a little that night. Dreams of warm fires and lighted trees, the laughter of children and the embraces of loving women couldn't break through the reality of the cold, the blood and the frostbite. There was no escaping the sickening terror each time an artillery shell whined overhead.

Glenn heard footsteps approaching his post. He looked and saw his friend from Fort Hamilton, Captain Cummings. They had been assigned to the same company.

Glenn smiled. "A little early, aren't you?"

"I couldn't sleep."

"I feel the same way. I'm glad to have the watch."

Glenn was also glad for the darkness. He doubted Cummings would be able to see that his eyes were wet from tears. Captain Cummings sat down beside him on the narrow bench.

"How about this?" said Cummings. "A couple of captains, taking the night watch. Pretty soon you and I will each be commanding our own platoon."

Glenn smiled. "Maybe the French will respect us better for taking our lumps before all the poor sap foot soldiers from back home arrive.

"I suppose you're right."

"What difference does it make? We're no safer from the shells out here then we would be behind the line."

Cummings pointed toward the pair of gas masks hanging from Glenn's belt.

"Still got 'em both, I see."

"I don't want to offend anyone." Glenn managed a small laugh at the ridiculousness of it. Arguing over whose gas masks worked better, both the French and the British issued their own model to every American soldier.

"Which one did you decide on?" Glenn asked.

"I'm using the French one, but only because it fits better. They're both lousy. I don't know if the mustard gas could be any worse than trying to see and shoot in these things."

Glenn nodded in agreement. "Besides, there aren't any British in this particular hell-hole of ours."

Cummings made himself comfortable on the bench and inched closer to Glenn. "Here. I've got something I want to share with you," he pulled a small, paper-wrapped packet from his inside pocket. "Call it a Christmas feast."

He unwrapped the paper from a sticky block of toffee. One small square had already been cut out. Cummings cut two larger squares with his pocketknife and handed one to Glenn.

"My mother makes this each year. I couldn't believe it when I opened her package last week and this was in it. I'm surprised they let it through, with everyone starving over here in France."

Glenn held the sticky lump between his fingers, savoring the sight and smell of the candy. Cummings playfully lifted his chunk and looked at Glenn. "Cheers." They both bit in. Mrs. Cummings's toffee was easily the best piece of candy Glenn had ever eaten. Sweet, and sticking between his teeth, it really did feel like a Christmas feast.

Cummings leaned back against the cut dirt behind their bench. "Mom sent me a block of this toffee last year, too, when we were at the base. I didn't share it with anyone. I savored it slowly, cutting off smaller and smaller pieces until it was gone." He nudged Glenn with his elbow. "And it isn't like we were poorly fed at Fort Hamilton."

Glenn laughed. "We complained enough at the time."

"If we only knew what we were in for out here."

"So why did you share it with me this year?"

"Because what I miss now aren't luxuries like a piece of candy, a nice juicy steak, or a swig of whiskey. What I miss is sharing those things with friends and family. This right here," he cut off two more pieces of toffee, "is the closest thing to home . . . to family."

"You're right."

Glenn thought again of the last Christmas he had shared with Dafne and Elsa. This little moment of unity with a companion made Christmas feel real this year, too. He placed his hand on Captain Cummings's shoulder. "Merry Christmas, Sam."

"Merry Christmas, Glenn."

The dawn came just like any other dawn, but without gunfire. Glenn thought the Jerrys must have wept too that night. It was a cold, dark morning. Unable to sleep, most of the men rose at first light. A tense silence hovered over the zone. At such times, a loud word spoken in one trench could easily be heard in the other. That morning, few were willing to break the awful silence of their own memories.

When the sound first rose toward them from the German trench, the Allies clutched their rifles with a confused and heightened sensation. Then they relaxed, for this new weapon struck straight to the depths of their hearts. The heavy baritone voice, timid at first, rose in volume as its power swept over the entire landscape. The notes were slow, the vibrato perfect and smooth.

> *"Stille Nacht. Heil'ge Nacht.*
> *Allis Schläft, einsam wacht.*
> *Nur das traute hochheilige Paar.*
> *Holder Knab' him lockigen Haar.*
> *Schlafe in himmlischer Rue,*
> *Schlafe in himmlisher Rue."*

The following silence was even heavier than before. No man dared to look at another. Five minutes or more the holy silence lasted before a reply came from a tenor in the Allied trench. Glenn doubted he had ever heard a more beautiful voice.

> *"Nuit de Paix, Sainte Nuit.*
> *Dans l'etable aucun bruit.*
> *Dans le ciel tout repose en paix.*
> *Mais soudain dans l'air pur et frais.*
> *Le brilliant Coeur des anges*
> *Aux bergers apparaît."*

He paused for a moment before repeating the first verse. The German baritone was only a moment behind him. The two languages melded in the fraternal unity of the music. More voices and a third language entered. The German slipped into a bass line, leading others into the parts they knew from boyhood choirs. Dozens of voices, led by the beauty of the French tenor and the power of the German baritone, slowed in joint reluctance as the last line concluded and the magical peace necessarily ended.

The following silence was broken only by the tears it no longer seemed a shame to cry.

There was no fighting that day—only a lasting stillness and the enchantment of unforgotten music. How could any fire their guns, knowing they might kill one of the two men who had given such an unforgettable gift of peace?

But the next day war resumed with heavy shelling at dawn. The faceless German baritone and the faceless French tenor became soldiers again. None knew whether their heroes lived or died.

# CHAPTER TWENTY-TWO
# THE SUFFRAGISTS

When Elsa came home, Dafne was drunk.

"Miss Graham!" Elsa was more sad than angry.

"What's the matter?" Dafne tried to correct her posture, brushing her hair back with her hand.

"Look at yourself."

"Oh, I see. Now *you're* going to start in on me. I bet you think you're too good for the likes of me."

"Don't say that."

"It's true! You all hate me because I'm not fun like I used to be. But it's not my fault. I didn't start this war. Don't lecture me."

"When have I lectured you?"

"When Hal and I got together."

"That was different."

"Oh, yes, it was different, so different. You act so pious but you had Glenn long before I had Hal."

Elsa glared at her. "That is not true, and you know it."

"I've seen the letters. I know you went to see him."

"It has been a year and a half since you left him." Elsa refused to feel ashamed of her correspondence with Glenn. "I am sorry Hal does not write you. I never thought he would. But do not blame me. You made your choice."

She walked back to the door.

"Where are you going?" Dafne's tone changed quickly from anger to worry.

"I will come back when you are sober."

Elsa didn't intend to go far, but her feet carried her quickly south on Park Avenue. She was tired, having just walked back from Sonja's home—what was left of it.

Dafne's outburst angered her, especially in the face of what other people were really suffering in these times. Look what Sonja and Christof were going through. Look what Glenn had to endure. Elsa had slim patience for Dafne's little problems. What right had Dafne to take out her sadness on her?

But then again, perhaps she did have some right. Her accusation may have been false, but how could Elsa argue? She *was* in love with Glenn, and Dafne knew it. Glenn was out of Dafne's life now, but her jealousy of Elsa could still fester. Today was only a drunken outburst, but perhaps gave a glimpse of Dafne's true feelings. Those feelings could lead to real consequences.

Earlier today, Elsa had given all of her savings to Sonja and Christof, hoping it would be enough for them to repair and restock the bakery. Although they tried to refuse her charity, Elsa made them accept for the sake of the children. Ultimately, they called it a loan to placate Christof.

Through her years with the Grahams, Elsa had managed to save most of her small salary. She had considered it a luxury to be paid at all. Her lodging, meals and all her basic necessities had been provided to her. She had no reason to spend the little extra she was paid. Although she had sometimes indulged dreams of what she might have done one day with the money she saved, she could not think of a better use of it than to give it to her sister's family in their time of need.

Yet she wished she was not so reliant upon Dafne, now of all times. Until yesterday, she could have made it on her own for a little while, if something had happened. Now, if Dafne decided to move on from her, she would have nothing.

The sound of a crowd lured Elsa west to Fifth Avenue. When she got there, she saw a line of people along the side of the street and past them, women marching down the center of the avenue. This march sounded very different from the other marches Elsa remembered. The shouting she heard was happy and jubilant. This was not a march of protest or of demands. This was a march of celebration.

Elsa immediately realized what it was about and smiled. She hurried to join the crowd, hoping her mother was marching and that she might catch a glimpse of her.

New York State had just granted women the right to vote. It was the first eastern state to grant suffrage and seemed sure to portend national suffrage soon. So said the papers, and Elsa's mother had told her the same. As New York led, the country followed. Elsa had been glad to see her mother involved in the movement again, so as to be able to share in this triumph.

Elsa looked over the bodies ahead of her as the women marched passed—high class women and working women marching together in the unity of their shared cause. Elsa felt inspired. She had seen so many marches—for women's factory rights, for women's voting rights, protesting the war. She had even participated in a few, walking beside her mother. A day like this showed that unity of purpose *could* bring change. Seeing this was an encouraging contrast to the tragedy she saw earlier at her sister's store.

She spotted her mother, walking beside Rachel Shapiro, holding a banner between them. Elsa waved, trying to get their attention, but they didn't see her through the crowd. She began to walk on the sidewalk parallel to the march, glancing through the line of onlookers to keep in step with her mother. After a few blocks, Elsa felt as if she was a part of the march. She may not have participated directly in the suffragists' cause, but this was her success too. She had fought for this in her own way, through her ambition and tenacity.

Elsa was less afraid than just a short time ago when she left Dafne at the apartment. She might soon lose her position with Dafne, either because Dafne no longer wanted her or couldn't afford her, or—the thought came to her for the first time—because she no longer wanted to work for Dafne. Whatever happened, she would be fine. She didn't need Dafne. That tenacity that had brought her this far would bring her even further, even if she no longer had a penny to her name.

The march led downtown. Everything was so familiar, yet also so changed. Elsa had mixed feelings about New York City. She didn't have many good memories here. But being here had taught her priceless things about herself. With everything this city tried to throw at her, for all the times it tried to break her, she had succeeded. She had mastered this place. Whatever it threw at her next, she would take it in stride.

Feeling strong, Elsa allowed herself a moment to indulge her dreams. It had been a long time since she'd done so. For a few years, in Lindenhurst, she felt her dreams had come true and did not think much about the future. After coming back to the city, everything started changing at a rapid pace. It was all her emotions could do to keep up. Recently she had felt she was hanging on to what she had achieved, rather than hoping for more.

She did have more dreams, ones she had not let herself indulge. The feeling of love, which came on her so suddenly before Glenn left for the war, opened new doors in her heart. The serving life was not the final goal, it never had been. What had become of those dreams she and Sonja talked about that day at Ellis Island?

Even in their tragedy, she found that she envied her sister, with the fullness that her children brought her. She envied the bond Sonja shared with Christof, that they could face their tragedy together. Elsa wanted the kind of love that would last through everything.

For the first time, she let herself imagine Glenn as that partner to her. She imagined children with him as their father. It was a foolish dream, but she did not push it away from her mind. She allowed herself the enjoyment of the fantasy.

After all, she thought, looking back at her mother, with Rachel and the other suffragists, where would they all be if a few women had not allowed themselves a foolish dream? It was foolish for them to have believed they could beat the factory bosses and make reforms, but they did. It was foolish to believe they could win the vote—the right having to be voted on by men—but here they were, celebrating that victory.

When the parade ended, Elsa slipped through the crowd and found her mother. Nina was overjoyed to see her there. They walked back to Nina's apartment in the Lower East Side and made dinner together.

Elsa told her mother what she had done for Sonja and Christof. She would have preferred not to tell—*and your heavenly father who sees in secret will reward you*—as the scriptures had taught her. But she knew her mother had been worried and she looked so relieved after Elsa told her. Giving her mother that relief was itself a part of her charitable duty. With that strain soothed, Nina talked all evening about the march and the victory of suffrage.

Elsa loved hearing her mother's enthusiasm. When she visited her mother last year with Glenn, for the first time after returning to the city, she had noticed how much she had aged in their years apart. Now she seemed younger, more energetic. She still worked at the same job, but had found another purpose. Elsa also supposed that Nina's mother's instinct was awakened by Sonja's recent plight. She had always fought to protect her daughters. If Elsa ever found herself in need, she had no doubt her mother would be there for her again too, in any way she could.

Elsa spent the night with her mother and took an uptown train in the morning.

Back at the apartment, she found Dafne in a panic. Dafne had never been alone overnight before. Elsa thought it might have done her good. She could see from the disaster in the kitchen that Dafne had tried to cook for herself. Her bedroom was a complete mess too, with clothes and toiletries strewn about.

Dafne apologized for her outburst, explaining that a message from her parents had upset her. Elsa listened understandingly and forgave her. They embraced. But one more measure of trust had been lost between them.

Elsa resumed her work, cleaning the kitchen and preparing for the coming day. Her tasks were familiar, but it felt different. She felt a fresh independence after yesterday. Even the act of giving away her savings seemed to free her from reliance on it. She would serve Dafne to the best of her ability. She did love her mistress. But she no longer had any illusions that this would last forever. When the change came, she would be ready, and she would succeed again, just as she had done before.

# CHAPTER TWENTY-THREE
# THE PRICE OF WAR

Glenn had heard of Floyd Gibbons long before the famous reporter visited the front lines. As one of the first American officers to see action, Glenn had been sought out by Gibbons for an interview.

Floyd Gibbons was as much a soldier as a reporter. They said his pen was his weapon, with which he drew fire from his enemies and fired back through the sentiment of the people he influenced. Glenn knew he had come to Europe as soon as the United States declared war. When his ship was torpedoed by a German U-boat off the coast of Ireland, he wrote a fantastic account for the stateside newspapers. He was on hand to greet General Pershing and the first American soldiers.

Sitting in Floyd Gibbons' well-outfitted tent, a safe mile behind the reserve trench, Glenn enjoyed his cup of tea for the first time since arriving in France. He'd *had* tea but hadn't enjoyed it. There was plenty of tea in the camps . . . as long as you didn't mind a little dirt in the water, or leaves that had already been brewed twice, or the taste of tin from the army cups. Gibbons had new tea imported straight from England, served in porcelain cups. He even had fresh milk.

Glenn had looked forward to this interview, but hadn't anticipated what he felt as he sipped his tea. The lack of fear was incredible. He now realized that for weeks, every single moment had been colored by an immediate and crippling fear of death. Even at the reserve trench, the fear was constant. As long as he was within shelling range, every moment could be his last.

They sat in padded folding chairs at a folding table, all perfectly designed for the nomadic comforts of a war correspondent.

"Tell me a thrilling tale about the battles you've seen," said Gibbons.

Glad for the opportunity, Glenn related the story of Christmas morning, with the emotional singing across no-man's-land. He told every detail he could recall. Gibbons listened respectfully but without eagerness. Glenn didn't perceive the reporter's ambivalence until he was finished. Only then did he notice that he hadn't written a single word on his pad.

"You're not interested, are you?"

"Sure I am."

"Has somebody already told you about it?"

"No."

"What, then? Don't people back home want to read about this sort of thing . . . humanity in the midst of the carnage?"

Gibbons sighed. "As I said, I am interested. It is a beautiful story. But I cannot write about it for the American people."

"Why not?"

"Captain, I don't want to stifle your enthusiasm, but I must be honest with you." He paused. "You and I know this war in all its terrible truth. I understand why you grasp at the good in the midst of the evil . . . even the good of the men on the other side. But I am a soldier, just like you. If I write this story, I am striking a blow for the enemy. To people back home, the Germans must appear evil, even inhuman. Once folks stop believing that, they will begin to doubt the war. Do you have any idea how important the support from home is to winning a war?"

"No."

"It is everything. Germany will lose this war, and let me

tell you why. After three and a half years, Germany is starving. You think things are bad here in France. Imagine a similar state, but with a complete naval blockade against them. Not only are the Germans limited to the resources they can get from their own land and the small area they have conquered, they have no one to harvest those resources. All the men are either dead or shivering in that trench over there. The soldiers still have meat while the citizens try to make soup from the bones. The people are beginning to hate Kaiser Wilhelm for what he's brought upon them. Soon the people will pull Germany down from within. It happened last year in Russia. It happened in Austria. It's happening right now in Turkey. So now those poor soldiers who sang with you on Christmas don't even have the support of their wives and mothers.

"Meanwhile, in the States, civilians are volunteering to sew uniforms and build weapons. Families are proud to buy liberty bonds to pay for the war, and let me tell you, war costs a lot of money. Do you think German families are buying war bonds right now?"

Glenn sipped his tea in silence, already anticipating his grim walk back toward the battle lines. Gibbons continued.

"Sentiment and propaganda are the most powerful tools of war. Germany has lost its power to use them, for the reality has become brutally obvious to its people. But our people believe every word I tell them. The food, supplies and fresh men coming from America is the only hope the Allies have. It is the work of men like me to keep that flow coming across the Atlantic. Meanwhile, Germany is headed for the same fate as Russia and Austria. If the American people feel the agony of the German people, or the humanity of the German soldiers, they will doubt. Now do you realize why I cannot print your story?"

Glenn's face fell. He didn't know what to think.

"Cheer up, Captain." Gibbons stood up and clapped him on the back. "That's the price of war, my friend. Be inspired by the people who stand behind you. Anyone who fights in this war begins to separate the men from the idea. But remember, you are fighting against an idea—the imperialism of Germany. Those soldiers across from you may not themselves be evil men, but they are tools of evil and must be brought down. You are protecting your friends and family back home, as well as the French and British, from the encroachment of this evil. At the same time, you are helping to bring the promise of the American idea here to Europe."

Glenn left the tent in despair. He had come hoping to show his homeland a light in the midst of the darkness— proving there was hope even for the men in the jaws of death. Now he was being told to forget that small light of hope.

Gibbons was right . . . he was merely the tool of an idea. And what kind of idea? It was America as a shining beacon that would first sweep away evil, then starvation and poverty from war-torn Europe.

Glenn began to see clearly America's role in the world after the war. Gibbons said that Germany could no longer win. But neither could France or England. Only America could win now. With its economy still intact, all of Europe would rely on American resource and philanthropy in the postwar era. The economic invasion would be much more effective than the military one Germany had attempted.

But the war had to be painted as moral in order to win the support of the people. Floyd Gibbons probably understood that reality even better than President Wilson.

Glenn wondered whether there had ever been a moral war.

As he walked back toward the reserve trench, the familiar fear crept back into his body. He felt it in his blood, his muscles, his gut. It made it difficult to think about anything else, but Glenn had to keep thinking. It was what kept him human.

He shouted a silent prayer at heaven as he reached his

post. How could God allow civilization to so thoroughly rend itself apart? How could God take away hope? Losing hope was worse than death. Even a sign of humanity such as the music of that Christmas morning was stifled and silenced.

Dafne watched the luster of New York fade away in the winter of 1917–18. The United States had only sent a handful of divisions to France, but two million draftees had entered military training, mostly in the Deep South. Toward the end of winter the deployments would begin in earnest, with ships sailing almost daily out of the New York Port of Embarkation on the Hudson River and from Fort Hamilton in Brooklyn. There was an urgent need for fresh bodies in France.

The New York City that Dafne had come to love so dearly was hibernating. It irked her that everyone felt the need to suffer in support of a war three thousand miles away. She was willing to do her part and live simpler. But there was no reason for the city to go to sleep. Even the women stayed home now.

It shouldn't have been so dull. Most of the soldiers returned to the city for a night or two before sailing. They were never recognizable or memorable except for their new, sharply pressed uniforms. But despite the soldiers, the city had no energy. Dafne hoped Hal would let her know when he came north before deployment.

Each evening at about six o'clock, Dafne grew restless. She would dress up, make a few phone calls to encourage her friends to come out, then either go out by herself for a drink at one of the hotels or put herself to bed early. By the end of winter she felt lonely and depressed.

Her own family's finances were tightening. Her father's practice had suffered badly in the buildup to the war. Anti-German sentiment forced him to abandon many long-term clients. As the war began, he managed to get some new work with the government, thanks to his knowledge of German legal matters, but his income wasn't nearly what it had been. She didn't want to think about the cost of housing for herself and Elsa here in New York, but she knew it was a significant drain. She feared being asked to return to Lindenhurst.

Thelma Sanderson called Dafne when she returned to the city in February, having spent Christmas and January with her family in Lindenhurst. Having a friend reach out to *her* for a change made Dafne's week. They had tea together the next day at the Carlyle.

Dafne sat down, beaming at her friend. It was so good to see Thelma, who looked beautiful and wise to her. She clutched her hand.

"I've missed you, dear. I'm so glad you called."

"Poor Dafne. You must be so lonely. Does Hal write you?"

"He only wrote me once. His camp is in Kentucky. I wrote him every week at first, but I stopped. I don't know. Maybe once he's in France he'll write. For all I know he's there already."

Thelma smiled compassionately.

"It's even worse because I know Elsa gets letters from Glenn."

"Oh, my dear, I'm sorry. That must be so hard."

"I don't blame him for writing her. They became good friends, and I don't think it goes further than that. But it's tough. I feel like when I lost Glenn, I started to lose Elsa, too. I don't think she ever forgave me for what happened. Elsa and I used to be able to talk about anything. Something's changed."

"You really love that servant of yours, don't you?"

"I do."

Without having realized she was on the verge, Dafne started to cry. Thelma slid toward her and wrapped her arms around her, stroking her back. Dafne's head sank onto Thelma's bosom.

After a few minutes, Dafne sat up with a sniffle. She took

a handkerchief out of her purse to wipe her eyes. She smiled shyly. "I'm sorry. I can't help it. I've been very emotional."

Thelma placed a hand on her leg. "Don't apologize, love. I know. I'm here for you. Whatever you need." She looked deeply into Dafne's eyes. "*Anything* you need . . . call me."

Dafne put her own hand on top of Thelma's and squeezed it gratefully. "Thank you."

When their tea came, the conversation lightened. Thelma told Dafne about her two children. Her husband Michael was at a camp in South Carolina. He *had* been writing, but still not as often as Thelma thought he should. Dafne bemoaned the slowing nightlife of the city. After tea they agreed to go to a dance together the next night. Even if there were no one to dance with, they would get dressed up and have fun together.

Dafne took a cab home. The postman was arriving just then and handed her a letter. It was for Elsa.

She didn't have to look at the return address to know it was from Glenn. At first glance it was obvious the letter had been sent from abroad. That handwriting was familiar; it had penned sweet notes to her in the early days. Now it wrote out Elsa's name.

Going inside, she sat on the couch with the letter in her hands. It had strange stamps and blue markings. She wished it were hers. She didn't know whether she wished Glenn were still her man or not. She missed their times together more than she missed *him*.

Where was he? Was he in danger? She still cared for him. And where was Hal? Would she see him when he came through the city? Would she even know when Hal finally sailed? The loneliness was unbearable.

She who had lost two men to the war didn't even have the comfort of one who remembered her. She laid Elsa's letter on the counter. It would be obvious when Elsa found it that Dafne had seen it.

Dafne had lost more than her two men to this war. She

was also losing Elsa. Their friendship was fading. It had been the two men that came between them, certainly. But as time passed, Dafne realized that Elsa had become more precious to her than either Glenn or Hal had been. Even though Elsa was with her every day, Dafne felt that she missed her. What would she do if Elsa were really taken away from her?

Despite her loneliness, Dafne cheered herself up by anticipating the dance the next night. Later that evening Thelma called again and suggested they make a whole night of it, with dinner at the Carlyle before the dance at the Biltmore.

Dafne decided to wear a sleek black dress she'd bought last year but hadn't yet mustered the courage to wear. It had a plunging V in the front and the back. The skirt had a nice flow and hugged her hips and legs, despite all the folds of fabric. It was a bold, modern dress. When she slipped it on she felt beautiful and sensuous. She wanted to work the room just like in the old days—so recently past yet seeming so far away in memory. She put on a white lace cap that hugged her crown, letting her blonde hair flip out beneath it. Dark, smoky eyes completed her look. Examining her reflection in the mirror before leaving, she was quite satisfied.

That night was the most fun Dafne'd had since the war began. Thelma treated her like they were on a date . . . she paid for dinner, hailed their cab, even opened her door. She told Dafne she looked ravishing, and her eyes told Dafne she really meant it.

At dinner they talked about their past together in Lindenhurst. Dafne told Thelma she had once been horribly jealous of her. For her part, Thelma admitted she hadn't been able to stop thinking about Dafne after she walked into that dance at the grange wearing a man's coat and hat. They both laughed at the memory, which seemed so different in hindsight than it had on that night five years ago.

The dance at the Biltmore was sparse. All the men were

older, and they all wanted to dance with Dafne. She danced mostly with Thelma, however. Thelma knew the leading steps to most of the current dances, which surprised and delighted Dafne. She enjoyed dancing with Thelma, who held her with more sensitivity than the men. When they danced together the men fidgeted uncomfortably at the sides of the floor. Dafne loved it.

After the dance, Thelma accompanied Dafne back to her apartment before continuing to her own home further uptown. Dafne laid her head on Thelma's shoulder in the cab as Thelma wrapped her arm around her. They hugged warmly in the cab before Dafne scampered inside. She went to bed glowing from champagne and companionship.

# CHAPTER TWENTY-FOUR
# TERROR AT CHEMIN DES DAMES

*Dear Elsa,*
*Spring has come to France, and with it comes for me the relief of a change.*

*I am with a full American division now. After a long march north, we have taken up a position behind the British army near Amiens. We hold the reserve behind a strategic ridge that the Germans keep trying to take. I have included my new contact, but I do not know how long we will be here. The armies are moving much more now than they did last year. When you write to me, list my division and company numbers, as that is the surest way to reach me.*

*It seems Germany is intent on winning the war this spring. They have concentrated all their force here on the northern front. Thank God I was not in the path of their first assault. So many of the Americans who are finally arriving died in their first action of the war. It is all so sad.*

*I am relieved to be here, as I am not presently on the front lines. No longer do I fear being killed in my sleep. No longer must I sully my soul by joining in the daily slaughter that was my life in the front trench.*

*Since coming here, all I have been required to*

*do is dig. But that, indeed, is the primary task of a*
*soldier in this war. Before a battle, we all dig. After a*
*battle, we dig. But I am not complaining. I would*
*much rather dig than fight.*

*How long the respite will last I cannot say. The*
*German army is on the move. But I am glad for a*
*chance to catch my breath out of the line of fire . . .*

Glenn paused with the sheet unfinished. There was so much
he wanted to say to Elsa. He wanted to comfort her after the
uncertainties her last letter expressed. He wanted to assure her
of his own spirits, fragile as they were. He wanted to tell her
how much her thoughts meant to him.

But he couldn't bring words to his mind or his pen. This
war wasn't an easy thing to write home about. How could one
describe the details: the shelling, the gas, the bodies of
comrades torn apart, the persistent stench of death? By not
writing these things down they could be kept at arm's length,
like terrors seen on a motion picture show. But how could one
write about something else?

His emotions were numbed by the horror. If he let himself
become emotional he couldn't endure the things he had
seen . . . and would surely see again soon. So he left his letter
as it was, reading like a military correspondence.

The morning postman was about to leave. He quickly
finished the letter, signed it, and sent it off.

Leaving the tent, he looked east to the ridge where the
British army was camped two miles away. For now his
position seemed safe, but he knew the German army was close
beyond that Chemin des Dames ridge.

It wasn't difficult for him to see what was happening. The
papers called the Germans' spring offensive the greatest
display of firepower the world had ever seen. Glenn could
only hope this was their last effort. Kaiser Wilhelm knew

Germany needed to win before millions more Americans arrived in France. The U-boats had failed to stop them. Germany poured every man and boy who could hold a weapon into the surge on the Marne. The problem for Germany was that to win the war, it needed to conquer; the Allies only needed to defend. The goals that brought Germany into the war had become obsolete. Now, Germany had to take Paris or lose everything. But just as in their initial onslaught of 1914, the advance on Paris was limited by lack of resources. Exhaustion and delayed supply trains forced the army to slow. Did the Germans have enough left to finish the surge?

As if a foreboding answered his own question, Glenn saw puffs of smoke rise over the ridge. Moments later came the deathly sound of cannon fire. Another battle was starting. He sprinted back to his company.

Even here in the reserve, two miles behind the ridge, Glenn quickly surmised that things were going badly. He had learned to recognize the sounds of battle and knew the British army on the ridge had been taken off guard. The German artillery was ripping apart the tightly packed troops in the front trench. They had probably preceded the shelling with a mustard-gas drop. Glenn shuddered to think of the casualties the British division was suffering.

He clutched his rifle and waited for orders. It was better not to think at all in these moments. The company commander organized them into defense position. Glenn looked at his old friend Sam Cummings beside him. Their look was brief. Neither wanted to show their fear. They were positioned next to a small wood bunker in the rear line.

German troops came pouring over the vital ridge. Allied artillery and machine gun fire rained down on them. The rush was unfazed, despite heavy German casualties. Desperately, the two Americans retreated to the open door of the bunker, sharing the frame as a makeshift shield as the Germans reached the range of their rifles.

Orders were being shouted somewhere but instinct had taken over. Glenn could barely hear his own rifle amid the din. Bullets began to rip into the walls of the bunker. What poor protection a doorframe was, when one had grown accustomed to a trench.

Captain Cummings fell. Glenn saw the scream of agony on his face, though he couldn't hear him yell. Glenn's fear gave his emotions no space to process sorrow for his friend. Soldiers were falling all around as the Germans got closer. If anyone sounded a retreat, it wouldn't have been heard. Intent on survival, men began to run back.

A line of machine gun bullets slapped Glenn's rifle out of his hand. He could feel the wind from the shots blow the hair on his fingers.

In the split second he had, Glenn looked around. Men were running back and falling all around him. Even if he could outrun the Germans, he couldn't outrun their bullets. For a moment he knew he would die, but refused to accept it. He ducked inside the bunker. Bullets and shattered wood flew past his face.

A single beam supported the interior. He could think of only one plan to live. He had never climbed a bare beam before, but the jaws of death inspired him. He scaled the beam as if he had done it a hundred times.

At the top, he tried to punch through the roof but his position gave him no leverage. He only succeeded in bruising his hand before starting to lose his grip on the beam. He jumped back down to the floor of the shed.

Time was running out. He had certainly lost the chance to flee. He had to hide here or else surrender and hope this was a convenient day for the Germans to take prisoners.

He had a small grenade on his belt. Hurrying to the back side of the shed, he threw the grenade onto its flat roof, hoping to blow a hole he could climb through and hide. He waited, with his revolver in his hand. The grenade exploded, sounding like a dull pop amongst the deafening shells all around him. But instead of merely blowing a hole in the roof, the entire shed quickly crumbled around him.

*Idiot.* Glenn couldn't believe his stupidity. This was life or death.

He burrowed into the pile of shattered wood, ignoring the splinters that scraped at his hands and face. The boards shifted on top of him, pinning one leg, but not crushing him. He laid still. Through the cracks of the pile on top of him he saw bodies everywhere on the field. His sweat made a puddle of the hard ground around him. He didn't know if he was well hidden or not. But he had taken his chance and it was too late to do anything else.

A pair of boots tramped by. He saw them not ten feet away from his eyes. Then another pair, then a dozen, a hundred, a thousand pairs of gray boots. The ground shook from them, the massive German infantry, parting and merging again for a pile of shattered wood. The air was heavy with the smell of gunpowder, hot metal and thousands of dirty men.

Glenn waited, hardly daring to breathe, for what seemed like hours. Still, the army came. Having escaped from the first men in no way eased Glenn's fear. Those who followed would be more eager to kill than those who had already killed today. His fingers shook around his pitiful Colt revolver with its six bullets. All it would take would be for one man to carelessly stumble into the ruins of the shed and he would be found. But no soldier stumbled. The Germans were well trained. They knew how to march efficiently through ruined forests, abandoned villages or vanquished battlefields.

The stampede finally passed. Glenn felt as if he could breathe for the first time in hours. Shellfire sounded from further down the valley. Now that the troops were past he could hear the horrible cries of the dying. He waited another hour or so, he couldn't really tell, then climbed out of his hiding place. Bodies were strewn as far as his eye could see.

The field was oily and slick, reeking of fresh blood.

Six months ago, he would have worried over the men who were still alive. But not today. He wasn't a medic; these were beyond his help. He only hoped he had the strength to save himself.

He ran north.

To the west was the onrushing German army and to the east was Germany itself, with whatever reinforcements might come after the advancing front. He didn't pause to think what hope there might be to the north—it was German held territory—but he couldn't stay still. A hostile army separated him from the nearest ally.

The stretch of front the Germans had broken through in the battle was startling. It must have been twenty or thirty miles wide. Now they would have a clear path toward Paris, rushing forward with three hundred thousand men, four thousand heavy artillery guns and Big Bertha, that horrifying cannon with a thirty-mile range.

Glenn's path traversed the corridor of death the Germans had cut across the countryside. He tried to shield his eyes from the stilled faces and mangled bodies, but it was impossible. Some of the dying moaned and reached out toward him. He ran on in terror. He didn't think to gather supplies or even to pick up a fresh rifle from one of the dead. The sight and smell of the field sickened him too much to think straight.

Medics began to appear among the bodies. Though German soldiers and armed, they had no interest in accosting the lonely American. Their job was to save lives, not take more. Still, Glenn saw their uniforms and feared them. He ran in wide circles around anywhere the medics worked.

Most of the dead were German. The Americans had inflicted heavy losses in their brief stand. He didn't venture near the trench. He knew the British IX corps had been in it. His only hope was that the Germans had captured a few and not killed them all. He could still hear guns in the distance, moving farther away but still loud and clear.

As he came into areas where the battle had passed less recently, the medics were no longer soldiers but Red Cross volunteers.

Though he ran straight, it felt as if he stood still, while death circled closer and closer. As if in a dream, his feet seemed rooted to the ground in a vast field of death. No matter how far he ran, he couldn't escape the field of death. Tears and sweat were indistinguishable to him.

His paranoia swept into a new fear. Figures were moving parallel to him about fifty yards away. These men weren't medics.

There was nowhere to hide. Trees no longer grew anywhere near the front. In a panic, he dropped to the ground, hoping to hide among the bodies.

It was too late. They had seen him.

Sweat poured through his clothes and down from his helmet into his eyes. He tried to stand up but his knees buckled. He lifted himself to his knees and tried to slip his finger around the trigger of his pistol but his soaking fingers couldn't grasp it. He dropped the weapon.

The shapes of four men swirled in his weary eyes, coming quickly toward him. He still couldn't stand but tried to crawl away.

Arms reached around him and held tightly, not in capture, but in embrace. His whole body shook violently.

"He's been through the ringer," someone said.

"It's all right, mate," said the man who held him. The soothing Scottish voice, so recognizable as an ally, broke through Glenn's panic. He wept on the Scotsman's shoulder. Finally, Glenn controlled his hysteria and stood up.

"So, it was no better for ye than for us in the trench?" the man asked in his thick brogue.

"Bloody Francs should have been up front with us," said another of the men. Glenn saw that all four were in British uniforms.

"How many of you survived?" Glenn asked. It was a stupid question, but it felt good to speak again.

"They did take some prisoners, thank God. But you're the first survivor we've seen since we got out of there. It was a good routing."

"I'm sorry for my panic, gentlemen," said Glenn. The human contact brought him fully back to his senses. "I suppose you've been just as frightened as me today. Where were you heading when you saw me?"

"Don't know," said one of the men.

"Well, we can't stay here," said Glenn. "More Germans will be coming through here by tomorrow."

"Where, then, Captain?" asked the Scott.

Glenn looked at each man in turn. There was one sergeant and three privates. He realized that, as an officer, they were looking to him. He felt ashamed for having been found in such hysteria. He hoped this wasn't their first encounter with an American soldier. He determined to earn their respect and trust.

"We must stay out of sight until we can determine the position of our own troops."

"If the French make a stand and force even a partial German retreat, they'll fall back on us," said the English sergeant.

"You're right," Glenn agreed. "The farther behind the front lines we get, the safer we'll be, even though it puts us deeper in German territory. How badly destroyed is your camp at the front?"

"The men are all dead, but we could gather some supplies and ammunition."

A sudden bombardment of artillery thundered to the west. Though it was miles away, they all shuddered.

"Let's move across the trenches, gathering what we can, and get far from this battlefield by nightfall. In the future we should move at night. Who knows how long it will be before we find our companies again."

Glenn put his pistol back in his belt as the others slung their rifles over their shoulders.

"Since we are to be companions," he said, "we should get to know one another. I'm Captain Streppy, from New York."

"Sergeant Fulwider, from Cornwall."

"Private Hageman, London."

"Private Sanders, Stratford-upon-Avon."

The Scotsman offered Glenn his hand. "I'm Private MacLeod, from Dundee. But call me Fergus."

Their time in the British trench lasted longer than they expected. There were still a lot of wounded in and around the trench. The German military medics moved closer behind their army. The decimated British trench was being serviced by Red Cross, as well as some civilians. Private Hageman had some medical knowledge and stayed to help.

Others who had wandered east after the battle returned to tell that German reinforcements were on the way. These, along with any lightly wounded who could still march, joined together. Now a company of twenty-one, they journeyed southeast as night fell, well behind the German front, with a vague hope of finding their way to the French army stationed at Reims.

# CHAPTER TWENTY-FIVE
# BEHIND ENEMY LINES

After the German surge on Chemin des Dames, French soldiers and civilians fled in a mass exodus before the onslaught. The Germans advanced to within thirty miles of Paris. People made plans to evacuate as Big Bertha rained shells on the outskirts of the city. Many on both sides sincerely believed France would fall, and then the war would finally end.

But the Americans had arrived. They made a brave stand at Chateau Thierry on the Marne River. If the Germans were to cross, they would have a free run toward Paris. Throughout the night, the Germans charged the bridge, spending lives thousands at a time. The American guns held firm. Not a single German soldier crossed the river alive. The assault checked, the Americans counterattacked and drove the Germans decisively back. Just as at the beginning in 1914, the Marne proved impossible to cross, when France seemed sure to fall.

This defeat left the Germans demoralized. In the spring offensive alone they had lost almost a half million men. After four years of fighting, they were faced with a fresh and motivated enemy. By then some French had openly suggested surrender, willing to accept German mastery if it would bring an end to the war. But the Americans came ready and eager to stop them.

Glenn's small band of Allies behind the German front had no grasp of the action in front of them. They moved in counter to the German troops, remaining out of sight of their enemy. Soon they lost track of how many days had passed since their isolation. The German army had advanced swiftly, but few reinforcements or supplies followed. This push represented Germany's final expenditure of men and resources.

On the north bank of the Aisne River, the fugitives found an abandoned camp from which they were able to restock their own supplies of food. They hid in what was left of the forest. Most trees were burned to tall stumps, and nowhere could a fresh blade of grass be seen, although it was early summer. The countryside of northeast France had been completely ravaged. But at least the dead tree trunks and riverbed offered some seclusion. If an army either advanced or retreated their way, it would be more likely to go around rather than through their position. They knew the Allied army at Reims was close, but the German front was solidly in their way.

Soon they sensed the Germans beginning to accumulate forces for an attack on Reims. Each night the stranded band tried to find a way to rejoin friendly forces, but there was no way to cross the German position. Captain Billings, an English officer they came upon in the abandoned trench, had assumed command of the tiny company. He resolved to wait while they were reasonably secure.

"Perhaps when the attack comes," he told his men, "we will find a way to help our side from behind the lines."

With this goal, Glenn took a small party out each night to record the positions and number of German divisions. Glenn was well suited to this kind of mission. He could move silently through any terrain and had unusually good coordination. He had never realized these skills until the weeks of secretive movements.

Sergeant Fulwider was a mapper. They had recovered a notebook at the trench, and he created detailed diagrams of the area as they scouted behind the enemy lines. With Private MacLeod and a Private Cook they marked their way west. The

Germans had assembled a huge army along more than fifteen miles facing Reims. It took the whole night just to record the westward flank. Dawn surprised them, still two miles from their camp.

"We'll take shelter in this creek bed," Glenn said. "We cannot risk walking out in the open after all the wagons that came through here yesterday."

They found temporary seclusion in the dried-out creek bed. They didn't have to hide well—just out of the direct path the troops would take. Nor would Captain Billings worry about their absence. Glenn had prepared him for this possibility. Even if they were discovered, their friends in the wood couldn't help. They were on their own. The four soldiers slept sporadically through the morning.

Close and irregular gunfire woke them.

"Where is that coming from?" Private Cook whispered.

"Could they have found our camp?" said Fergus.

"No," Glenn said. "Those shots were from the north. Our camp is east. Something is happening."

He climbed the side of the creek bed and poked his head over the charred landscape. With his eyes just above the ground, all he could see were sticks and dead grass. Then a runner came into view in the distance. Another shot rang out, and the man lurched, stabbed by a bullet in his left shoulder. Wounded, he kept running. Although he was still far off, Glenn could see by the color of his uniform that he was an American. He slipped back into the creek.

"There is an American running this way. He's wounded. I can't tell how many are chasing him."

"I hate the cruelty of it," Sergeant Fulwider said, "But we can't afford to rescue him. If he has any sense he will let himself be captured."

"You're right," Glenn agreed. "It would be too risky."

Fergus poked his head up to see the race that was coming toward them. "There are only three Germans chasing him," he whispered. "We could take 'em!"

"No," Glenn said. "It hurts me to leave him alone, but it is not only our lives we would risk but also those of our companions in the wood. If we start popping away they'll send a whole company after us. It's too great a chance for one man."

The voice of the American shouted from above, less than a hundred yards away. "I give up. Don't kill me."

The man's voice stirred Glenn. He raised his head, feeling his heart twist with a complex array of emotions.

The American had fallen to his knees with his hands in the air, facing his pursuers. He had thrown his pistol to the ground. He slowly pulled himself to his feet with his good arm. Blood oozed slowly from his shoulder. The three Germans tossed their rifles over their shoulders as they reached him. Suddenly the American ripped out a knife and stabbed one of the Germans in the throat. The other two threw him to the ground, kicking him into submission. The obstinate American tried alternately to protect his wounded shoulder and his groin, as the two Germans aimed their kicks at those areas. He cried in defiance and agony.

Glenn dropped back into the dry creek, his face sweating profusely. He began to remove his coat.

"I have to go fight for that man."

"You're crazy."

"I'll go with ye," said Fergus.

"No." Glenn pointed his finger authoritatively at the Scot, then the other two. "You are all to stay here. If they overwhelm me, do not come out to help, even if they kill us both. That is an order."

Glenn left his rifle and took only his Colt revolver.

"Is he a friend of yours?" Fulwider asked.

Glenn paused at the top of the creek.

"No."

He ran at a low crouch across the field, angling to make sure the Germans both had their backs to him. The one who had been stabbed was dead. The American had stopped struggling. One of his adversaries held his arms down while the other playfully brushed a knife across his neck. The American had lost his chance to be taken alive. Glenn knew he had to hurry. He ran silently, undetected by all three.

He stopped running thirty feet away and walked slowly forward. He could not miss his first shot or he would be dead. He had practiced his shooting diligently since joining the army, but he knew he wasn't the most accurate of shots. Fifteen feet away a twig on the ground betrayed him. The Germans turned quickly. Glenn sprinted forward and fired at the one who had been holding the American down and hit him in the chest from point-blank range. He died instantly.

The wounded American brought his free arm up and hit the other German in the face with his elbow. The German dropped the knife and twisted away, pulling his pistol out of his coat. Glenn shot at him but missed. The German got one shot off, but it wasn't well aimed toward either American. He started to run away. Glenn steadied his arm and aimed carefully. If this man escaped, they and their company in the wood would all be found. He shot and missed. Taking a slow breath to concentrate, he aimed again, fired his fourth round and hit the German in the back.

The wounded American ran up with his own pistol and shot him twice more where he lay on the ground, then the American collapsed from exhaustion and loss of blood.

Glenn grabbed him by the good arm and half supported, half dragged him back to the creek bed. Fergus came up to help for the final stretch. As soon as they lay in the shelter of the ditch the wounded man vomited three times before relaxing. After a few minutes, his body became calm and his eyes cleared.

Glenn sat, exhausted and shaken with his back to the slope as Fulwider dressed the wounded shoulder.

The American's eyes were fixed on Glenn. Nobody spoke.

The three British soldiers could feel a tension in the air that they didn't understand.

"Why did you save me, Glenn?" asked Hal, unable to bear the silence any longer.

"Is that the thanks I get?"

"You can't help being a do-gooder, can you?"

"That's how you explain it?"

"It's what I never understood about you."

"On the contrary, I think you were right about me all along. I did it for selfish reasons. Bitter as I am to have risked my life for you, I would have hated myself forever if I had hidden here and watched you die."

Glenn buttoned up his coat and picked up his things.

"We need to move on. I hate traveling in daylight, but those shots were probably audible from the front. Once they find those bodies, they will hunt us down. The others in the wood are not safe, either. Private Halifax, can you travel two miles quickly?"

"Yes."

"Good. We'll help you."

They dragged the three dead Germans into the creek bed. They would have preferred to bury them, but there was no time. At least the bodies would be out of immediate sight. Then they moved on toward their camp.

Hal and the Brits introduced themselves. Fulwider and Cook eagerly heard the tale of his harrowing flight from the battle at Belleau Wood. At first there had been five companions. Hal was the only survivor. Fergus stayed ahead with Glenn, who had entered into a solemn melancholy.

Throughout their campaign together, Hal and Glenn never again acknowledged a special acquaintance with each other. To Glenn, Hal was an audacious and daring private. To Hal, Glenn was a shrewd commanding officer. The men who saw the exchange in the creek bed later wondered whether they had imagined the entire episode.

# CHAPTER TWENTY-SIX
# COMPANIONSHIP

Dafne read her father's note a second time. He was right, she knew. But that didn't make it any easier.

It had been two weeks since her outburst at Elsa. Though they had resumed normality, something was different. Their relationship was now almost purely professional. Dafne missed the friendship they used to share.

She folded up the letter and looked around her bedroom. How she loved this little apartment, even though it had hardly provided the life she dreamed of finding in New York City. She would be sad to leave it, more for what could have been than for the memories she'd actually made here. The best times—those first few months—had been so brief.

In these times, everyone had to give a little. Now it was her turn.

Her parents had asked her to come back to Lindenhurst. Elsa had to be let go. She understood; she had expected it. But she also determined to do all she could to find a way to stay in the city. She couldn't give up. New York symbolized all her dreams, even if Lindenhurst held her best memories. Why go back to the place of her memories when those years were finished and beyond renewal? She had to stay and prove she could make it in New York. Somehow.

She would have asked her parents to take Elsa back into their employment, but her father had anticipated this and addressed it in the letter. Katherine was now working in the house beside her father. There was no need for translation work anymore, thus no place for Elsa. Still, Dafne determined to help Elsa find another position. She—and her parents—owed Elsa that after she served their family faithfully for six years. Dafne had grown apart from her servant, but she still loved her dearly and wouldn't see her working in the factories again. Elsa would come out of this okay.

Would *she*?

Dafne sighed and walked to the window. She looked out at the green trees lining the busy street. How she loved the energy and pace of these city streets.

Life without Elsa frightened her. Even though she had been cross and cruel with her lately, Elsa steadied her and helped her in so many little ways. Dafne knew how to cook a little, and she could figure out how to do other things. Perhaps her father would let her take a smaller, cheaper apartment. Or at least come back to the city after the war. But there were so many other voids than cooking and cleaning that Elsa's departure would create. Dafne was afraid of being alone.

How she wished the war would end. Then New York could return to being the city she loved. Strangely, Hal didn't play a very large role in her postwar vision. Would they still be together after the war? She didn't know, but if New York became the vibrant city it used to be, she could build her place in it once again. Her charm and her beauty would be enough. She didn't need Hal any more than she needed Glenn. As the months passed, she found she hardly missed either of them anymore. She missed the *life*.

She didn't have the courage to talk to Elsa yet, but she needed to talk to someone. She called Thelma and went over to her friend's home that same evening. Sitting together on the couch, Dafne told her everything, then started to cry. Thelma pulled Dafne's head down onto her lap.

"We've grown apart recently. But I love Elsa, and I need her. Without her I'll feel so alone. I've never been alone before."

Thelma stroked her cheek. "Dear Dafne. Sweet Dafne. You never need to feel alone."

"But I am alone now. I don't know what to do. I can't bear the thought of returning to Lindenhurst."

Thelma turned Dafne's face with her hand and looked down at her earnestly. "You are *not* alone."

Dafne smiled up at her friend. She understood what Thelma meant, and it comforted her.

After relaxing a few more minutes, Dafne got up and retrieved a handkerchief from her purse. She wiped her tear-stained eyes, feeling much better.

Thelma sat back on the couch with her legs crossed and arms out over the back of the furniture.

"Everything will work out okay," she said. "Trust me."

Dafne smiled, reassured by Thelma's confidence.

"You know, Hal hasn't written a single letter since he left for France. I only found out secondhand that he had really gone. I don't care anymore."

Thelma nodded.

"For all Glenn's faults, I know he's a good man. He wasn't right for me, but he's a good man. With Hal I'm starting to feel like I was just one more girl he can brag that he bedded."

She sat back on the couch beside Thelma, and saw her friend's inquisitive eyes.

"No wonder he kept pursuing me so hard after that night at the Biltmore," Dafne continued, answering the question Thelma was too shy to ask. "I didn't sleep with him until much later. I thought I wanted to, despite the risk to my reputation. I always thought I wanted to with Glenn, too."

"And?"

Dafne just shrugged. That single word was a loaded question, particularly from Thelma. She didn't want to discuss the experience further.

"You must be starving," Thelma said, and Dafne knew that she understood. "Let's go have dinner together."

Dafne looked down at her day dress.

"In this? I couldn't."

Thelma laughed. "I'm not taking you to the Ritz Carlton. I know a casual place close by where you'll be the best-dressed girl there."

Dafne chuckled. "Okay. Let me fix my face, though. I can't let you see me like this."

Thelma, with her children and their maid, lived in a large apartment on 88th Street, toward the river. It wasn't the most prestigious neighborhood, but that allowed the Sandersons to have more space for the price. They walked to a restaurant in the nineties that Dafne could only describe as a dive. She had never been this far north on the island. Sure enough, Dafne, in the dress she couldn't *possibly* go to dinner in, looked more formal than anyone else in the place. They ate greasy meals and drank beer. Dafne thoroughly enjoyed it. She felt ready for a new adventure—for something fresh and exciting.

Throughout the meal they talked easily. Dafne felt she could tell Thelma everything. She couldn't believe she'd once felt jealous of this wonderful woman.

After dinner they walked hand in hand to a nearby nightclub where a four-piece band played jazz music. Dafne had never been in this kind of club. It was very dark inside, but still felt warm and inviting. She didn't recognize any of the songs. This music was too new to have made it down to the dances at the big hotels yet. They sat in the back, at a table lighted by a single candle, and ordered two more beers. Thelma rested her hand on Dafne's leg under the table as they listened to the band.

Dafne asked Thelma to dance with her. Although they were the only two dancing, nobody gawked at them the way the men had watched at the Biltmore two weeks ago.

When the band took a break, they sat back at their table in the shadows. Thelma looked at Dafne and held her eyes, then tenderly placed her hand on her cheek. The scant inches between their faces dissolved into the darkness of the club.

Dafne closed her eyes and waited hopefully . . . welcomingly for Thelma's kiss. When her lips touched hers they felt soft and smooth. Thelma began to pull away, but Dafne grabbed the back of her head and made her kiss her for a few seconds longer. They smiled at each other and laughed shyly together. Dafne knew if there had been light to show it, her cheeks would be flushed, but inside she felt warm and happy.

Returning to Thelma's apartment, they both felt sleepy from the heavy food and beer. Dafne borrowed a nightgown and shared Thelma's bed.

She awoke in the morning disoriented. Sunshine poked through the cracks in the curtain to light the unfamiliar room, the big bed and the warm body beside her. Then she remembered everything and felt happy.

Thelma, seeing her eyes open, leaned up on her elbows and smiled at her. Dafne saw herself reflected in Thelma's smile. She felt lovely and loved. She reached up her arms and pulled Thelma down to her, hugging her tightly.

Until that night, Dafne hadn't consciously realized what was happening between her and Thelma. She couldn't point to a moment when, once past, *this* became inevitable. But now, in each other's arms, she knew that it had to be . . . and this had been true for some time.

She could have lingered in bed all day but knew Elsa would worry. She dressed in yesterday's clothes, hoping to make it home without being seen by anyone. Before allowing her to leave, Thelma put both hands on her waist and looked earnestly in her eyes.

"Dafne, love, write to your father. Tell him you are coming to stay with me. Be my companion."

"What about Michael?"

"Don't worry about Michael. That is a matter for another day . . . after the war."

"Okay."

"I'm not letting you get away . . . now that I've found you."

How good it felt to Dafne to be spoken to that way. How different this assurance was from Glenn's timidity and Hal's frivolity. She wondered why she had been wasting her time and her heart for so long. She trusted Thelma and wanted to let her take care of her.

They kissed again on the doorstep, both hands held at their sides and their bodies pressed together. Dafne closed her eyes for a moment before stepping back with both of Thelma's hands still grasped in hers. They exchanged a look that meant more than any words could have said.

Elsa and Dafne both cried on the morning they said good-bye.

Despite promises to keep in touch and to see each other from time to time, Elsa knew that wouldn't happen. She wouldn't have much free time in her new position, and Dafne would never come out to Queens. As she left Dafne in the boxed-up apartment, Elsa knew the possibility was very real that she would never see her long-time mistress and friend again. She left early with her single suitcase of possessions. Dafne waited with all the boxes marked either to be sent back to her parents' house or to come with her to Thelma's.

Elsa took the new subway train under the East River from Grand Central Station, stopped two stations into Queens, walked half a mile, and checked in at the building indicated on her telegram.

She had been hired by a maid service that employed a dozen other girls. The agency had both residential and commercial clients who didn't need someone on their own staff but still required maid service once or twice a week. Above the office was a dormitory she would share with the other girls. Dafne had been instrumental in helping secure her the job.

After signing the necessary paperwork in the office, she took the stairs up to her room. She didn't mind sharing the facility with the other girls but was glad to have a small bedroom to herself. Perhaps she would make new friends. Setting down her suitcase, she looked out the thick glass at the street below and the warehouse building across from her. It wasn't much of a view, but the room was well lighted.

Today certainly lacked the excitement of the last time she took a train east from the city for a new job. Yet she felt glad and even relieved. She had needed to move on from serving Dafne, and she was good at this kind of work. It was better than sewing uniforms in the factories. Furthermore, something told her this was only a temporary position for her.

She reminded herself of the pride she felt that first night in the Graham house, when she realized that she had earned the right to call herself a career woman. Her hard work had earned that opportunity and would earn her another. Her emotions were frayed right now, but she still had that strength within her. She still believed in herself.

So ironic, that she had saved for years for a time just like this, and now her savings were all but gone.

She had no regrets about helping Sonja and Christof. They had already started on the repairs of the bakery, and thanks to her, had been able to restock and open for business in the least damaged part of the building. Elsa couldn't imagine a better reason to have saved.

Everyone was struggling to support this war, either directly or indirectly. She was lucky to have a new job. For her and her family, the first thought had to be surviving the war. Once it was over many things would change.

How these changes would impact her life, she could only imagine. After the first indulgence in her dreams about Glenn, it was hard not to keep imagining a future with him after the war. This new job would allow her to dream quietly without risking her security.

She wanted to write to Glenn immediately, to tell him her new address and to describe her new home. She always wanted to tell him everything. But this afternoon she couldn't start. She was afraid.

Although she wrote to him at least once per week, she hadn't received a letter from him for over a month. She feared he was dead. The papers spoke of large battles in France. She always read the names of the dead, but in war there were unknown casualties. She had no assurance that he was alive.

Almost worse, however, was the fear that he had forgotten her. His last letter had felt short and distant. Then nothing. Had he come to his senses and talked himself out of his brief fancy for a servant girl who wasn't even all that pretty? Had he used her to help himself get over Dafne and now was ready for a new romance in his own class?

So many times, growing up, her mother warned her not to let herself be swept off her feet by a man. Others—girls in the factory and elsewhere—had told stories of "swells" talking pretty to working girls, only to leave them with broken hearts . . . and often a baby to provide for as well. Elsa had never thought of herself as the kind of girl to be taken in so easily, yet here she was, her heart as vulnerable as could be.

She knew Glenn was a good man and wouldn't hurt her intentionally, but these things happened.

She still had no idea whether Glenn thought of her the same way. She could have imagined the tone she read in his early letters. Maybe it *was* only friendship to him.

Her free time was almost up. She was expected downstairs in the office in half an hour. She sat down and forced herself to write the letter to Glenn. Hard as it was to write to someone from whom she had stopped expecting a response, she would continue for as long as it took. She had taken her chance. If he *were* dead, or *had* forgotten her, then her heart was already doomed to be broken.

It had only been a month. She tried to keep hope. Deep in her heart she felt he needed her love and prayers now more than ever.

# CHAPTER TWENTY-SEVEN
# THE WAR TO END ALL WARS

Glenn didn't flinch when he heard the artillery assault begin.

The position of his vagabond company was eight miles behind the battle, though it could easily spread to their position. They all listened intently for any change in the gunfire.

"What are ye thinking?" asked Fergus, who sat with him against the wall of the abandoned farm shed that had become their home.

"I'm feeling guilty for hoping the Jerrys win this battle."

"Why?"

"If they retreat they'll fall back right to us and kill us. But if they push on to the Marne, we may be able to slip back to our side of the line."

The Scotsman nodded. "Ye're right. But ye *should* be feeling guilty that we're sitting here with bellies full of sausages, green beans, and brown beer!"

Glenn laughed. "How did we get so lucky?"

That morning, after traveling through the night, the group had stumbled upon a heavenly bounty in the farmhouse where they now hid. The Germans had used it for their officers' quarters until the most recent advance. Leaving hastily, they left much of their supplies behind, including enough for the wanderers to have a breakfast fit for kings.

None of the gun ammunition was useful to them—the German officers' weapons were of different issue. But they had found a good quantity of explosives that they planned to take with them. The store that had been left made Glenn think they planned to use this place again. It would be dangerous to stay long whatever the outcome of the battle.

"We've got it good," said Fergus, patting his stomach. "I'm sure glad I ain't up in the trench for this one."

"I don't think there have been trenches in these last battles."

Both sides had figured out how to circumvent the trench stalemate. The Germans did it with a huge concentration of men, but their push wasn't sustainable. Now it was matched by the Americans, whose numbers *were* sustainable. Meanwhile, the English had introduced a new invention that Glenn expected would eliminate trench warfare for good: the armored tank.

"Can you believe I enlisted for this?" Glenn asked at length. "They would have sent me anyway, but I *wanted* to come."

"So did I. They never say what it'll be like. Ye have to see it for yourself to know there's no glory in it."

"I find it hard to care who wins anymore. I just want to stay alive."

"Do ye have someone to stay alive for?" Fergus asked.

"Yes, I suppose. There's a girl I've been writing to, but I don't know what will come of it when I get home ... if I get home. Would you believe she's my former fiancée's servant?"

"I've heard stranger things."

Glenn briefly closed his eyes to allow a vision of Elsa to come into his mind. He had thought about her so much during these weeks of wandering.

"Do ye love her?" asked Fergus.

*Do I?* Glenn wondered.

"I don't know if I'll get through this war alive," said Glenn, not answering Fergus's question, "but if I do, I'll probably have to forget about her. Still, the thought of her gives me peace."

"If ye love her, there will be a way. There always is, if ye have enough courage."

Glenn smiled. "She must be so worried right now. So must my family. No word from me in . . . how long has it been?"

"I lost count of the days. Out here even night and day blurs together."

"What about you, Fergus? Any special lady to stay alive for?"

"Only my dear mother." He lifted his nearly empty bottle of beer. "Here's to getting out of here alive."

Glenn inclined his own beer forward then drank the last of it. How funny that he'd always disliked the taste of beer. But this morning's warm bottle had been the most refreshing beverage of his life.

The sound of distant movement penetrated the countryside: engines, wheels on cracked mud, and thousands of feet. The gunfire continued more sporadically, joined by fire from farther away.

"You hear that?" said Glenn. "The Germans won the first fight. They're advancing."

He stood up. "Let's get ready. Billings will have us on the move soon."

As the German army advanced through the next few days, Captain Billings led his two dozen men well behind the enemy army, moving mostly at night. They hoped either to find a way to break through to their own army or to somehow disrupt the German supply lines from behind. The main reason the German spring advance had stalled was a failure of their supplies to keep up with the army's advance. Captain Billings hoped to have a hand in similarly handicapping the summer advance.

It was clear to Billings and his men that the front had finally been broken. If they could have known exactly where, they might have been able to slip around the advance and rejoin their own army. But there was no way to know and instinct pulled them west. They followed the German army on its western surge as it neared the Marne River for the second time in the war.

On the third day of the advance, a convoy of eighteen German supply trucks rumbled dangerously close to the makeshift camp of Captain Billings' men. They drove in single file on the battered road. After the last truck was past, the small band followed at a distance until the trucks stopped. The men hid until nightfall, then crept forward to investigate.

The supply convoy had stopped at an abandoned trench. It appeared they had started to build a temporary bridge to cross it, but had stopped their work to wait for morning.

Billings and his men had been monitoring this area closely since the advance and knew there was nobody left in this trench. It had been the German front line earlier in the war, before the advance. They circled around the trucks and dropped into the dark cavern.

"Tonight we can finally strike a blow for our comrades," the captain said. "The trucks are poorly guarded. We have almost as many men and plenty of explosives."

It was a dangerous proposition. The men all looked around anxiously. But after weeks of wandering they were all ready for some action.

"String the dynamite together on a long, loose wire," he said. "Look at how the trucks are parked, all in a line waiting to drive over their little bridge in the morning. With a charge under each truck we can take them all out with one fuse."

"That's crazy. How would we place the charges without being seen and killed?"

"A man would have to carry the charges from one truck to the next, staying underneath them." Captain Billings paused as several of the men worked on stringing together the dynamite. "I know there is one of you who could do it."

They all looked at Glenn.

"Captain Streppy," Billings said at last, "You are the man for this job. I've seen how you move. I think you could do it without being seen or heard."

Glenn said nothing.

"I can't order you to take on a mission like this. But think of the difference this could make for our men at the front. It would be worth all our lives to destroy this convoy."

"I'll do it."

"Thank you for your bravery. We will back you up from the trench. If anything goes wrong, we'll open fire."

The dynamite was prepared, as was the igniter to light the fuse from the trench.

Glenn got himself ready. He was eerily calm. Hal came up and patted him on the back.

"Good luck, buddy."

Glenn and Sergeant Fulwider crept through the trench, stopping beneath the nose of the first supply truck. Boards were stacked nearby, ready to build the bridge in the morning. Fulwider carried the igniter while Glenn had eighteen charges of dynamite wrapped around his shoulder.

"If anything goes wrong," Glenn whispered as Fulwider set his position, "don't hesitate to set it off. Taking out a few trucks is better than none. Don't worry about me. I'll get out of there in time."

He climbed the trench and slipped under the first truck. Breathing slowly, he saw boots close by. He slowly set the first charge beneath the gas tank. Waiting until the boots walked past, he ducked out from the back of the truck, scampered the few steps to the next one and dropped under it. His breath grew quicker. His face was sweating, but his hands were steady as he set the second charge, ducked out and under the third truck.

Now the boots stood behind the truck. He waited anxiously. The truck above him moved slightly as a man leaned his hips onto the bumper. How long would he have to wait, Glenn wondered, and would Fulwider think something had gone wrong? It was too soon. Only three charges had been set. Glenn waited, wondering what he should do. But he could do nothing but wait and watch. A cigarette butt dropped next to the boots. The truck wiggled again as the man stood up, stomped out the cigarette and walked off. Glenn exhaled deeply, then scampered to the fourth truck.

Five . . . six . . . seven . . . without a problem. He was getting into a rhythm and moving quickly. But not too quickly. It remained imperative to be silent as he attached each charge. Although there weren't as many boots here as he saw at the front of the convoy, he had to be just as careful between each truck. Eight . . . nine . . . ten . . . the trucks were spaced farther apart now, carelessly. He had to skip one charge since there wasn't room on the fuse.

He set the eleventh, checked the space and ducked out toward the twelfth.

Suddenly he was grabbed from behind. For all his care, he missed the soldier just coming around the corner.

*"Was gibt? Ein Feind!"*

Glenn wrenched his body around and hit the German in the face with his forearm. Their arms locked together as they struggled between the trucks. Sounds of shouting and running approached. Quickly the first shots rang out from the trench . . . then the first explosion.

Fulwider had ignited the fuse.

Glenn struggled to free himself from the German. He still had five connected charges wrapped around his shoulder. The second explosion . . . then the third. It would reach him in no time.

He jolted his right arm free from his enemy and flipped the dynamite off his shoulder, losing track of the explosions as they rang out in quick succession. Still held by the German, Glenn tugged them away from the convoy. The German saw the string of explosives on the ground and realized the danger. Unwilling to let go, he ran with Glenn a few paces in mutual desperation. As Glenn stumbled away, the German fell on top of him.

At that moment, the charge on the closest truck ignited. He had set that one perfectly—the gas tank exploded. A red fireball shot toward the two struggling men.

Glenn saw the flame rush at him as if in slow motion. Everything became red, then everything was black, then there was no color at all.

Time stood still.

An image appeared to him of a small boy standing on the beach. It was himself, in some unremembered summer. There he was, too, in his restless adolescence, in college, with Dafne, in Hal's hotel room . . . the images of his life seen from omniscient eyes, detached and distant. Then he was there on the bench in the Fort Hamilton courtyard, seeing through his own remembered vision Elsa's warm brown eyes, wet with tears, open wide with love for him.

Glenn felt death reaching out for him, and his heart reached back out of this hell toward her.

*Come back in tears, O memory, hope, love of finished years.*

A small spark of energy returned to him in the darkness, and with it the will to fight off death for a moment more. He could see nothing, but struggled to regain his other senses.

With life came pain—terrible pain. His face was hot as if in a furnace. The German lay motionless on top of him. People shouted all around in confusion. Gunfire continued a little longer, then stopped.

Glenn fought back against the agony that tempted him to give up. He writhed on the ground, struggling to free himself from the corpse that pinned him down. Finally free, he crawled away, blind and bewildered.

Arms reached down and grabbed him. He almost could have believed they were heavenly arms, but the searing pain in his face reminded him he was still alive.

And he knew these arms. They had reached down for him once before.

"Ye've done good, Glenn," said Fergus. "Now help me to save ye."

The familiar voice stirred his will. He ran under the Scotsman's guidance until they both tumbled into the trench.

Gunfire sounded farther away as the Germans chased their friends down the trench. Fergus lifted Glenn and they ran in the opposite direction. Glenn ran as best he could without sight as the Scott guided him through the abandoned trench. Every few minutes they stopped as Fergus looked for a medical kit. Finally he found one.

"Lean against this wall here. I'm going to put something on your face."

Glenn waited, expecting a sting. Instead, a cool balm soothed the burning. Fergus also rubbed some on his hands and legs. Glenn's lower trousers had been burned off, and the skin along his legs was singed as was his entire face.

"Come on," Fergus encouraged. "I know ye're tired, but we've got to go on."

They ran on through the night, finally climbing out of the trench into the shelter of a deserted barn. Fergus told him it was dawn. Glenn could see nothing. Finally allowed to rest, Glenn lay on the hard barnyard floor and began to cry. They were desperate, emotional tears—the kind no soldier ever wanted to cry. Fergus compassionately held his shoulders.

"I cannot see. I'm blind."

"Once the burn recedes your eyes will open again."

Glenn moaned incoherent words. He doubted his eyes would ever open again. They felt like they had been completely scorched off.

"But ye're alive!" said Fergus. "And ye're a hero."

"It doesn't matter," he cried. "No one will know of our heroics. We're going to die. All of us. We're going to die!" A new wave of tears stung the burn through which they spilled.

"I will not let ye die, Glenn. God sent me to your aid twice now. It's not just to let ye die."

The image of Elsa came again into Glenn's mind's eye, giving him renewed strength. Oh, to see her one last time. He couldn't bear the thought of losing his life before he had a chance to fulfill his love.

What a fool he had been.

How could he not have realized how much he loved Elsa? All the conventions and expectations of society that had blinded him now seemed like pure vanity. He wanted to give her his whole heart, even if his family disowned him for it. Nothing but his love mattered now. But the chance already seemed gone.

"Let me save ye for her," said Fergus. "Don't give up now. If we die, we die, but if we give up, we're cheating ourselves, and God. Ye'd be cheating that girl, too, who's loving ye and waiting for ye. Just live one more day. Then another day. That's how we'll get through this."

Glenn leaned his head back on the dirty floor of the barn. He tried to ignore the burning, and worse, the dawning knowledge of his blindness. Even if Elsa loved him before, how could she love him now, blinded, broken and half-dead? He waved his hand frantically in the air until he caught Fergus's hand.

"We're safe here," Fergus said. "So we're going to wait. And pray. We're in God's hands now."


Without sight, Glenn couldn't know how many days or even weeks he followed Fergus away against the German retreat. It seemed to be coming at them from all sides. Sometimes he knew they'd been spotted, but the panicked Germans didn't seem to care. Glenn found it difficult to care anymore too.

Glenn understood what was happening. Germany had thrown the last of their men and resources into their spring offensive, only to be pushed back in the summer by a million fresh American soldiers. Germany had exhausted the reserves and morale of both their soldiers and their citizens. They wanted to rest. All of Europe wanted to rest.

"The war's ending, Glenn," Fergus said to Glenn. "I can see it in their eyes. The Germans no longer believe they can win."

Delirium clouded Glenn's thoughts, jumbling his memory of those weeks. Without sight he had no way to distinguish the events in his mind. He only remembered the fear, the pain and the despair. The realization of love had convinced him to care about his life. Now that he wanted to live, the fear of their plight made each day a sightless nightmare.

Early on, Fergus offered continuous encouragement, describing the retreat of the Germans and the hope of victory. But as the days wore on, even Fergus struggled to maintain his spirit.

They were very hungry. Foraging was practically impossible. Thousands of retreating men were desperate for each scrap of food on the desolate land. Both Glenn and Fergus were sick, dehydrated, and infected.

Glenn was delirious when at last he heard Fergus's voice shouting, following weeks of whispers. There were more arms and words spoken in French. At first he thought it was a dream. Then came water, food, medicine and a cot. Glenn knew that his war was finally over.

# CHAPTER TWENTY-EIGHT
# HOMECOMING

Elsa remained in an emotional agony all summer. She was glad for the steady work that provided just enough distraction to keep her mind and body busy during the day.

Every night she read the newspapers' account of the war. But how could the movements of hundreds of thousands give her any clue to the fate of the only one she cared about?

By then, Glenn could have been dead for months. She had no way to know.

How she wanted to contact his family. She'd had good rapport with his sister Jeanette, from back in the days when she and Dafne were friends. But she didn't dare write to Jeanette. How could she explain why she was so worried— that she had been receiving letters that had suddenly stopped? What if he was fine and had forgotten her? Then Jeanette would know Elsa's feelings for her brother, in all their impropriety and foolishness.

By September, the loneliness of her new life had begun to wear on Elsa. It had been three months since she'd left Dafne's service. There was little consistency in her work. Occasionally she cleaned the same house repeatedly, but she seldom saw the tenants, and when she did, few words were exchanged. Although she had forged some friendships with the girls who lived with her at the dormitory, they weren't deep or sustainable relationships. She had little in common with the others.

She had one full day off per week. Most Sundays she

attended church early, then took a train to visit either her mother or her sister's family in Manhattan. One time she took the train farther east in Queens to visit her old friend Josephine. She considered visiting Dafne, but as of yet she had not. She was afraid it would be awkward. Perhaps one of these Sundays she would.

These trips were good for her. She needed to stay connected with the people she cared about. Getting away once per week reduced the monotony of this new life.

She took satisfaction in knowing she was good at her work. Clients would ask for her specifically because they liked the care she took when cleaning their homes and offices.

Although she enjoyed working as a maid and was treated well by her employers, this life seemed only a small step up from her life working in the shirtwaist factory. She was grateful for the opportunity, but this wasn't the life she had dreamed of and worked for. The joy she had experienced working for the Grahams showed her what was possible. Only until the end of the war, she told herself. If it ended without word from Glenn, she would look for a more fulfilling position.

According to the newspapers, the war *was* ending. How long would it be before the men started coming home? And then how long before she faced reality—that her dream of a life with Glenn was a fantasy that she should have never even dared to think about.

The season was beginning to change; it had been a hot summer. Finally, a pleasant breeze cooled the brick and concrete of these streets that had become her home. She walked home from the day's job, smelling only urbanity on the early autumn breeze. How different from the fresh breezes in Lindenhurst, or even on the Upper East Side of Manhattan, when the wafts of air from the park had brought freshness through the open windows of their apartment. Even the neighborhood she grew up in on the Lower East Side had more interesting smells that filled the season's winds. They were not always pleasant, but they contained a complexity born of the life of many diverse cultures. Her new neighborhood had the industry without the complexity.

The city was changing rapidly. This afternoon she walked past three new construction sites . . . being dug down first so the buildings could rise higher. Even before the treaties were signed to end the Great War, New York City—the pulse of America—was readying itself for a new surge of industry and economic boom.

She climbed the stairs to her bedroom and opened the door.

A yellowed envelope with blue markings sat on her counter. Her heart leaped! She had come to know that yellowing—the color of an envelope that had traveled by sea. She dropped her bag and rushed over. It was indeed sent from France, but it wasn't his handwriting on the envelope. Her momentary joy turned to terror. She ripped it open. The letter was in his hand, though sloppy. The date on top was from two weeks back—the normal time for it to arrive.

She clutched it to her breast, filled with relief. He was alive.

Now that the worst fear of these months was gone, she took her time to read the letter. She kicked off her shoes, sat up on her bed, and read the two pages.

*My dear Elsa,*

*I hope you have not worried too much for me . . .*
[Ah . . . how little he knew her heart!]

*I have been through hell, but I am safe at last. For me the war is over. It is only a matter of time now before the war is completely over. The Germans are defeated. But the war has been won at a terrible cost.*

*How can I describe what I have endured and what has become of me? I wandered for weeks behind enemy lines, faced each day with the threat of death. I will not go into what I have lost in terms of sanity, dignity and belief in man. Most significantly I have lost my sight. I was blinded by an explosion that I set myself. I wonder if it is God's punishment for me. I have killed and sinned enough this year to deserve the hell I have been through, along with this crippling that is mine to bear for the rest of my life.*

*I hope this letter is legible. I cannot see the page. Thankfully, all your letters reached my division. They were forwarded to me here at Calais where I slowly recover. My friend and companion through this misery read them all to me. As soon as my body is able, I will sail home.*

*The love I feel from your letters has been the best medicine for my recovery. It means so much to me that you continued to write to me despite nothing but silence in return. You must have assumed I was dead. My love for you has sustained me through all the dark days of this war.*

*I am blind now but feel I finally see what I was blind to all those years. I love you, Elsa, and have loved you for so long. But I let myself be blinded by so many things. I let myself be told I was supposed to marry a woman such as Dafne, even though we had nothing in common, and my heart was elsewhere. But now it is too late. I am a broken man, both in body and in spirit.*

*I am rambling, my dear. I hardly know what I want to say to you. I want to give you so much. But now that I realize it, I have nothing left to give. It would comfort me to hear your voice once more, even if my eyes cannot see you.*

*Yours, Glenn*

Elsa read it again, and then a third time as tears poured from her eyes. What sorrow, yet what joy! He said he loved her! What did she care if he were blind and broken? The love she had carried through this year—and longer—was reciprocated. She hadn't been able to believe it until now. *"I love you, Elsa, and have loved you for so long."* Even by saying he had nothing left to give, he told her that he wanted to give her something.

She lay back on her bed, feeling giddy. She didn't care if he could give her nothing. She had *everything* to give to him.

She needed to tell someone about this joy of love that bubbled up in her heart. Her first thought was to tell her mother, but she had spent so many years preparing her daughter to live as a spinster. She would have warned her to beware of a broken "swell" returning from war and wanting a warm bosom to embrace. So that Sunday she took a train east and showed the letter to Josephine, who was still, after all her hardships and loss, one of the most positive people Elsa knew.

She had already told Josephine about Glenn and her own feelings, so she didn't need any new explanations. Elsa simply handed her the letter and let her read.

"Oh, the poor man," said the older woman, quickly reading the pages.

"What should I do?" asked Elsa after a moment.

"Go to him. He needs you. You can be for him what Miss Graham never could be. You have a servant's heart. This is what God has called you to do. What more could you want from life than to serve the man you love in his disability?"

"I'm scared," said Elsa. "My position. What will his family think?"

Josephine nodded. "But if you do not go to him now, when he most needs you, it will become the biggest regret of your entire life."

Elsa nodded, frightened but eager.

"You can help him to recover his peace," said Josephine. "His loss of peace is far worse than his loss of sight. But fortunately, peace can be recovered—with prayers, and with love."

Josephine smiled, with a wise twinkle in her eyes.

"Who knows? You may help him recover more than peace. God has a way of giving miracles to those whose love is strongest."

"This is it, my friend," said Fergus on the dock in Calais.

"My year in France seems like an eternity," Glenn said. "I can't believe you've been here four years. Somehow I still get to leave first."

"Ye've given more in one year than I gave in four. Allow yourself to be proud of what ye've done."

Glenn sighed. Since his blinding, his hearing had become incredibly sharp. He would always remember Fergus's Scottish brogue fondly, even though he could barely remember what the man looked like.

"It's hard for me to be proud of this war," said Glenn. "There were no winners. Only destruction and sorrow."

"How long will it take for it to simply end?"

"I hope and pray it is soon. But most of my countrymen just got here. I fear what they're doing now in Germany. It's not the way to start an era of peace."

"How do ye mean?"

"I heard in the hospital that Kaiser Wilhelm has offered surrender, but President Wilson won't accept it yet, so the American army is pressing forward into Germany. Wilson has demanded a complete dismantling of the German imperial government and democratic elections. Now they say revolution swirls in Berlin."

"But that's good. The Kaiser must be punished for what he's done."

"I suppose you're right. But it worries me, how this war's ending. New seeds of bitterness are being sown throughout

Europe. Nations are often rebuilt on bitterness. Even in conquering, I fear we are creating a monster in Germany."

"I hope ye're wrong, Glenn. After this, Europe deserves many years of peace."

"I hope so, too. Time will tell."

Fergus lifted Glenn's bag and guided him toward the ship. After one week at an inland military hospital, they had been sent together to the port city of Calais to complete their recovery. Both had been closer to dying of infection and malnutrition than they'd realized. They had now been here three weeks. Glenn was headed home, while technically, Fergus awaited reassignment. His division had been practically annihilated at Chemin des Dames. With the army pressing toward Berlin, he didn't expect to be reassigned before the war ended.

After repeated inquiries, they had finally learned the fate of their companions behind the German line at Reims. Hal, Captain Billings, and several others were reported to have survived, while Sergeant Fulwider was dead. Whether he'd died the night they attacked the supply trucks or later, Glenn would never know.

"Promise me one thing," said Fergus, stopping with Glenn at the gangplank. "Promise ye will give yourself a chance with that girl."

Glenn said nothing.

"All the things that made you worry before . . . none of that matters after what ye've gone through. She loves ye. I read her letters to ye, remember. I know it. Ye need love now more than anything. I'm sure she'll make ye happy."

"Look at me, though. I'm a shell of the man she once knew."

"I don't believe that. Ye say ye're not worthy of her because ye don't want to face the objections ye'll hear if ye marry her. I told ye that night to stay alive for her. Ye did. Nothing else mattered that night. Nothing else should matter when ye get home."

The ship moaned its final invitation. Fergus reached out and embraced him.

"Good luck to ye, Glenn. I'd hope to meet again, but I doubt I'll leave the highlands after this. I don't expect ye'll be traveling much, either."

"I'd be happy never to leave my home town of Lindenhurst again. But we will write. God bless you, Fergus. When you see your mother, thank her for sending you to my aid."

The Scot laughed. "Ye're a good man, Glenn."

Glenn took the arm of another American and followed onto the ship.

On the homeward voyage, he thought back through all the time since his enlistment. He remembered how worthwhile he had felt in his early days as a soldier. In retrospect, the reality of war had been so far from his mind. Going through training, none of them ever thought of watching one another be ripped apart, as he would watch his friend Sam Cummings die beside him that day at Chemin des Dames. He remembered how fervently he had believed in this war up until he had killed men. He remembered the voice of the German baritone on Christmas morning. That man was probably dead now. If he was still alive, he was likely living in destitution and bitterness.

What had Glenn's sacrifice been for? He would never again be free to move without a guiding hand. He couldn't run, he couldn't dance. . . would he even be able to work?

He had lost more than his sight. He had lost his innocence and his peace. He would always be guilty for what happened in this wicked and pointless war. He himself was a finger on the hand of death that cursed Europe. He feared he would carry that guilt for as long as he lived.

Would Elsa forgive him for what he had partaken in? Would she want to see him, even though he couldn't see her? He wondered how badly his face was deformed. Fergus had told him it wasn't bad, but how could he trust his friend? It would be in kindness that he tried to spare Glenn knowledge of deformity.

What future could he and Elsa possibly have together? He didn't deserve to ask her to spend her life with him. He hadn't known he wanted to until it was too late. How could he ask her such a thing, when he had nothing to offer her? Elsa was smart, educated and determined. Why would she want to take on the challenge—for half a man? Better to let her carve out her own life free of the dependence he would create for her.

He didn't try to open his eyes anymore. He feared what was there behind the lids that had quickly forgotten even how to blink. But damaged as they were, his eyes hadn't lost the ability to cry. He spent many nights on the ship in tears.

When his ship landed in New York, Glenn was greeted as a hero. Captain Billings had recounted the story of Glenn's bravery, which turned out to have had a significant impact on the German supply route. Later convoys, fearing ambush, took roundabout routes to the front, further delaying progress and giving the Allies time to prepare the counterattack. Once Billings learned Glenn was alive, he recommended him for the Medal of Honor to go with the Purple Heart he had earned. A full-page account of the story was published in the *New York Times* the day before Glenn's ship arrived.

Glenn was polite on his arrival. He shook all the hands of the people he couldn't see. He posed for pictures and tried to smile, wondering what he looked like.

But all he wanted was to go home.

# CHAPTER TWENTY-NINE
# ON MOONLIGHT BAY

After reading the story in the *Times*, Elsa knew where she would take the train the next Sunday. She rose early and boarded the Long Island train instead of attending church. She hadn't been back to Lindenhurst in two and a half years.

The streets looked exactly the same. While the city changed so rapidly, here there was a comforting stability. The sea breeze blew softly against the cool, fall morning, stirring so much nostalgia in her heart. How she loved this little town. She felt like she was coming home.

Yet the familiarity could not dispel her fear as she walked from the train station toward the Streppys' home. What right had she to presume this town was still her home? The role which first brought her here was long gone. So much had changed for all of them since that day. While Lindenhurst may have *looked* the same, everything was different since the war. Nobody could escape that fact.

She was different, too, Elsa reminded herself, as she mustered the determination to go on. She was no longer the girl who could be so easily frightened. It was time for her to be brave.

If going to see Glenn at his camp had been bold, going to see him at his family home was much bolder. It was presumptuous. But she had to. Her whole life pointed her toward this moment—all her hard work, all the dreams she had barely dared. She refused to let her fear defeat her. *He* needed her, too. That knowledge strengthened her. She had nothing to lose—nothing except her heart, and that was already committed.

She approached the house, wondering whom she should hope would greet her at the door: Mrs. Streppy, who was kind but very conservative, with a firm sense of propriety? Mr. Streppy, whom she had only met once or twice and had never exchanged words with? Jeanette, who would grasp everything at once and be fiercely protective of her wounded brother, or perhaps if she were lucky, it would be a servant who didn't know her.

Her heart pounded in her chest. Elsa only paused a moment on the porch before knocking.

It was Mrs. Streppy who opened the door. Elsa hadn't seen her since the tea at the Graham house when Glenn announced his enlistment. Today she looked exhausted. There was both relief and pain written over her whole body. Elsa's heart went out to the mother who had endured the same fear and uncertainty as she had this year.

There seemed to be a lot of activity in the house, apparent through the open doorway, but Elsa saw no one else behind Mrs. Streppy in the hall.

She hardly knew what she should say, finally managing only "Hello."

"What are you doing here?"

Elsa thought Mrs. Streppy's tone spoke of her exhaustion more than anything, so she forgave the harshness of the words. She remained bold. "I hoped to see Mr. Glenn." She almost forgot to include the "Mister," which would have been much too bold. "Is he here?"

"Oh, dear, this is too much." Mrs. Streppy looked as if she would burst into tears. "I feel for you, Elsa, I do. I know the Grahams had to let you go, but we cannot afford a servant, and neither can they. We had to let our own girl go, too. These are new times. Glenn is badly wounded— I'm sure you've heard—but we will care for him ourselves.

We cannot afford a servant or a nurse."

Elsa was taken aback. "No, Mrs. Streppy," she stammered, "it is not like that. I . . ." But what could she say? She couldn't tell Glenn's mother what she *really* wanted. Who did she mean by *we?*

Mrs. Streppy looked at her fiercely. "Please leave us be."

Elsa wasn't ready to give up. Mrs. Streppy demeanor was merely a misunderstanding. It had to be.

Just then, her eyes were drawn past Mrs. Streppy by the movement in the hall. A woman walked past from the drawing room. Could that be Mrs. Graham? What was she doing there? Then another figure came into view through the open door. No, it was impossible. *Dafne!*

Elsa couldn't breathe. Her knees grew weak. She stared in shock as Dafne's head turned slowly toward her. Their eyes met, and Elsa felt her total defeat.

Of course. How could she have ever presumed to take Glenn from Dafne?

"Who's there, mother?" Elsa heard Jeanette's voice from inside, just before the door closed sharply in her face.

Elsa took a step back from the closed door, a wall erected firmly between her and everything her heart yearned for. She hung onto the porch railing to keep from collapsing. In an instant, all her dreams had crumbled to dust. She could not even cry, so numb did she feel from both heartbreak and shame.

She began to retrace her steps to the street. Even crying for her loss would be foolish now. She never should have fancied such an impossibility. It had been rash to come here.

It was Glenn's place to invite her to his home, not hers to impose. For all the ways the world had changed since the war, some things would never change. She was still a poor, homely serving girl, she thought. And Dafne was still Dafne. Everything her mother used to warn her about had come true. What a fool she was.

She did not blame Glenn, but it now seemed he had used her love, if inadvertently, as his comfort through the difficulty of war, perhaps talking himself into believing he loved her, too. But naturally now they would all seek to reestablish order to their world: the two mothers, Dafne, even Glenn himself. It would be comforting to them all to go on as if nothing had changed.

Finally her tears came in a torrent. She quickened her steps, suddenly eager to get out of this town, away from all the memories. There was nothing for her here. There never was.

Footsteps sounded behind her. "Elsa, wait."

She didn't stop or turn. She wanted to disappear from these people, to sink into anonymity and try to rebuild her life.

Jeanette ran up and grabbed her arm. "Elsa!"

She blinked back her tears and looked up into Jeanette's eyes.

"Come back, please."

She tried to say something, but nothing would sound right. Jeanette had only known her in a certain role. With Dafne and her mother there, wouldn't it just feel like a big happy reunion with Elsa coming back, too? Maybe Jeanette thought that she could be Glenn and Dafne's serving girl.

"The Grahams were just leaving," said Jeanette. "They had no right to impose."

Elsa didn't understand. *She* was the one who was imposing.

"To think they would waltz in and assume everything could be like it was. After Dafne betrayed him, and now with these Sapphic murmurings coming out of New York. Honestly! My brother won't be a mere path back to respectability for that woman."

Elsa felt so confused. Jeanette took both her shoulders in her hands and looked at her earnestly. "I'm so glad you came. I hoped you would."

Elsa took a breath to steady herself and looked into Jeanette's eyes. She saw warmth there, even a welcoming friendship. In the past, Jeanette had known Elsa only as Dafne's serving girl.

"He's blind, you know. We had to unpack all his things. I saw his packet of letters from you. I didn't read them; don't worry," Jeanette continued. "And I didn't let Mother see them. . . she wouldn't have understood. But *I* do. *I know.* I trust you with him."

"Thank you." Elsa's nerves were tossed by waves of emotion.

"The war changed so many things. It's not so unusual anymore that you and Glenn could love each other. Don't worry about my mother; she will accept you in time."

Elsa was amazed. Was this the same Jeanette who had resented Dafne's relationship with her brother? Elsa had expected the same reaction toward herself. But Jeanette's eyes showed her the truth: she cared more for character than station, and she had spent enough time around Elsa to know hers.

"My brother needs love so much right now." Jeanette took Elsa's arm and led her back toward the house. "You can give him that. Dafne never could and certainly has no right to try now."

Elsa retraced her nervous walk to the Streppys' door, but this time took courage from having a friend and ally beside her.

Jeanette opened the front door. "Glenn's in the parlor."

Elsa left her coat in the hall and walked quietly forward. Jeanette slipped away.

Her heart filled when she saw Glenn, sitting alone in a padded chair. His eyelids were closed and scarred, but his face had survived the burns reasonably well. His frame was gaunt. How he had changed since she'd first met him, as the stocky college student who filled out his suits. Sadness was etched on his mouth. She wanted to cry for him . . . to somehow share in his sorrow, even though she beheld him with joy. She wondered how long it had been since he'd smiled.

She waited another minute, then walked silently across the room and knelt beside him.

"Hello, Glenn."

His face leaped. His neck strained in her direction. It was sad to see him instinctively look for her though he couldn't see.

She laid her head on his knees. "Welcome home."

"Elsa, is it really you? Give me your hand so I know it's not a dream."

"Here is my hand. Here is my heart. I am here to love you and care for you."

He took her hand and brought it up to touch his face. She sighed. Glenn's voice and movements seemed sharp and nervous to her, unlike the steadiness she always remembered from him.

"I dreamed of this moment so often during those dark days of the war," he said. "I can hardly believe this time it's real."

"I had to come to you, as soon as I knew you were home." Elsa felt like her heart would beat out of her chest.

Glenn pressed her hand against his face. Her touch seemed to calm his nerves.

"I wanted to believe you would come to me, but I didn't know. I wanted to ask you to come, but how could I, now? Look at me. I'm a broken man."

"Let me help you to become whole again."

"I had wanted to give you so much, dear Elsa. But I can do nothing for you now."

Elsa could hardly believe the daring she found. She lifted herself from his knee and brought her face close to his and kissed him firmly on the lips. He took a moment to realize, emitting a quick gasp before responding to her touch. She held a second longer, delighting in this first kiss for which she had barely dared to dream. She knelt and laid her head back on his knee.

"You do not have to," he said as he softly stroked the top of her head. "You have your whole life in front of you. I have nothing to give you in return."

"I love you, Glenn. Let my eyes guide you through anything you want to see. Nothing could make me happier than to be with you, serve you, see for you, and most of all . . . love you."

They remained for several long moments in silence. Glenn breathed slowly. When he spoke again, he had regained some of the calm thoughtfulness Elsa knew from him. She hoped her presence was already helping.

"My dear Elsa, I have been through such hell this last year. While I begin to learn how to live without sight, I also feel I need to learn how to be a man again. But through all the horror, you were there with me every moment. My love for you strengthened me and helped keep me from descending to the depths this war might have led me to. In the last days, when I was half-dead, when every day should have been my last, your love kept me alive. I felt it across all the miles— actively and energetically—I felt your unwavering love."

"Yes, Glenn. Every day, even when I feared you were dead."

"The moment the explosion took my sight was the moment I realized how deeply I loved you. For a second I thought I *had* died, and I was filled with regret. Once I knew I had a chance to live, I held onto it in hopes of this—in hopes of hearing your voice again and touching your hand. Perhaps I cannot see you, but in the eye of my heart I see you clearly before me now. Many images have become blurred to me, but the image of your face is the one thing that is completely clear."

He lifted her head and with both his hands began to feel the lines of her face.

"I remember every curve of your face, every hair of your head, the shape of your eyes, everything as if I were gazing at you with seeing eyes right now."

Elsa suddenly felt shy, as if she were being stared at. She had never been accustomed to being looked at. But his eyes were still closed.

Glenn moved his hands to her shoulders and pulled her up to him. She hugged him where he sat, sitting on and pressed her face against his cheek. He clasped her tightly. His hands moved on her back as he tried to pull every inch of her toward him. Elsa felt her love being pulled into him . . . comforting him, healing him.

"How I wanted to hold you like this," he said. "Beautiful Elsa. I love you so much."

Elsa could hardly believe the words she was hearing— words she had never dreamed she would hear from a man.

After several contented minutes Elsa stood up, bending toward him as she again looked at his face. "How can I make you smile?"

"You have already done so much. But it will be hard for me to smile."

Smiling herself, she walked to the nearby gramophone. She spotted the record to which she had danced with him on their last night in Lindenhurst. Dafne and Jeanette had fought long about the possession of this record. When Dafne moved to New York, Jeanette finally won.

Elsa placed the needle. As the music began it had the opposite effect from what she had hoped. Glenn's face darkened with sorrow. "This music makes me remember how much I loved to dance. I will never be able to dance again."

She walked to his chair and pulled him to his feet. "You can try."

Sensing his resistance, she shaped his arms around her. "I do not know the steps. You will have to lead me, but I will keep you from running into things."

He hesitated for a moment before taking a first step, then another. The rhythm was still in his feet.

> *We were sailing along,*
> *On Moonlight Bay.*
> *We could hear the voices ringing,*
> *They seemed to say . . .*
> *You have stolen my heart,*
> *Now don't go 'way . . .*
> *As we sang love's old sweet song*
> *On Moonlight Bay.*

She clutched his hand as they embraced and directed him. "There's a lamp there. Oh . . . that's the wall."

When the song was over Elsa wished he could see how she beamed at him.

"That didn't go so bad. If you teach me more of the steps, we can dance even more."

"Thank you. It feels so good to dance."

She touched his lips with her finger. "You smiled."

With the smile still on his lips, Glenn pulled her close to him. She melted into his strong arms, delighting in being held by him. How far away this dream had seemed mere moments ago and now it is real.

"Elsa, my love, if you will have me, broken and all, will you marry me and be my wife?"

"Yes, Glenn, yes."

"Feeling you here, hearing your voice, you have brought me back out of the darkness. I never want to let you go."

She took a deep breath, still unable to believe this was really happening. . . to *her*, not to some character in a story.

"It may take my parents some time to accept it, so be patient. Just today my mother and Dafne's mother tried to put our engagement back on. My mother is very conservative, but once she gets to know you, I know she will love you as I do."

"I will wait as long as it takes. I want to be with you no matter what. I can be patient and understanding—as long as it takes."

"Today you pulled me back out of my nightmare. You gave me back my hope and my courage. I will find a way, even blind."

She pulled back and looked at his face. "Can you open your eyes?"

"I don't know."

She smiled compassionately. It sounded so simple, so childlike, yet she understood the difficulty. "Try."

"I'm afraid of what you'll see. I'm afraid I have no eyes left."

"I am not afraid. I want to love all of you, even the scars. Just because you cannot see, do not deprive me of the joy of seeing your eyes."

Glenn's face contorted in concentration. It took him a moment to open eyelids that had been shut for months. The muscles had grown weak. At last they opened.

Elsa's own eyes swam with tears of joy. His were still the same eyes she knew, remembered and loved. His eyes were dull and distant, but there was no death in them.

"You still have beautiful eyes, my love. They are not so damaged. Keep them open a little bit each day. Let them search for light. Perhaps one day, my love can teach them to see again."

Looking at those eyes, Elsa saw mirrored in them the depth of the horror Glenn saw in the war. It must have literally turned off certain parts of his mind that he didn't want to revisit. Could it be that the pathway to sight hadn't been irrevocably damaged, but merely turned off by the terror of that waking nightmare? If so, what better than love to re-forge that path? She would pray for a miracle, just as Josephine suggested.

"Come to the window." She pulled him by the hand.

The window of the room looked out to the houses and trees of the neighborhood, all of which must have been so familiar to him. She opened the pane and saw him breathe deeply of the crisp fall air.

"Look out there. Do you remember? The trees are almost bare now. No, keep them open. Let yourself see through me."

He did.

"The sky today is dark, but it is not one of those dull, gray fall days. There are a few clouds that are almost black—rain clouds, maybe even snow, though it still feels too early for snow. Then there are lighter clouds, soft and white. Sometimes these pass in front of the dark clouds. I even see a few glimpses of blue."

She saw Glenn point his open eyes upward. Just then, the sun broke unexpectedly from behind one of the darkest of the afternoon clouds.

"How lovely! The sun just burst through. It will only last a moment, but try to remember how the red brick houses look in the sunshine, with all the bare tree branches throwing spidery shadows on the street."

"Yes. I *knew* the sun had broken through a moment before you said it. I felt it even though I didn't see it."

Elsa looked at him eagerly. "Was it the light? Did you see light?"

"I think so. At least I felt it."

The sun moved back behind the cloud.

"Be patient, my love. Let the light be the first step. I believe one day when I look at you, you will look back."

Elsa leaned her head against Glenn's shoulder. The moment had given her such joy, and made her feel ready for the patience his recovery would take. Good things always took a lot of work—she'd learned that from a young age. Also, the good things in life were always tinged with a little sorrow. She felt closer to Glenn now since he knew that, too. She did not mind that their lives still had a little pain—this war could not be dispelled quickly. Its mark would remain, both on their house and on the world. Joy was not in having a perfect life. True joy was to have your own bit of happiness and someone to share it with.

She gazed at Glenn's face, his eyes open in the cool air of the open window. There was not sight in his eyes, but she did see something different in his face from when she'd first come here an hour ago. It was hope. With hope, Glenn's belief in the world and his place in it would come. Elsa knew this. Perhaps his sight would return, perhaps not. Either way, he would find his purpose again. She knew this man she loved would find a way.

# THE END

## IS ONLY BUT THE BEGINNING...

# SUGGESTED QUESTIONS FOR BOOK CLUBS AND DISCUSSION GROUPS

1. How has the immigrant experience changed from the 1910s compared with today? In what ways is it similar?

2. In what ways does Elsa resist the expectations that are placed on her: by her parents, by society, by herself?

3. How does Elsa's experience as an uneducated immigrant in America differ from Sonya's? Why?

4. Was the women's general strike a success? What can we learn today from the women in the garment industry in the 1910s?

5. Elsa experienced two drastic changes, first moving from Germany to the United States, and later moving from the Lower East Side to the high society of Long Island. How did these changes prepare her for what was to come? Have you ever experienced a change so extreme and if so, how did that change you as a person?

6. What changes and why with the dynamic between Dafne, Elsa and Glenn when they move to Manhattan?

7. What do you think motivated Dafne to cheat on Glenn? Did she simply get carried away, or was something deeper going on?

8. What allows Elsa to come to terms with her feelings for Glenn? If she hadn't been through the earlier experiences, do you think she would have had the courage to act on those feelings?

9. Do you think the United States was right to join World War One? Why or why not?

10. What do you think it would have been like to be an ethnic German living in America during either of the World Wars?

11. What inspired Glenn to save Hal's life, even after he had been betrayed by him? Would you have acted the same way in that situation?

12. How have the expectations of their families and society changed for Elsa and Glenn after the war? How has his injury changed both of their idea of what's most important?

13. Do you think this is a timely read? Does it reflect some of the issues that immigrants are currently experiencing?

# ABOUT THE AUTHOR

*Love of Finished Years*, a debut novel by Gregory Erich Phillips won the Chaucer Award in historical fiction, as well as the Grand Prize for best book of the year across all genres from Chanticleer Reviews while still in manuscript form. It was then picked up by the Sillan Pace Brown Group to be published January 2018.

Some people have called the author a renaissance man, because of his diverse life experiences. He works by day as a mortgage banker, and in his spare time plays the violin, sings in cathedral choirs, and moonlights as a tango performer (He has danced on stages in San Francisco, New York City and Seattle).

Writing novels has been his passion since he was in high school as he was inspired by his literary family. He enjoys researching historical context for his unforgettable characters to explore.

He lives in Seattle, Washington with his wife, Rachel: his wife, his tango partner, and his muse.

# Discover More

Author Events
Book Signings & Book Tours
Video & Audio Clips
Historical Research
Interviews
New Works
and much more

We invite you to visit the author's website at
www.GregoryErichPhillips.com

Find Gregory Erich Phillips on Facebook:
www.facebook.com/gregoryerichphillips

Follow Gregory Erich Phillips on Twitter: @by_gep

For more information about ordering this novel or to arrange
an author event,
please contact JA@SillanPaceBrown.com
or visit:
www.SillanPaceBrown.com